Renata

Books by John Buell

THE PYX

FOUR DAYS

THE SHREWSDALE EXIT

# THE
# SHREWSDALE
# EXIT

## John Buell

FARRAR, STRAUS AND GIROUX | NEW YORK

Copyright © 1972 by John Buell Associates Ltd.
All rights reserved
Library of Congress catalog card number: 72-81009
ISBN: 0-374-26342-6
First printing, 1972
Printed in the United States of America
Published simultaneously in Canada
by Doubleday Canada Ltd., Toronto
Designed by Dorris Huth

# THE
# SHREWSDALE
# EXIT

# 1

They decided to pull in at the Howard Johnson's.

It was an innocent enough decision. They had been driving for over two hours, and when they saw the big orange sign and the crisp lights in the young evening, she said, "Let's stop and get something to eat," and he nodded, reluctantly, for he wanted to keep going, and had just enough time to signal, check behind him, shift lanes, brake and get into the exit at 50 m.p.h., which was faster than he intended. He relaxed, let the station wagon drift down to 30, to 25, time out is time out, no point rushing it.

"Can I have some M & M's when we come out?" asked the little girl.

"We'll see," said the woman. "You don't want to be sick in the car."

"I won't be sick."

"We'll see."

"Well, can't we just get them?" She was six years old and very persistent.

He grinned at the enormous importance of the M & M's, turned right at the traffic light and began looking for the driveway to the motel.

"Sure," he said. After all, they were on holiday.

From the throughway the spotlit restaurant looked airy and spacious, but now they were passing through a cluster of signs and overhanging wires and poles, three gas stations, competing hamburger stands, a chicken counter, the hardly discernible entrance to a shopping plaza, a Dairy-Bar, a liquor store, some close to the road, some far, all with parking space at a premium, and finally on the right he saw the motel sign, pulled into the uncrowded parking lot and stopped in a clear strip near the restaurant.

He got out and stretched, deliberately noticed the clear, darkening evening, waited for his wife, who was putting tissues in her purse, while the little girl ran ahead. They locked the car, it was full of holiday equipment, and started inside. They didn't look around too closely outside, they had no reason to.

He was in his mid-thirties, she a little younger. He was tall and heavy-boned, going slightly to weight, which made him look shorter. He was wearing tan cotton pants and a golf shirt. He had hair just long enough to be combed, with sideburns as far as the ear lobes, a bony pleasant face that would have looked hard but for a straight nose and clear blue eyes, almost washed out to gray, the sort that catch light and look watery. They made him appear boyish.

For a woman she too was tall, a natural redhead with hair worn long, touched up and dressed in varying tones.

4

She had a long thin face with the regular features of makeup ads but without their emptiness, swift intelligent brown eyes, a rounded but muscular body, breasts firm and high, long legs topped by noticeable buttocks. She wore a short dress about the size of a one-piece bathing suit and wooden-soled sandals that made her take short steps, a fashion that emphasized a sexiness she was probably not aware of. It made her get looked at.

The restaurant wasn't crowded at that hour, although it had quite a few customers. The little girl picked a booth unselfconsciously and her parents joined her. She had light hair, pony-tailed, mostly her mother's face, eyes just like her father's, red jeans raggedly cut at the knees and a T-shirt colored like a barber's pole. She went well with the crisp cheerfulness of the place.

They ordered sandwiches and beer, a Coke for the little girl, and were served in good time. They weren't in a hurry. They were going to the coast, to work their way along the ocean, camping where possible and staying in boarding houses when necessary. They talked as they ate, and in a short time they were about finished.

"I forgot to tell you," he said. "I did get that kid's tent, they don't need it right now," referring to the friends he'd borrowed it from.

"For me?" said the little girl.

"Yeah, and for the friends you're gonna be meeting. Like a dorm, it's fun. We'll all have a little more room."

His wife looked at him and her expression added: and privacy. And he raised his glass in exaggerated self-satisfied glee. She laughed.

"Did you get Bill's long lens?" she asked.

"And a clamp, I didn't have room for the tripod."

"What's a long lens?" asked the little girl.

"For the camera," he said. "It makes far things look close."

"Oh."

He got up, left a tip, and went to the cashier while the mother made sure the little girl went to the washroom.

When they joined him, he bought the M & M's.

Outside it was darker, a little cooler, the lights brighter and obscuring the dim glow of the sky. In the dark and under the lights, less clutter showed and things seemed farther away than they were. The road was busy with unhurried traffic, people coming back from supper or going bowling or just going, big trailers that would work all night, restless kids gearing up for the evening's fun. The stand-up eateries were busy, cars parked askew, stopping long enough to pick up a computerized hamburger, everything from heavy men in Cadillacs to youngsters on bikes who thought the food was great. At the edge of the Dairy-Bar lot, close by, three helmeted and weirdly costumed toughs sat on big motorbikes and drank milk from waxed cartons.

At the car the woman said to the little girl, "You might want to go to sleep later," and began clearing the back seat, with some difficulty. From the inside it was just another domestic chore, from the outside it was squirming long legs and wiggling buttocks at a low angle, and finally a straightening up with a toss of hair and a two-handed brush-back that thrust her breasts forward. It was visible and watched, in silence, from the Dairy-Bar, as usual and normal as ice cream on a Sunday afternoon fifty years ago.

He made sure they were belted in and eased the wagon

through the parking lot as he put on the lights and checked the gauges. He slid into the casual local traffic, pacing it slowly so he wouldn't have to brake or stop too often, took the green light, and a short distance away swung into the ramp, where there was no traffic, and onto the throughway. He let the car gain little by little and relaxed into the pace of the driving. The noise of the airstream made talking difficult and the radio hard to hear, but the M & M's were asked for, some given, and the rest tucked away out of sight. They settled into the ride, watching the road and the signs, and talking every now and then in a semi-shout.

It started happening about fifteen minutes later.

At first it didn't seem like anything. He saw one headlight behind him in the distance, one light in both mirrors. He thought it was a car, one light obscured by the way he was sitting. He moved a little. Still the one light, and still the idea that it was a car, a one-eyed car. He didn't think any more about it.

The next time he looked he saw two lights. They were too far apart to be a car, and he wondered vaguely what size truck would have lights that wide. He entered a long curve and the rear view went black. He forgot about it. He felt like going faster than the posted 65, but he had a fully loaded wagon, at night, with a family.

A little while after he came out of the curve he looked behind and saw three lights taking up the entire width of the throughway and gaining on him. Motorcycles. Something made him feel uneasy—the nudge of an idea that they weren't going to pass. He didn't say anything. He sat up a little higher, watching front and back alternately. His wife sensed his movement and looked at him. She thought he might be getting ready for a speeder, and she turned away, but not immediately.

They came up fast, well over 80, got behind the wagon and stayed there. Their bikes roared. Their lights filled the inside of the wagon. The woman turned, first to one side, then the other, and saw the three lights spread in a row across the road, pacing their car.

"What's that?" she asked, her raised voice quavering.

"Motorbikes."

"What are they doing?"

"Playing games," he said. "Is Patty asleep?" He hadn't heard the little girl and he didn't want to turn around.

"Yes."

"Check the doors, make sure they're locked."

The toughs held their formation, swaying now and then to put light into the car and barking their horns.

He held his course. He felt unreal, quiet and icy, suppressing what he knew to be a useless and dangerous anger, his mind sorting out the possibilities, none of them good: get to an exit, try to out-race them, car-fight them, attract attention, hope for the police, or . . .

A sign said the next town was twenty-five miles away. The throughway going back was far to the left behind bush and cut rock. They were on a desolate stretch, and not by accident.

He put on his emergency blinkers, floored the pedal and raced ahead at 75. The car was smooth at 80, and became a furious vibration at 85. He dropped back to 80, he could do twenty-five miles in something like twenty minutes. He checked his watch: it was 9:40. It was also no use.

8

They came up behind again, zigzagging, and honking, and this time the two outside toughs moved up alongside the front windows while the third one stayed behind. The noise was deafening.

"Close your vent," he shouted to his wife. He didn't want them tossing things into the car.

The toughs were visible now. Adorned helmets, the one on the right with horns, sleeveless jackets studded and riveted and covered with graffiti, straggly hair and stubbles like beards scissored in the dark, insignia of all sorts, metal armbands, gauntlets that were probably metal-painted gardening gloves, and fixed grins like psychotic grimaces under what looked like yellow-tinted shooting glasses.

The tough near the woman was making obscene thrusts into his saddle and beckoning her with jerks of his head. The one near the man was signaling him to pull over by pointing to the side of the road. When he didn't pull over, the tough on the bike showed a heavy chain and threatened with it. As if on cue, a heavy clangy thump rattled off the end of the wagon, then another. The tough in the back was hitting the fender, or at the blinking light.

The little girl was awake by now, bemused and terrified, sitting up stiff and wide-eyed. She only uttered, "Daddy!" in a soft sharp despair. It almost unnerved him. The woman reached over and touched her.

"Don't take off your belts!" he yelled as he saw his wife going to comfort the child.

He'd made up his mind now, without choice. There was no exit to take, he couldn't race them, and there were no police. He jammed on the brakes. At that speed it didn't stop the car suddenly, but it did slow it enough to cause the back tough to heave into the wagon and go off balance. He didn't spill. But he had to fall back to regain control.

Then he put the pedal to the floor, edged the car to the left and swung as quickly as was possible to the right, hoping the lash of the wagon would upset the bike on his left. It didn't, the tough had had more practice, he swung the bike out and fell slightly behind.

The wagon swayed to the right on its own, almost out of control, causing the bike on that side to fall back, and continued its swerve into the stopping strip. He drove on the strip until things were steady and finally got back on the asphalt.

He was covered with sweat, his wife was rigid with her two hands on the dash. The little girl had buried her face in the back seat. No one spoke.

He watched the three lights cluster in the distance, saw them pick up speed and separate across the road. His wife turned to see. In seconds they could hear them again.

They were passing this time, slowly, grimacing and dancing in their saddles, two on the left, one on the right, until there was a bike in front and slightly to the side of each headlight and one ahead on the far left. Then they held steady, a grim, relative motionlessness. He tried to ease the car back imperceptibly, he was expecting something.

It came.

The two toughs ahead of the car suddenly turned in their seats and threw something at the windshield, two containers which burst and spread an ooze over the glass. Oil. The woman shrieked.

He couldn't see. He eased on the brakes, holding on a

remembered course, quickly flicked on the wipers and the washing jet, but that only spread the oil evenly. It would take too long, he'd have to stop. A blind car, the bastards, I wish I had a gun. He felt the wheels crunch over the stopping strip, he was going off the road. Then something soft, and he knew the car was on grass. It tilted slightly and rolled to a stop.

He jammed the lever in park, snapped off his belt.

"Keep everything on, lean on the horn, lock up."

He got out and quickly slammed the door after him. He was shaking with anger and fear, over-aware of everything, for a moment surprised how far down the embankment the car had come. The horn started a steady whine; the headlights shone askew along the grass and into the bush, weak against the night, the blinkers and wipers keeping time.

Two of them up ahead were off their bikes and approaching with chains. The third was closer, just getting off his bike. There was no use standing still for it. He ran to the third tough, crashed into him in full stride, grabbed hair in two hands, pulled down and brought his knee up hard into the tough's face. He felt teeth loosen.

He gripped him by the lower neck, still two-handed, and was going to swing him against the other two, but a heavy chain struck him across the shoulder, lashing also into the tough he was holding. "Ya dumb fucker, you're gettin *me!*" He tightened his grip, felt the flesh tearing, tried to heave and turn. The chain came down again, this time right, on his head and neck and shoulders.

He heard glass breaking, the screaming of woman and child, and sank to nothing under heavy kicks, hoping distantly not to live.

# 2

Maybe, his own voice said, maybe if you called the manager. Maybe, his voice answered, but the motel shouldn't be this goddam cold, they don't even have blankets here. Furiously he fumbled in a long languorous reach for a phone, but there was no phone, and then there was no motel but only some confusing thing that was cold and dark and stretched forever. Still he kept reaching and reaching, no object in mind, it was just important somehow to ignore the pain and keep making gigantic efforts, huge decidings to heave past some point, some edge, past a strange and environing nothingness, a tightening fear that was casually natural and utterly hateful. Then it all went away, and what seemed like the cold night entered his stirring consciousness.

He was on all fours in tall grass. He was clearly aware of his posture, could feel the grass, knew that it was night. He felt cold. He didn't move, he waited. He sensed that something wasn't right, that soon he would understand where he was and why. He felt remote from himself somehow, as if he could step aside and watch the scene.

Then he moved his head to look up and sharp pains jolted his whole body, and with that, like a sudden image on the screen, he remembered everything and leaped to his feet with a crying moan.

Instinctively he turned around to go "back" to the car—the opposite of his last remembered direction. He stumbled and fell. Something slipped off him, a rope he thought and let it lie. It was dark, moonless, the stars clear in the non-city air. He got up again and tried to see better. Vague shapes and lumps of black that seemed closer than they were surrounded him and ended at the not totally darkened sky. The tall grass he could see as something there, but without detail.

He remembered the embankment, and tried to run "up" to get to the throughway, desperate to hurry. But it was like taking a step where there are no stairs. He fell and rolled and lost his imagined direction completely. There should be lights, he said inside, headlights, our headlights. He didn't let the implications surface—he felt cold again, and started shaking, and the pains came back. He struggled to his feet and stood still, listening. There could be no hurrying. What he heard was the thumping of his heart and the faraway screeching in his ears. Then the night sounds came through, chirps, and warbles, and calls. Finally, from far off, he thought he heard a motor.

He waited, then shifted to hear better. The noise of the high grass was like brush fire. He froze in mid-shift to find the motor again. Nothing. Painfully he turned his head slowly in a careful sweep of the dark. Suddenly the motor was back, louder. He cupped his hands behind his ears in two tries and the motor faded, but as he kept turning he heard it better and better. He was twisted like a gymnast to his left. When he was sure of where it was coming from, he corrected his footing noisily and quickly without losing track of the sound. Loud now, a diesel, a truck, he could hear the tires. Somewhere above his head, it seemed, the truck passed, and he thought he saw the glow of lights. He had a direction.

He started walking, stumbling again through the grass and losing his way. He stopped. He had to be sure he was going straight. He looked in the only direction he could, up, to the sky, and his eyes rested primitively on a bright object almost directly to his right. He moved through the dark. Before long the tall grass disappeared abruptly, and he stopped to feel the roughly mowed surface: he was on the embankment. He checked the sky and ran up the embankment, stumbling and falling as he went. Soon he saw the flat, less black surface of the throughway. He got on the shoulder, paused, and holding panic down he turned suddenly to look down the embankment. There was nothing, only the darkness and the sound of his gulping breathing.

Without stopping to decide, he simply began walking against the traffic direction, watching the dark slope intently. Any time now, he thought, and couldn't keep down the flood of possibilities that attacked him like pain. He began seeing forms in the dark, once he investigated, and later he stopped, rigid, because he thought he heard the little girl calling him. He couldn't see from the shoulder, and realized he wouldn't see. He took to walking down the embankment, then along, then up again, combing the area.

He grew weaker and less steady and finally fell on all fours, in despair, knowing time was important and fighting off the images that panic made in his mind. He sat back on his haunches and rested as well as he could.

But not for long. Without warning, the sound of a car, distant but clear, cut the air. At first he was going to run up and try to flag it, but he knew few people would stop to help. More important, he needed light, and he estimated that there would be some light spill this time because he was higher on the embankment. He knelt upright, shielded his eyes, and waited, looking wide-eyed into the blackness. The car came into range, there was light, some spill, and it sped on. About thirty yards ahead there was something, a glisten, and he was sure. He made his way to it.

He was surprisingly close before he could see the car plainly, and had to get even closer to see the oily windshield, the smashed driver's window. There was no sound.

He opened the driver's door. There was no one inside. Without even thinking of broken glass, he leaned over to the dash compartment and took out a flashlight. Still leaned over, he tried it. It showed candies all over the floor and seat. Then with quick grimness he shone it into the back seat and on the floor. Nothing. He turned it off, got out of the car, left the door open. Something half-noticed made him open the second door and take a better look. The seat belt had been cut, the buckle was still tied to the loose end.

He straightened up. He felt hollowed out inside, and cold, what he knew he knew with his whole body.

With mechanical efficiency, he checked around the car, and proceeded farther down the embankment. As sure as a blind man in his own room, he walked a short distance, stopped, played the light in a short arc along the grass until it caught something whitish. He went over.

Their torn clothing was strewn around. They were lying roughly side by side in each other's blood, naked and motionless, in slightly unnatural postures. Their lower stomachs and throats had been cut.

His face stiff with disbelief, knowing it was no use, he examined them for signs of life. No, she hadn't called him. They were both dead.

# 3

As if, with the grim search done, he were now free of emergency duties, he sat down heavily and clumsily and began to wail and rock to and fro like Vietnamese women on the TV news. He couldn't stop. He was a different person, untouched by social niceness and cultural habits. He sent his wails up into the night and noticed, with a feeling of cosmic strangeness, that he was facing the star that had been his guide earlier. He touched his wife's arm and rocked and cried out loud. He couldn't leave the place, couldn't leave them.

Remotely he knew he'd have to get to the police—but it was useless and pointless—yet, so was staying here. They're dead. And his crying gushed out again and shook him like strong hostile arms. "For shit's sake, don't go to pieces," he said aloud in a broken voice, using a younger vernacular. "It's less than half a mile, five minutes maybe." He surprised himself by saying that. It just came out, and it was true: there were emergency phones every half mile on the throughway. He hadn't thought of it until he said it. If I'd stopped and used one while . . . . no, they would've jumped us before I could get to it.

He turned off the flashlight and sat trembling in the dark, looking at the dim whitenesses before him. His sobbing was becoming a reflex and he tried to check himself. "You've gotta get on your feet," he said in his still broken voice, "and tell somebody." "Yeah," he answered himself, "I gotta do that." He didn't move. On the throughway, a car went by, then two more. They seemed to throw an awful lot of light. He saw his own car not very far up the embankment, starkly silhouetted in the moving glow. A sharp feeling of unnaturalness came over him, there are places not meant for being.

He stood up and went to his car, and doing everything with an eerie precision he opened the gate, neatly moved some of the baggage and took two blankets from a kit bag. With these he went back to his wife and child and covered them. He did this slowly, and he didn't pause at all. He straightened and walked up the embankment to the highway and went left on the shoulder. Then he stopped suddenly and turned directly around. He couldn't bring himself to believe what he knew.

He went all the way back to them and fell to his knees and kept saying, "No, no, no," in a very low voice.

After a long while, he returned to the highway and kept walking. It was all unreal. He had to fight off the urge to turn back. His actions now were acknowledging their deaths, but everything inside him made them seem so alive.

Less than a half mile away he finally came to the yellow

phone. He got it open, with two hands, and picked up the receiver. He looked for some sort of dial, but a voice said: "Highway Patrol, Holland speaking."

"You gotta get out here. Something terrible . . ."

"What happened?"

"You gotta get out here." He couldn't use the words that would say it.

"Mister," the voice said, "get a grip on yourself, okay?"

"Yeah."

"What's the number on that phone?"

"Number? You've got to come out . . ."

"Gimme the number on that phone," the voice said sternly.

"There's no number."

"On the box, mister, right in front of you, or on the outside. You got a light there?"

"Yeah." He looked, and found the number. "It's 43."

"Okay. What's your name?" the voice said in a kindly tone. Then to someone who was there, "Forty-three, guy calling, seems upset, may be something, can't or won't say."

"Grant," he said in a broken voice.

"What was that?"

"It doesn't matter." He was shaking, beginning to sob.

"Cran?" the voice said.

"Grant. Grant. Like in Ulysses S." He didn't know why he said that.

"Mister, are you being funny?"

"Get out here! For–the–love–of–Christ–will–you–get–out–here!"

"Stay by the phone. It'll make things easier all around."

He replaced the receiver, left the box open. Easier. All

**1 9**

around. It kinda depends on your point of view, doesn't it. You see, it's like this, there's a . . . His brain was running away with him, he felt faint. He slipped to one knee, and landed hard on the hand that had the flashlight. He pulled himself to a sitting position and leaned his crouched back against the phone post. He turned off the light. Won't it be funny, he felt his brain saying, and then laughing, when they get here and find it's all not true, how the hell am I going to explain . . . and what was that thing I had on me when I . . . Just a baby. Shit, you'd think. What . . . what would make people . . . ?

He snapped alert. Cars were swooshing by. The last one's brake lights came on, but it reconsidered and kept moving. They'd seen him, he knew. He jumped up, yelling, "A-a-a-h, no!" They'd seen him, they might look for something else, they might find the car, and— He began running back to them. He fell down in the dark, got up right away, put on the dimming flashlight and kept running and running until, after he had fallen, he imagined he was still running. But he was down, mainly unconscious, struggling in twitches to get up, life protesting against their dying.

When he was aware again, strong hands were holding him up on his feet.

"Can you make it to the car?"

He turned his head and saw the trooper in the amber flasher. He nodded. He was helped into the front seat.

"Where?"

"Just ahead. Coupla hundred yards."

When they were close, he pointed through the windshield. The trooper pulled over on the shoulder and stopped, idling.

"Can you tell me what happened?"

**2 0**

"I—they—"

"I'd like to know, just the general idea, so I won't disturb too many things."

"They killed my wife—and my little girl."

"I'm awful sorry, Mr. Grant."

Then the trooper asked, "Your car's there?"

"Yes."

"Where did you go off the road?"

"Little farther up."

"The others, what were they driving?"

"Motorcycles."

"Okay. You can stay in the car, take it easy."

"No, no, I want to go with you."

"Mr. Grant, you're not in very good shape. There's no use making it harder for yourself. You stay here."

The trooper took the car keys, a big flashlight, and went to the edge of the grass, where he played the light on the station wagon, found its tracks, and circled widely down the slope until he was past the wagon. He found and checked what the blankets covered. He shone the light in the disturbed grass, but didn't walk in it. He returned to the patrol car.

Into the microphone he identified himself and said, "It's a code 3, multiple. Man here needs medical attention. Approach for markers." The trooper looked grim, grateful for the neutral jargon of work. He said nothing more.

From the trunk he took spiked fluorescent markers, like long flares, and went over and put two of them in the wagon's tracks. From there he went ahead on the shoulder, looking for and placing markers on the disturbed areas he could see. Then he moved the patrol car off the road onto the grass just at the edge of the wagon's tracks. He got out again, taking the keys, and stood on the shoulder waiting for the others to arrive. He had tried to do his work as delicately as possible.

The man in the car, Grant, was weeping quietly, and the trooper tried not to think of his own family.

# 4

From the patrol car he kept staring into the dark beyond
the station wagon, waiting for society to arrive. There was
nothing he could be allowed to do, nothing he could do,
except feel more and more unreal. The first arrivals were
two more uniformed men. The trooper waved them to the
entry side and made sure they stayed away from the
marked-off space as if it were sacred and not to be entered
without privilege or purification. They stood talking in the
white light of their cars slapped by amber flashers: molded
broad-brimmed hats without wrinkle, the same clean official uniforms, casual and comforting and ominous with
heavy-caliber revolvers and belted supplies of bullets.
They were strangers. They were there because of a phone
on the highway, a contact with society whose only human-
ity was the sorrowful response of the men kept hidden behind faces as expressionless as their clothing. The fragile

extensions of his heart, the human that was so despised, lay unlit beyond the wagon.

The new troopers came over to him and explained that they had to take down basic information. One of them had forms on a clipboard. He sat in the driver's seat, the other stood by the open passenger door.

"May I see your identification?"

He extended his wallet to the standing trooper.

"Just take out your driver's license, please."

"You do it, you do it."

The trooper simply opened the wallet and shone his flashlight on the plastic holder.

"Joe Grant?" he said, confirming, not waiting for an answer. "This the correct address?"

"Yeah, it is."

He read it off for his partner.

"Joe," he said gently, "what are the names of . . . ?"

"Sue, my wife. And Patty . . ." His voice broke.

The man with the clipboard shook his head, and the standing trooper touched Grant on the shoulder.

"Okay. Take it easy. We'll get it later."

Two more cars were pulling in, both unmarked, no flashers. The lone trooper waved an imaginary stop line for them. Motors and lights stayed on and made more glare and more shadows.

Two men in summer jackets emerged from the dark of one car and went to the trooper. One was tall and massive with muscles in his face and a blond close-cut head that looked bald in that light; the other was older, shorter, big-boned and lean with a mess of wiry hair the color of cold ashes.

From the second car came a short fat man with windblown gray hair, coatless, in a shirt and loose tie, sleeves partly rolled, looking as if he hadn't changed in a week. He carried a medical bag into the light and waited.

The trooper indicated the dark behind the station wagon.

"There. This side of the markers is clear. We go round that way."

They went to the covered bodies and held light for the doctor. He removed the blankets gently, handed them to the trooper, and set about examining the dead woman and child. It didn't take him long.

"Pretty obvious," he grunted in a flat disgusted tone. "Any one of those wounds could've been fatal."

"Molested?" said the massive detective.

"Guess, probably. I need them in the lab to answer that."

Very carefully he examined the grass around the bodies.

"Lot of bleeding," he muttered. Then more clearly, "I want all this ground brought in too. I'll mark it."

"After the pictures," said the older detective.

"Course."

"Time?"

"Can't tell here. Warm night, cooling air, blankets, bring those in too. He can probably tell us."

"We'd like it from the physical evidence as close as possible."

"Find out when they last ate."

A big van like an elongated camper, with windows all around, flasher and spotlights, was directed down the embankment. Two men in uniform began setting up photographic equipment. Another man, also in uniform, went to the older detective and the doctor for instructions. The

**2 5**

trooper gave this last man the blankets, he put them in a clear plastic bag.

An unmarked light-green panel truck parked in the background, its lights and motor off. The two occupants in white work clothes got out and settled down to wait.

Bugs were gathering more thickly around the lights. The lone trooper showed the detectives and two of the lab men around the entire perimeter of the site. The doctor went to the patrol car where Grant was sitting.

"Shame," he said.

Grant barely nodded.

"I'm Dr. McLintoch. Call said you were hurt."

Grant nodded again.

The doctor began examining him, eyes, pulse, heartbeat, the scratches and cuts, the scuffed and dirty clothes, his hands. He even swung his light on his shoes. Grant was missing the implications.

"You saw them?" Grant said.

The doctor looked at him with a steady gaze. "Yes, I did."

Grant had difficulty saying, "You're sure about . . . ? There's no possibility that . . . ?"

"I'm sure. No chance." And when Grant looked as if he were going to press the point, he added gently but firmly, "They're dead."

Grant once more barely nodded.

"What happened to you?"

"I fought, they hit me with chains, I passed out."

"Where'd they hit you?"

Grant waved absently at the back of his head, and the doctor looked that over carefully.

A voice by the car was explaining, "There's too much

ground, we'll have to use an open shutter. So all lights off. We'll take more from upstairs in daylight."

"Is everything all right, doctor?" said the big detective.

"He's pretty shaken up," he said and moved aside to let the big man stand next to Grant.

The older detective seated himself on the driver's side. "I'm sorry about all this, Mr. Grant, it's tough."

Grant looked at him in acknowledgment.

"I'm Captain Sparrs. That's Lieutenant Ketner. Do you feel well enough to tell us what happened?"

Grant's head turned involuntarily toward the station wagon.

"Here?" he said.

"Some of it has to be told here, Mr. Grant. We have to find out what to look for."

Lights were getting turned off, motors stopped, until only the two spotlights on the van were left on.

The detective lit a cigarette.

A voice commanded routinely, "No matches. Lit cigarettes okay."

"There were three. Followed us on motorbikes, then moved in, tried to get me to stop. Wild-looking guys. I tried everything, going fast, swerving at them. Then they heaved guck at the windshield, oil it looked like when I put the wipers on. I couldn't see, I had to stop."

The spotlights went out. They all waited to adjust to the dark. On the site a flashlight came on, went off, a voice said, "Now," and a flash gun exploded. The whole thing was repeated, this time with the flash in a different place. They kept doing this until a voice yelled for lights and the spotlights came on. "Take it all again without the markers."

"What happened when you stopped?" the captain asked.

Grant didn't answer.

"Are you all right?"

"No, I'm not all right."

"Doctor."

"Never mind," said Grant. "I got some Scotch in . . ."

"Where?"

"The wagon."

"We better leave it, they're working there."

"Here," said the doctor and handed Grant a small bottle.

"What is it?"

"Brandy."

Grant took a swallow and shuddered, gave the bottle back.

The spotlights went out again. Grant talked slowly in the dark.

"I got out. Told my wife to lock up behind me. They were up a ways, in front, coming toward us. One guy was getting off his bike. He was closest."

The flashgun began its routine.

"I grabbed him, fought with him. Then I got hit with the chains they had. They knocked me out."

Silence for a while, darkness, flashes.

"And then?"

"What you just saw. That's all."

"I mean with you. You regained consciousness. What did you do after that?"

"That's not important."

"It might be."

"I don't see how. Those three guys are loose. That's important."

They realized he was speaking from shock. They waited

in the dark until the spotlights came on again. The doctor had Grant drink more brandy.

"Those three in question," the captain said slowly, "did certain things, left traces. You came to, did certain things and left traces too. We've got to subtract yours from theirs. Do you understand me?"

"Certain things. Like what?"

"Well, like the blankets. They—"

"I did that!" Grant said furiously. "I covered them!" He couldn't continue for the tears that choked him.

"Easy now, easy."

"I'm sorry. I'm . . ."

"That's all right. We understand."

"I came to. I was lost. It was dark and I was on my hands and knees in hay."

"Hay?"

"Hay or big weeds or tall grass, anyway it was high, it was higher than me—you know, when I was down. I couldn't see anything, the headlights were off, and I had to find them, and then the noise of the truck and I was able to get out of the hay and on the short stuff and then on the road."

"You'd left your lights on?"

"Lights, blinkers, wipers, everything. The horn, I told my wife . . ."

"Okay."

"I kept going back and forth around here, you know, in a pattern, and I got to the car. And got the flashlight from the dash."

"The car doors were closed?"

"Yeah, closed."

"Lights off?"

"Everything off."

"You left the two doors on this side open?"

"I must've. I saw the cut seat belt in the back. I . . ."

They let him stop. The big detective detached himself smoothly but quickly and went to check the seat belt. He gave instructions to the lab men and came back to the patrol car.

"We hadn't spotted it," he said.

"You say you *saw* the cut seat belt," the captain said.

"Yeah, yeah."

"You looked back there?"

"Yeah, sure I looked."

"What made you look there?"

"That's – where – my – little – girl – had – been. This is beating me down, Captain. Is there much more to go?"

"I hope not. Can we go on with it?"

"I suppose so. Look, it'd be easier if you asked me things."

The captain thought it over and said: "You found them shortly after you got the flashlight?"

"Yeah."

"You checked for signs of life?"

"Yeah."

"Did you move them at all?"

"No."

"Then you covered them?"

"Yeah."

"Where were the blankets?"

"In the wagon."

"In the back?"

"Yeah."

"You moved stuff to get to the blankets?"

"Yes."

"Had anything been disturbed back there?"

"I don't think so."

"The tailgate is worked by the ignition key?"

"That's right."

"Did you get the key from the ignition lock?"

"No, I had it on me."

"Was there a key in the ignition lock?"

"Didn't notice."

"After that you went to phone 43 and called us."

"Yes."

"And that's *all* you did?"

"Yes. That's all."

"Okay. Thank you, Mr. Grant. By the way, that oil they threw at you, how did they do it?"

"They had some kinda containers."

"How soon after that did you stop?"

"I dunno. As soon as I could when I saw it wasn't cleaning off."

The captain got out of the patrol car and instructed one of the troopers to search for the containers. Then he and the big detective began examining the ground ahead of the wagon. Presently the big one returned.

"We'd like you to show us where the struggle took place."

Grant went. He walked unsteadily.

There were very few signs and they were hard to see even with strong flashlights: scuffed grass, depressions, a skid mark as though someone had slipped.

"Think you can find where you were when you came to?"

"I dunno. It was over there and I came out toward the road."

"Let's go that way."

The captain signaled a lab man to come over and the four of them walked up the embankment and parallel to the throughway. By standing off from the higher grass they were able to play light along the edge where the mowing had ended. They found a vague opening, and what looked like crushed stems. The lab man went to it, followed the marks, and stopped.

"Something," he said.

He emerged carrying a length of rope in his gloved hand. "Grass is all crushed there. I'll mark it for tomorrow's shots."

"Did they tie you?" the captain asked Grant.

"No."

"Did you have rope in the car?"

"Yes. In the back seat. On the floor in a plastic bag."

"Any way of telling if this is yours?"

"I'd whipped the ends with fishing line."

The lab man examined the rope. It was whipped.

They walked back along the flashlit grass. On the slope, busy men with equipment were still moving like rescue workers under the close lights. Only there was no one to rescue. A tow truck had parked on the shoulder and was waiting.

While the captain talked to the troopers and then to the doctor, the big lieutenant showed Grant to the back seat of the detectives' car and got behind the wheel. Finally the captain got in and they pulled away. The last thing Grant was able to see was two men in white clothes lifting a green plastic bundle into the panel truck.

# 5

He thought it was some sort of conference room. It never occurred to him that it was also an interrogation room. There were large grilled ventilators but no windows, two long fluorescent fixtures, grayish pale green walls unadorned save for an uninformative diagrammatic map of the area and two color prints of landscapes stiff with consumer beauty that probably came from a hotel corridor. A large wooden table roughly in the center had a microphone on it and was pitted with cigarette burns and surrounded by institutional chairs that were supposed to be form-fitting. The room was clean but not neat, as neutral as a junkyard, a place no one could ever give character to, no one would stay long enough.

It made Grant feel it was all temporary, that he'd be home soon, just a feeling, not even a conscious desire, a normal feeling so basic and human that he couldn't prevent it from arising and holding together the three people who were, even now, still home.

"Mr. Grant—" the captain started to say.

"Call me Joe, will you?"

"All right, Joe."

The captain looked bonier in this light, his hair whiter, his face tired and distantly kind. The big lieutenant's muscled face was alert and alive, as if he'd much prefer to be jovial. He was smoking a thin cigar with a plastic tip and putting the ashes on the floor. There was no ashtray, an ashtray is a possible weapon. The captain, who was standing, continued.

"Joe, so far, from what's around, we haven't got much to follow up. They don't seem to have left anything behind. There's no usable tire marks. Chances are they left no fingerprints."

Grant's eyes went to the table in disappointment.

"Right now," the big man said, "you're the only one who can provide anything. That's why we're here."

"Yeah," said Grant.

"Did you get a good look at them?" the captain asked.

"No, not really."

"Tell us what you did see."

"Three bikes, that's for sure," he said and went on to describe their maneuvers.

"Do you know what kind of bikes?"

"No, I don't know anything about motorcycles."

"Were they big?"

"Oh yeah, big regular bikes, not like those little things."

"What kind of handlebars?"

"Just handlebars."

**34**

"Not those high ones? You know, like kids have on bicycles."

"No, just the bars you'd expect."

"Noisy?"

"Yeah, lots of noise."

"And they were able to go faster than you?"

"Very easily, all I could do was 80 without vibration."

"Did you notice their licenses?"

"I didn't have a chance to see them that much, they kept crowding me in front. I don't even know if they had licenses."

"Did you notice any color?"

"No. They were any color but white. Dark colors if anything."

"Did they have windshields?"

"I don't know. Could have. I assume they did, but I'm not sure."

"Saddlebags?"

"Could be. They looked bulky when they were in front of me."

"Any doodads, ornaments?"

"Yeah, lots all around, but I can't pick one out." Grant stopped and then added in self-reproach, "I should've noticed all that, eh? I knew they were trouble as soon as I saw them, I should've paid more attention."

"Ordinary citizen on vacation with his family," put in the lieutenant, "fighting three bikes. What's he supposed to do, take pictures?"

"I could have," said Grant, taking the rhetorical question seriously.

"While driving?"

"My wife is good at—" He stopped himself.

"It wouldn't have done any good. They would've known from the flash and they would've taken the camera." He fixed his muscled face on Grant's and said with a slight change of mood, "As it is, they probably don't know you're here."

"What do you mean?"

"How the hell do you think you got so far away from the car when you were out? They dragged you. And they weren't hiding you, they were hiding your body."

Grant thought about that and wished they had killed him.

"Yeah," he said, "that's probably the way it was."

The captain resumed the questioning. "Can you describe the three men?"

"Not them too well. Just some of what they were wearing." He told them as much as he could remember: the helmets, jackets, insignia, gauntlets, hair.

"Regular crash helmets?"

"Don't know. If they were, they were made over into what they had."

"Beards?"

"No, stubbles, like three, four days' growth."

"Goggles?"

"No, glasses, like sunglasses, the kind pilots wear, but not green, plain or maybe yellow, light yellow."

"Shooting glasses?"

"I wouldn't know."

The captain sat on one haunch on the edge of the table. "Did you see these three guys earlier?"

The question caused Grant to sift through his memory.

"It could be," he said reflectively, searching the floor for an image. "We'd stopped at the Howard Johnson's . . ."

"When?"

"It was getting dark, about nine o'clock. Sky was still bright."

"You had supper?"

"No, sandwiches, things. I bought some candy . . ."

He stopped again, his eyes looking at nothing.

"Oh, oh, Christ!" he moaned.

"Hang on tight, Joe."

"Yeah, yeah." His eyes were wet and his voice was broken but he retained his composure.

"When we came out," he continued, "I looked around, more gawking than anything else, and my eye caught three bikes in the other parking lot. Just a glance, I didn't pay much attention to them."

"No guys?"

"Oh yes, they were on the bikes. They seemed to be drinking something."

"Which Howard Johnson's?"

"The first one coming back this way, on the edge of town."

"We know where it is. Drinking, you said. What were they drinking?"

"I don't know. They were holding something white."

"What's at the other parking lot?"

"I'm not sure. Either a hamburger place or an ice-cream bar."

"Were they at the bar?"

"No, at the side of the parking lot, this side, I mean the Howard Johnson side, up against some kind of railing or low fence."

"Were they looking at you?"

**3 7**

"It's hard to tell. They were facing us."

"Joe, do you think they were the same guys?"

Grant mulled it over and shook his head. "I can't be sure."

"Did they follow you?"

He shrugged and shook his head again. "I wouldn't know." The pressure of the questions was becoming too much, he was beginning to imagine they didn't quite believe him.

At the look from the captain, the lieutenant left the room quietly. Cool air poured in through the open door, it made Grant shiver. He sat back hunched and folded his arms, leaning forward as if his stomach hurt.

"Do you think you'll catch them?" he asked.

"We'll try," the captain said. "With what we've got. They're long gone by now."

Grant looked down at his watch. "What time is it, Captain? My watch is broken."

"It's two-thirty."

"That late?"

"Yeah, the wee hours. Can I see your watch?"

Grant slipped it off his wrist and handed it to the captain. The glass was shattered and pieces were missing. It read 9:50. Grant wasn't making connections.

The lieutenant came back with two flimsy plastic cups of machine coffee. He gave one to Grant, kept the other. The captain showed him the watch.

"Joe, you got any idea what time these guys got to you?"

Grant sipped the coffee, rubbed his face.

"I had twenty-five miles to go, it was twenty to ten when I checked."

"Twenty-five miles to go where?"

**3 8**

"To the nearest exit. When they were behind us, when they first started bugging us. I figured I could make it to an exit, so I looked for signs, and one said twenty-five, but it wasn't much use, the damn car couldn't move . . ."

"Okay, Joe, okay."

They waited till he drank more coffee. Then, the lieutenant: "Let's suppose you broke your watch either in the car or when they hit you. Nine-fifty. Your call came in at 11:22. That's over an hour and a half later."

"Yeah, yeah."

"Part of that time you were hunting around in the dark. Got any idea how long?"

"No."

"Well, we could pace it off approximately. After you found them, Joe, and . . . and looked at them, what did you do?"

"What did I do!"

"Yeah, what did you do?"

"I folded. That's what I did!"

"What do you mean folded?"

"I sat down there and broke open. I cried. What the hell do you think I did?"

"Okay, okay, Joe, calm down."

"Well, you don't have to be so goddam stupid about it! What would you do, eh? Light a smoke and play it cool?"

"Probably the same thing you did," said the lieutenant.

"Joe," the captain cut in with authority, "we're trying to establish time. Lots of guys are going to get picked up. They're going to be asked to account for their time. And we've got to know what to look for. Okay?"

"All right, all right."

"Drink your coffee."

When he did that, the captain said, "I guess we can hang it up for now."

As they were making motions to leave, the lieutenant turned to Grant. "That fight you had with them," he said, "you remember how it went?"

"I ran right into him full tilt, I don't remember what happened after that."

"I guess that's how you got the blood on your right hand."

"I dunno. It's blank."

"Mind if I lift some of that?"

"No, I don't mind."

He took enough samples to leave the hand clean. He was all equipped to do it. Grant looked puzzled and still wasn't making connections. They left the room. And after the lieutenant got rid of his samples, they left the building and got into the detectives' car. Grant wasn't even curious.

They drove to a small motel that had some two dozen units and large neat lawns with evergreens planted along its wide curving driveway. The captain went to a door next to the office and rang briefly. A light came on and the sleepy owner appeared. He seemed to know the captain. He kept nodding his head at what the captain was saying.

Back at the car, the captain said, "Come on, Joe." Grant got out and followed him quietly into one of the units. He put the lights on and gave Grant the key.

"Get some sleep. We'll be back for you tomorrow."

"There's more to do?"

"Yeah. The site, the contents of your car, autopsy results. Sorry you can't go home, Joe."

"There isn't one to go to, Captain, not any more."

"Get some sleep."

He left.

Grant looked around the room idly as people do when they walk into a motel. He really didn't see anything. He had nothing with him, no car, no luggage, no people. He felt strange, remained standing, deciding vaguely to lie down. There was a discreet knocking at the door. He went over and opened it.

The owner, in a hastily put-on shirt, slacks, and slippers, came in carrying a towel-covered tray and pajamas in a store wrapper. He placed it on the dresser and revealed cheese and cellophaned crackers, ice, a small bottle of Scotch, utensils, and a card. He took the card.

"Could you sign, please?"

Grant signed.

"If you need anything, come to that door."

"Thank you," Grant said. "Thank you."

"That's okay," the man said, and left.

Grant opened the Scotch bottle and drank from it. The whisky burned and tasted bad and wasn't going to do anything for a while. He went to the bathroom and turned on the taps and stopped as he saw himself in the mirror: face drawn and eyes sunken, bruised and scuffed and scratched, hair mussed, and a look of faraway emptiness that had never been there before. He washed and went back into the room.

He sat near the dresser and drank from time to time until the Scotch was finished. Then he went to the bed and stretched out like a man expecting to get up at any moment. It was going to be a bad night. And there'd be more after that.

# 6

In early morning he woke up quickly and fully as if he'd never been sleeping, as alert as a man in danger, dimly grateful he didn't recall the dreams that woke him. He knew where he was and what had happened. He was aware of precisely where he had left things, the untouched food, the Scotch bottle, the unused pajamas, his state of dress and lack of luggage, the fact that he'd slept clad, on top of the bedspread. Everything was continuing unchanged, except that he was less emotional. He was at the mercy of what he knew, he couldn't alter his awareness, couldn't reduce the intensity of his consciousness.

His broken watch told him nothing. He figured it was about seven or eight o'clock, bright sun on the closed venetian, it had been a clear night. He went to the bathroom, washed as best he could without gear, combed his hair roughly with his fingers. His expression hadn't changed. The bruises on his face and what he could see of his neck were colored and painful. His legs and one knee ached, his arms were bruised and scratched, the back of his head throbbed. The pain didn't matter, it didn't seem to bother him or call for the usual careful attention. It was just there.

He left the unit and found the dining room, an airy homey place that tried to look like a restaurant and served only breakfast. A girl about nineteen was setting places at the tables. She smiled at him and he only nodded his head. Behind an abstract partition an older woman was laying out food ready for the hurry-up cooking she'd have to do when the customers came in hungry and eager for instant service. She didn't look up, she had nothing to do with the public and her manner said she didn't want to.

Grant stood at the counter and waited, and found himself obsessively speculating about the counter. His perception was acute and his mind raced furiously. The counter was also a showcase, it was handmade, beautifully fitted, and for that reason looked homemade, there weren't any punched-out metal strips and prefab plastic, and if it was homemade it was cheap and therefore not desirable in the opinion of many people because it showed that the man who made it for himself couldn't afford a factory-made counter that would make a restaurant look like a real restaurant and not like something out of the back woods, and all that was silly because considering skill and labor and materials it was a hell of a lot more expensive and difficult to make a showcase counter than to buy one, but people don't like the human touch, so to hell with this goddam culture, so let people think their stomachs are kitchen drains and their hearts pumps that can't feel anything and their brains computers that have programmed them, so when they're sick they go to an engineer and not a doctor, and to hell with him too.

"You're up early," said the owner. He had come in from a door that led most likely to his living quarters.

"Yeah, that's right. What time is it?"

"Half past six."

"I thought it was around eight. I like your counter."

"Made it myself. How you feeling?"

"All right."

"You can have breakfast in about ten minutes, the girl can give you coffee now."

"I'm not hungry. Do you sell razors and stuff?"

"No, I don't. I'll get you one when the drugstore opens. In the meantime, you're gonna sit down and eat."

"Well, thanks all . . ."

"Don't argue, you have to eat. I know."

That was the end of the conversation. The owner left on the last words, and Grant wondered just how much he did know. He sat at a table, the first one he came to, and the girl appeared immediately with coffee. She behaved like a smiling nurse, she must have been told something. He ordered the menu's No. 2 breakfast, the one with only one egg.

The familiar routine of morning allowed him to think more normally, and thinking more normally made him expect to see his wife and little girl. It was that simple and that abrupt. Coffee, cream, sugar, sunlight, them. He wanted to stop existing. A real and actual nothingness seemed better than all this, and he hungered for it. His face ached with the reflex to cry, but he was in public and he held on stiffly.

The too hot coffee surprised him and he went through

**44**

over-elaborate attempts to keep drinking it. That put him over that hurdle. He knew there'd be more and he feared them.

Tastelessly he ate the breakfast, went to his room and sat back on the bed, gazing at the wall. It was neutral here, a little confining without a car, and he avoided thinking about that. He had no place he wanted to go.

Time drifted by on its own without touching him. Noise of people in other units, distant but audible plumbing, tinny canned laughter from a TV set, cars leaving. The sunlight grew into a definite day and made everything busy outside. The owner came by with a packaged razor and Grant tried shaving, using the motel soap. He couldn't do his neck, it was raw and blistered.

Around ten o'clock a trooper arrived to take him somewhere. Nothing was said except "Mr. Grant?" and "Will you please come with me," said as a statement, not a question. Grant paid his bill and was given a card advertising the motel which, to be polite, he put in his pocket without reading.

They drove to what looked like a recently built county hospital. The trooper led Grant through corridors and into one of the examining rooms of the outdoor clinic. A chubby crisp young doctor about Grant's age was waiting for them.

"Dr. Detoli?"

"That's right."

"This is Mr. Grant."

The trooper left.

"Mr. Grant," said the doctor, "how are you feeling?"

"Fine."

"You look pretty bruised. Do you hurt?"

"Yeah, I hurt."

"Well, let's take a look at you. Strip down to your shorts and get on that table. I'll be right back."

The doctor left and Grant stripped and sat on the table. When the doctor returned, Grant said: "What's the examination for?"

"To find out how you are."

"I'm fine, I don't need an examination."

"Well, then, to determine the extent of your injuries."

"I don't need that either."

"The police need it."

"What for?"

"For the record, I guess, I don't know."

"All right, go ahead."

For a little over a half hour the doctor peered and pressed and measured, head, shoulders, back, knee, hands, asking only questions that dealt with what he was doing. Blood pressure, heart, vision, pain, memory. He wrote it all down on a long form.

"You're very tense," he said.

"Yeah."

"You got it from all directions. Those are burns on your neck, friction."

"Yeah."

"Getting any dizzy spells?"

"No."

"Okay, that about does it."

"Fine."

"You're going to hurt for a while. I'll give you something to take with you."

"No thanks."

"Take 'em anyway, tomorrow you might change your

mind. Look, Mr. Grant, they haven't told me anything. I've got no background on this, I figure you were in some kind of accident."

"No accident."

"Oh."

He gave Grant pills and instructions and wished him luck as if without medical attention things would go bad. The trooper was waiting.

This time as they rode Grant said: "Where are we going?"

"Headquarters."

"What for?"

"No idea. It's not up to me."

"You're just chauffering me around."

"I suppose you can call it that."

"What do you call it?"

"Nothing. Nothing at all."

"Are they looking for those guys?"

"What guys?"

"The guys last night. On the throughway. Don't tell me you haven't heard about it?"

"Yeah. There's a bulletin out."

Headquarters was a big three-story building with a severely roman sign on the lawn explaining its function, two flagpoles, a long parking lot that was all driveway, grass that was always trim and beds of flowers that had a lonely official look.

Inside, Grant was left alone at a reception counter in the lobby, unlooked at by the man in uniform, who was busy at a desk with two phones and a stack of files. In line with the man's desk were two metal cabinets and over the top of one of them about three inches of shotgun muzzle stuck out. The man sat upright on a stool, a cushioned chair idle behind him, in order to accommodate the heavy pistol on his hip. His eyes never came to Grant. It was like a badly directed movie, he felt, but then so was last night. The wall clock with a sweep second hand said it was half past eleven.

Two men in sport shirts came in, one strapped with two cameras and a gadget bag. They spoke to the man at the desk, who obviously knew them.

"When do we get that story?"

"Ask the captain."

"Are you holding the husband?"

"What husband?"

"What husband! Like nothing happened, uh?"

"The captain," said the man at the desk emphatically, "wants quiet on this for a while. When he's ready, you'll get the story."

The reporter sighed and shifted about nervously, he was the go-ahead type. He turned to Grant and looked him over.

"You in a fight?"

"No."

"Oh. What happened?"

"Nothing."

"You here making some kind of complaint?"

"No."

The swing doors that led to a corridor opened a little but the officer saw the people in the lobby and went back in.

"Some kind of report?"

"No."

"Well, what are you doing here?"

"I need some information."

The phone on the desk rang, the man answered it with grunts.

"What kind of information?" said the reporter.

"About traffic regulations."

"You were in an accident?" The reporter was signaling the photographer.

"No."

The man at the desk said, "Okay," and pointed to Grant. "You can go on in. Through there."

Grant walked away before the photographer could take him. In the corridor behind the swing doors a young officer was waiting.

"I'm Sergeant Littledale. You're Mr. Grant?"

"Yes."

"This way, please."

They went along corridors, down one flight of stairs, along more corridors, and stopped in front of a heavy metal door, painted white. The officer hesitated.

"Uh . . . I'm with the lab," he said. "Your car's in there, and we'd like you to check the contents in case anything is missing. Okay?"

"Yeah," said Grant. It was better than the reporters. He braced himself for it as the officer slid the big door open.

The place looked like a diagnostic center, deliberately cleaner, tools gleaming as if new, supplies in neat order. Two men in white coats were working on a green Cadillac, it seemed to be bullet-ridden. The station wagon stood by itself like a dealer's display on the pale gray floor. Grant went to it and stood staring.

The officer started the work by asking for Grant's key and opening the tailgate. They took everything out, spread

**4 9**

it in reverse order on the floor, luggage, tents, camping equipment, camera in tote bag, a few toys, kit bags, last-minute odds and ends. Grant looked at it, and without a word began putting it all back. When they were finished he spoke.

"It's all there as far as I know."

"Okay." He paused and added, "Uh . . . there's a few more things."

"Oh. Well."

The officer went to the front passenger seat and removed a purse. He handed it to Grant.

"I don't know everything my wife had in here." What ordinarily would have been a source of humor wasn't lost on him, it was only painful.

"Money," the officer suggested.

Grant looked, flipped through some bills.

"It's here," he said. "I don't know how much she had. They would've taken it all."

"Car keys?"

"Didn't you people look?"

"Yes. There were none."

Grant handed the purse back, the officer put it in the wagon. Grant searched his own pockets, took his jacket from the car and searched it.

"Can I keep the jacket?"

"Sure."

"I can't find the other set of keys. I know I left them in the ignition when it happened."

"Okay. You want me to get that window repaired?"

"I suppose so. Is there time?"

"More'n likely. At least they can take the busted glass out."

"Fine. Go ahead. I'd appreciate it."

"I'll leave word at the desk where the car is."

He led the way out and back up into the corridors, swung away from the lobby, up to the second floor. At a door marked "25" the officer said, "Wait here a moment please," knocked and went in. After a few minutes he signaled Grant and left.

He walked into an airy office and recognized the two detectives. At a desk was a stout balding man with bifocals who was introduced as Dr. Rorsche, the coroner. At another desk was a thin middle-aged woman with a serious but pleasant face who could have been wearing a gray wig. They didn't introduce her, she was a stenographer.

"For the record this time," the balding man said, "we'd like you to recount last night's chronology of events beginning with—" he looked at some papers—"what you noticed at the restaurant at approximately nine o'clock in the evening."

"I did all that last night, for these two men."

"That was to enable them to proceed with their investigation," the man said patiently. "Now what is required is your deposition, that's a signed, sworn statement to be used in court when and if the guilty party or parties are apprehended."

Grant nodded and took the oath. He sat back and began to face the whole thing all over again. He spoke in a monotonous low voice, trying to keep his feelings under control. In the difficult places he had to speak louder to keep his voice from breaking. Captain Sparrs stood looking out the window, the lieutenant sat to one side of Grant and looked at nothing. The balding man listened attentively, scratching a few notes every now and then. Grant felt as if he were talking to no one, creating an official document to be used in some self-running process that seemed beyond the people involved. Without paper, what was so real to him could not be made real, much less true, to them. Without properly made paper, those three toughs would never come to justice. The apparent indifference of the gray-haired stenographer began to irritate him, he wondered of the persons in the room if long experience had dulled their feelings or only made them capable of hiding them. When his narrative came to the arrival of the police, the coroner nodded and held up his hand. The stenographer gathered her materials and left.

"Mr. Grant," the coroner said, "I regret that you have to go through all this, but in view of the circumstances your statement becomes rather important."

"What circumstances?"

"Other than your account there is no testimony or confirming evidence of the presence of the three men on motorcycles."

"There's no evidence!" said Grant. "Look at what they did!"

"I know, I know. But you must realize that the crime itself does not automatically point to three men on motorcycles."

"But they left tracks."

"Crushed grass, with nothing to say how it was crushed or when. Which indicates the importance of your testimony. Your own wounds indicate that *a* struggle took place with some person or persons, and again your testimony makes the difference. But of themselves your wounds do not prove *who* your aggressors were."

"You found nothing out there?" said Grant to the captain.

"Nothing. Just the milk cartons on the side of the road. You didn't see them when you went to the phone?"

"No."

"Tell me," the coroner said, "do you remember how the blood got on your right hand?"

"No, I don't."

"The presumption is that you acquired it in your struggle with your assailants."

"I must have, but I don't remember, they knocked me out."

"And," the coroner continued, "your wounds according to medical opinion were probably not self-inflicted."

"Self-inflicted . . . ?" Grant's voice was a low angry murmur.

"A reasonable assumption is that you continued to struggle even after you'd lost awareness, or that you are undergoing, quite commonly, a post-traumatic amnesia making you unable to remember events just prior to losing consciousness."

"Yeah, great," said Grant, "but why all this nit-picking?"

"The blood on your hand is the same general classification as your wife's. It is probably a coincidence, it's a fairly common type."

In the silence they all watched him closely. He knew now of course that they'd been building up to this. He felt let down by these men. He wasn't angry, just alone and disappointed, surrounded by society.

"That chauffeur this morning," he said, "was also a guard, eh?"

"Not exactly."

"Then what the hell was it?"

"Look, Joe," the captain said, "I don't know you. I don't know you at all. And in this job I can't pass up the chance you might be some kind of nut. Nothing personal. It was a check-out."

"And?"

"I believe your story."

Grant stared at the floor. He began to realize that his knowledge and his pain were uniquely his own. It was inside, it would have to stay there. There was no way to share it or communicate it. Proof was nothing compared to knowing, and justice would judge without really knowing. Considering their work and what they had to think, they hadn't dealt too harshly with him.

"Dr. Rorsche," he said, "I guess the autopsy is completed?"

"Yes."

"Tell me about it."

"Do you feel up to it?"

"I'll never feel up to it, but I want to know."

The doctor adjusted his glasses nervously. "There was a struggle," he said, stumbling through a choice of words, "of some proportion. Both . . . bodies had a lot of bruises. The condition of the girl's bruises is compatible with their having had to cut her seat belt. She must . . ."

"She what . . . ?" said Grant fast.

"I was going to give the opinion that she must have been too frightened to move and must have clung to the belt. Are you sure you want to . . . ?"

"Yes."

"They were molested."

"You mean raped?"

"Yes."

"They could have been unconscious at that time. Bruises about the head and neck indicate that they probably had

to be subdued. Which means they were, mercifully, unconscious when they were killed."

He took his glasses off as though he'd finished with it.

"Go on," said Grant.

"That's all, really."

"Knives," he said. That was all he could bring himself to
say.

"Look, Joe," said the captain, "you can get this some
other time when you're feeling calmer."

"No. Now."

The glasses went up again.

"The condition of the wounds indicates that the lower
wounds were made first and next the throat wounds."

"Lower wounds."

"Yes, Mr. Grant. I don't have to go into detail. It was an
act of sexual savagery. And at the moment it's unwise of
you to pursue this."

"*It* is pursuing *me*. I have no choice."

"That's precisely why it's unwise."

"Yeah."

The doctor sighed, slipped off the glasses, and added in
almost helpless human tones, "Time, Joe, for god's sake,
give yourself some time, let it settle."

"All right," said Grant. Time couldn't change a thing,
but he understood the logic of the doctor's remarks.

The coroner started to collect the papers on his desk.
They all got up.

"When," said Grant, "are you going to release the bodies?"

"Any time you want. Do you want me to make the arrangements?"

"What arrangements?"

**5 5**

"With the undertaker. We have a man who's good . . ."

Inwardly Grant gaped at himself in surprise: he hadn't thought of an undertaker or a funeral, he had only wanted to get them out of official hands, to have them under his care, to have them— The thought drifted into nothing.

"Yes," he said, "could you do that?"

"I would advise against having the usual wake, Mr. Grant."

"Oh?"

"It attracts the curious and even ordinarily well-intentioned people will ask too many questions. It will only add to your burdens. Mr. Doyle will know how to handle it."

"Doyle."

"The undertaker. Here's his card."

Grant took it, thanked him automatically, and left with the two detectives. At the desk in the lobby the officer with the guns inquired after him and gave him a note which read: Treer & Mast's Autowork, Ltd.

"Is the car still downstairs?" asked Grant.

"I'll check." He talked into the phone and looked at Grant. "It's gone."

"Can you get me a cab?"

The officer nodded.

"Good luck, Joe," the captain said. "We'll let you know if anything develops."

"Yeah," Grant said, and went outside to wait for the cab.

# 7

He went to Treer and Mast's Autowork, where he identified himself, dodged obvious questions and took his luggage from the station wagon. About a block away he paid off the cab in front of a car-rental agency, used a charge card to get a big green sedan, and with the help of a local map he went back to last night's motel, re-registered, dumped his luggage and went out immediately in search of lunch. He wanted to be nowhere. None of these places meant anything to him and the one that might, back home, was a full-empty center around which he was still revolving.

He stopped at a lunch counter in a shopping center, a busy place, hot and dusty, cars behaving like pedestrians, the sameness that was repeated all over the continent, alien with an air of meaningless familiarity. A good place to non-exist. It matched his feelings. He ate the food as if it was nice clean body fuel, which was the idea behind it anyway. Something wrong there, he thought, with a vague intention of exploring the notion some day, but it vanished as he watched the people and the overworked waitress, who was trying to smile as if happiness went with the job. He left her a large tip, money as a gesture, unyielding to message, would she think someone had understood, or had not noticed and was satisfied, or had just made a mistake, or had no other change and didn't want to look cheap. Despite himself his mind kept darting into everything, free to drop roles, illusions, pierce through appearances, unable not to see, touch the aching human. Mentally he tried to shrug it off.

In a phone booth on the walkway he looked down the list of Doyles and found the one he wanted. A receptionist got Mr. Doyle on the line and Grant tried to cut through the preliminaries but the man was being professional. Grant listened to the sympathetic words and waited for the business end to come up.

"I'll be in to see you later about details," he said finally. "What I'd like to know now is when will they . . . when will the wake begin."

"I see. Of course," said Doyle, solemnly polite. "Suppose we agree on nine o'clock this evening. We stay open till ten. However, I don't imagine there will be many people, and in that case we can perhaps stay open a little longer for you."

"That'll be fine, I'll be in later."

It was hot in the booth. He got out and stood by the open door. His next call wasn't going to be easy.

He watched the shoppers going by, mainly women and children, heard the cars and trucks and the continuous music to shop by, and tried to fashion words that would announce his news to someone who, like him, cared and loved with open helpless vulnerability. They were supposed to be away on a holiday, camping. The one phone call would change and shatter everything. Her father and mother. His in-laws, whom he liked, and in fact, now, loved. In a way he felt relieved that his own parents had died years ago. Time went by to ten, fifteen minutes and more, the thing happening in his mind but he doing nothing to make it actual. At last he shut himself in with the phone again and sank his dime in the slot.

He was put through to the right long-distance operator and he asked her to find the number of the firm called Consultants Twenty-Four and to reach a Mr. Steven Harrison, the vice-president. It took about a minute, he paid, and it was happening.

"Steve," he said, "it's Joe."

"Joe?" And then in go-ahead emergency tones, "What is it?"

"Something happened, Steve, something very bad. Get yourself ready, 'cause I can't nice it up for you."

"How bad?"

"As bad as can be."

"Sue and Patty . . . ?"

"Yeah. They're dead."

Silence, and a slowly uttered oath. "What happened?"

"It was on the road . . ."

"Did you have an accident?"

It was too unreal. He was in a glass cage surrounded by a shopping center in a strange town on a sunny day talking over miles of wire about things that were breaking two men and would break even more people.

"Steve," he said, "I can't kid you and I can't talk about it

**59**

too long. We were attacked, three guys, I was knocked out, and they did the rest, it was last night. I'll give you the story when you get here, I've been over it a million times with the cops. Maybe it's best to tell Betsy it was an accident, anyway at first. It's not . . ."

"All right, Joe, take it easy. Where are you?"

He told him, and explained how to get to the motel and to Doyle's.

"Get something for Betsy from her doctor. It's just crazy, Steve, just crazy."

"All right, all right, we'll be out there as soon as we can."

"There's no hurry, believe me. I mean . . ."

"I know what you mean."

"If you can't find me, call the cops, the troopers, I'll be with them, a captain called Sparrs."

"All right. And you, Joe?"

"I'm fine."

"You been eating, sleeping?"

"Yeah, enough. See you later."

They hung up.

He left the booth feeling as if he had committed an evil. Talking with Steve usually meant visiting with the family, lots of kidding and good talk, the feasts that Betsy served, beer and football on TV. And it was still all there in the act of phoning. It dogged him until he got to the rented car, where he had to concentrate on the unfamiliar dash. He resented the car but he was grateful it wasn't the wagon yet.

As promised he went to see Mr. Doyle, a big cheerful blond man with pink glasses who was helpful and practical, and without unnecessary unction or delay they got

**6 0**

through the details of coffins and hearse and back-home burial and price.

From there as though responding to a deep need for ritual he went to a men's shop and bought a suit, shirts and ties. They hadn't been included in his luggage. He left wearing the new clothes and felt more able to carry out the significant but ineffectual actions he could not avoid. At a nearby jeweler's he bought a cheap large-faced watch.

He found the throughway and joined the traffic following last night's route. Day was different, not ominous, not painful yet, things visible and bright, greens and hills and a clear warm sky, white on pale green signs pleasantly giving information, another civilization entirely, a way of life that was meant to work, to be clean and perhaps permanent. It was not without illusion. It was a dream that needed policemen to keep it from becoming a nightmare.

"Hayestown, 25 mi.," the sign said innocently. It didn't upset him. He half expected an emotional tug but he simply registered the message along with its significance. He didn't realize he was already at a high pitch of feeling. He checked the odometer and his watch, doing 60, and set the signal for a right turn-off. Cars passed him, drivers looking for his trouble because it was no place for a normal stop. He watched the half-mile phones, the fence, slowed more and more, saw the clearing and turned off and stopped. He was there.

It looked like a completely new place. Only his knowledge made it the place it was. Some of the grass was crushed and trampled, probably from the morning's investigation, but apart from that it was just an embankment, part of the scenic throughway. Not twenty-four hours ago. Living grass. He got out and walked slowly in the direction he knew. An earthen spot showed where the lab men had taken away the turf. He looked at it, knowing. He made no examination, no search. Professionals had been at it. This was no movie, no great clue was going to emerge. Just what was there, and it was all there was: late-afternoon sunshine and countryside and traffic on the road and something like an echo of a prayer in some region of himself, a desire embracing he knew not what. They were at a place called Doyle's, he knew, but they were here more than anywhere else. Presence, memory, love, a part of him, always.

He walked all over the area as if he had to bring presence to it and slowly went back to the car and sat in it with the door open looking at nothing in particular.

Over an hour later a patrol car came alongside him.

"Anything wrong?" the trooper asked.

"Nothing wrong. Just sitting."

"People keep reporting a car in trouble. We'd appreciate it if you kept moving."

"Sorry, didn't realize people would report it."

"Well, it's really against the law. Do you have a reason for being here?"

"It's all right, I'm going."

"This is a rented car, eh?"

"Yeah. How did you know?"

"From the license. May I have your name, please?"

"That won't be necessary, I'm leaving."

"I'd like it anyway, from your driver's license, please." The tone was firm and final, and Grant produced his license.

"Sorry," the trooper said, "but things have been happening."

"I know."

"I'll have to check you out. May I have your keys?"

Grant gave him the keys.

"Have you been in a fight?"

"Yeah. Look, ask Captain Sparrs about me. It's okay."

"We'll see."

The trooper went to his car and talked into the microphone, waited, talked again, and came back to Grant, gave him keys and license. He looked serious, perhaps sympathetic.

"Sorry," he said. "You could have told me."

"Would you have believed me?"

"You got a point there." Then: "If you're going back in, I'll take you to a U-turn, save you driving all the way to Hayestown."

Grant nodded. He followed the patrol car, took the turn and was honked at goodbye. Lots of action, after the event. He didn't blame them, no one can prevent tragedy. But it was like going to an empty theater and trying to reconstruct the play. Only the actors can do that, if you can get them all together. It was an idea he didn't quite notice, but it was beginning to take shape.

In town he stopped at the elegant bar-and-dining-room of a huge motor hotel and sat in a corner feeling hidden until his eyes got used to the gloom. He drank Scotch to no effect and couldn't decide on supper. It was now close to seven o'clock. He felt time pulling at him, drawing him on to more unwanted events. He ordered more Scotch and a sandwich, was told he couldn't eat in the bar, but a dollar bought him the privilege. When it came he ate half of it, tried more and couldn't, finished the drink, indicated to the waiter that payment was on the table, and left. Another oddball.

He went to his own motel and sought out the manager

**6 3**

to book a room for a Mr. and Mrs. Harrison arriving shortly. The manager gave them one next to Grant's and told him that Captain Sparrs had called and left no message except to call him back. Grant did that on the manager's phone, there were no phones in the units, and learned that they wanted him to go somewhere with them, no details, typically. He said he'd go if it wasn't going to take too long. When he hung up he turned to the manager and pointed to the registration card.

"You want to ask them to wait for me till I get back?"

"Sure thing."

He saw the newspaper on the counter as he was about to leave. His actions indicated he wanted to take it along, but before he could ask, the manager said, "They didn't cover it."

"There was a reporter at headquarters this morning. He had a photographer with him."

"They probably saw Captain Sparrs," said the manager, "and he asked them to keep it quiet."

"Would they do that?"

"For Sparrs, yeah."

"Why would the captain want it quiet?"

The manager rubbed his chin and looked as if he were trying to make up his mind about Grant.

"Well," he said, "if the people who got to you think you're all dead, they're gonna feel a lot freer, a lot surer of themselves. And that may give Reggie a break."

Grant presumed that Reggie was Sparrs.

"It might give me a break too," Grant heard himself say, with more of the idea taking shape.

"Yeah, you won't have them crowding you for news."

"You seem to know Sparrs pretty well."

**6 4**

"Some. I worked with him for fifteen years."

Grant almost grinned at this reticent man.

"No phones in the units."

"Cuts down on overhead," said the man.

"Cuts down on a lot of things," added Grant, feeling like grinning again.

He left and went to his room.

Sparrs and Ketner arrived just as he was emerging from the washroom after showering, clad in shorts and on his way to his clothes. They exchanged neutral greetings, nothing much was new, nothing much was being said. Grant reached for the dress shirt.

"Oh," said Sparrs, "could you dress as you were last night."

"Okay, but I'm expecting my in-laws, then, you know, to Doyle's."

"This won't take long."

"You playing mousy with me again?"

"No-o-o," said Sparrs in a long syllable, "I've already told you about that."

"But you're not telling me anything else."

"Habit," said Sparrs, filling in time, "years of habit. An investigator who talks gives people ideas, lets loose all kinds of minor information that he can't control, and interferes with the very job he's trying to do. The short of it is he buggers things up."

"Yeah. Makes sense. Surely you can tell me where we're going."

"This time, yes, 'cause I don't want you to get rattled. We're going to Howard Johnson's."

"Oh." It was soon going to be twenty-four hours. "You think it's worth it?"

**6 5**

Sparrs shrugged. Grant finished dressing.

At Howard Johnson's they parked where Grant had parked the night before, he and Ketner sat in the same booth while Sparrs talked with the manager. Presently he joined them, and the same waitress came over, this time not smiling. She remembered the nice family and had noticed the blue-eyed little girl, and Sparrs cut her off, had her ascertain the time within minutes and let her go. The cashier remembered the M & M's and that the little girl had not made a fuss about the candy. She confirmed the time.

Silently they went to the parking lot and stood by the car.

"Do you need me for all this?" said Grant.

"They fixed the time for us, they remembered," said Sparrs. "And now they'll remember us as well as the time. It's not just you guessing all alone."

"So?"

"So your three guys probably didn't bother to set their watches. They probably had no idea of the time, and gave no thought to it until much later. Which means they're gonna invent horseshit alibis to cover three, four, five hours. Okay. So when we hear that tune, we start pressing. Where did you see them from here?"

Grant pointed. They went over to the one-board white railing that separated the two parking lots. The detectives examined the general area, found nothing, turned to see the car which was plainly visible.

"When the lights come on," said Ketner, "this spot's not gonna be too well lit."

Sparrs grunted.

"Let's talk to the man."

**6 6**

There were five customers at the Dairy-Bar and a car was pulling up. Sparrs went to the glassed-in front and poked his identification through the serving slot. The man inside looked at it. He was short, tanned, jowly, and completely bald. His spotless white shirt gave him an air of surgical cleanliness. He nodded to Sparrs, spoke to a tall plump, rosy-faced, breasty young woman, also in germicidal white, a good advertisement for a milk bar, and came out the back way. He wasted no time on civilities and spoke only to Sparrs.

"Pin it down," he said, as if he were tired of being questioned by long-winded indirection.

"Last night, about nine, three wild guys, on motorbikes, over there."

"Yeah, but they came earlier, like eight. The sun was still up."

"Earlier?"

"That's what I said."

"And stayed?"

"No. They left. Then they came back. I kept an eye out for trouble. I gotta protect my Jeannie."

"Get their license numbers?"

"Didn't get that close."

"What kind of protection do you have?"

"It's okay, I'm all fixed up."

"The first time: did they buy anything?"

"No."

"How about the second time?"

"Yeah. Two quarts of milk."

"In cartons?"

"Yeah."

"Brand?"

"Home-Rich."

"Did they all come to the counter?"

"No. Just one."

"What d'he look like?"

The man guffawed.

"Look like? Hell, hair, funny painted helmet, big glasses, gloves, he took one off to pay, bare arms with junk painted on, maybe tattooed."

"Would you know him if you saw him again?"

"Hell, no."

"Why not?"

" 'Cause there was no *him* to know, just this clown thing, you know, and they're all like that. Crazy bastards, they even poured some of that milk out."

"Over there?"

"Yeah. I thought maybe they were gonna start throwing it at each other."

"What makes you think that?"

"They were giggling and horsing around and one guy choked on the milk at something funny. Then they got very quiet."

"Why?"

"How the hell should I know? Who knows what a punk feels?"

"I mean, did something catch their attention?"

"Don't know. Couldn't see. You wanna step in there and take a look at the angle I had?"

"It's all right. What sort of bikes?"

"Big, that's all I know. Not the small Jap things."

"The Japanese make the big ones too."

"So?"

"What happened next?"

**6 8**

"Nothing. They started up and went to the gas station over there, Frank's, the Shell. I kept watching."

"Why?"

"They weren't gone yet. And they didn't go to the pumps. So I figured if Frank's in trouble I'll go and help."

"And?"

"Nothing. They bought oil from the rack."

"How do you know that?"

"I was over there when I closed up and got gas and spoke to Frank. We kinda keep an eye out together."

"What did they do with the oil?"

"Took it with them."

"They didn't open the tins?"

"Nope."

"Which way did they go?"

"Down there, toward the throughway."

"Did they come back?"

"Not here."

"Any more bikes come by?"

"Maybe, can't be sure. I spot them when they stop."

"What time do you close?"

"Eleven, midnight if it's good."

"What time did you close last night?"

"Midnight."

"Okay, thanks. You didn't ask me what the trouble was."

"They never tell me, so I've stopped asking. You do it your way, and I'll do it mine. Then everybody's happy."

He left. It was over for him.

The man at the gas station had nothing new to add. Driving back to Grant's motel, Ketner said, "To hell with vigilant citizens. They had it in their palms, Captain."

"Yeah, surrounded by two dozen thumbs."

**6 9**

"Bet he has a sawed-off in a milk can."

The sun was gone behind the low hills when they reached Grant's motel. The sky was bright with the still strong declining light that caught the occasional bundle of red and white clouds. To Grant the fine weather was only a reminder.

"I shouldn't have come with you."

"I know. These things take time to end, and we're not letting it end. I'm sorry."

"It's not just that, it's . . . hell, I don't know what it is."

He was functioning despite fatigue and pain and emotional exhaustion, like the battle-weary who sleep as they walk.

Sparrs thought something over and spoke. "One of our men picked up something on a fluke. Drugstore here in town, stays open most of the night. Seems a motorbike type bought large Band-Aids, aspirin, the APC kind, and antibiotic ointment. Along about midnight. Could be just coincidence, but it got me thinking. You might have hurt one of them. It would account for the blood on your hand."

Grant's eyes drifted sideways as he tried to summon memory but things were blocked out by the bigger facts.

"Don't work at it directly," said Sparrs. "If it's gonna come, it'll come on its own. Good luck."

Grant watched the car curve almost silently past the evergreens and onto the highway, where it disappeared into the non-home countryside. Steve and Betsy would be arriving soon, from home. He went in, to change and get ready for them.

# 8

"It's awful, Joey, just awful."

She hardly said the words through her crying.

"I know, Betsy, I know."

He held her and looked at the ceiling in an effort to stem his own tears. She was gray-haired, green-eyed, with a clear complexion and tiny lines about her eyes and mouth, dignified and soft, matronly in her early sixties, the picture of benevolence.

"I told her what you told me," Steve said. "A rigmarole just isn't in the picture."

He was tall and thin, sparse-haired, even-featured, his daughter's father except that his brown eyes were now hard and hurt. Grant could hardly look at him when they first arrived. He had got them in the unit swiftly and smoothly, and had gone to Betsy immediately. Human contact was the only possible protocol.

Steve prepared drinks from the makings he had brought,

Scotch, ice, water, brandy. He sloshed the liquor around as though to neutralize its normally festive connotations. Every action was like an oath.

He led Betsy to a comfortable chair, handing her some brandy and saying, "Before we go . . . there, you give the details, Joe, all there is. We're as ready as we'll ever be, goddam it."

He sat on the bed, near Betsy. Grant stayed on his feet.

"Drink your drink and take your time. Don't mind me, I just want to have it done with."

Betsy was deliberately not saying anything, and Grant knew that Steve was blustering his way around his grief. For their sake he had to keep himself under control or they would all be overwhelmed with sorrow.

He spoke his narrative in the terse phrasal manner he had heard Sparrs use. It provided him with a needed mode of expression, a rhetoric that filtered out emotion. For most of it he didn't move, twice he shifted position, once he made a drink. He overrode Betsy's breathed-in oh's and her heart-rending "Patty." Steve uttered oaths of surprise and disbelief. Grant's voice became flat and hard, wavered in places, and was normal by the time he was into the details that brought them to the present moment.

The two men looked at Betsy, who seemed able to retain her composure.

"All right," said Steve, "let's go."

They went in the rented car, in silence. Mr. Doyle, who had been waiting, came down the front steps and took them in through a side door. "Reporters," he explained.

They went down a narrow corridor at the back of the building and avoided a crowded wake that was going on in front. Presumably the reporters were there.

**72**

"They came early," said Mr. Doyle. "They want to collect background for when the story does break. I haven't told them anything."

When they came to a plain door at the end of the corridor, he apologized for not using the parlors and pointed out that this wake was very private and brief. It was good diplomacy, it prepared them for what was inside and obviated later criticism. He held the door open for them.

It was large for a private room, carpeted, heavy drapes over its two windows, lit by floor lamps, decorated by discreetly placed flower stands, vague statuary in two corners, no pictures. The larger coffin was along one wall, the smaller one was alongside it at its base. The woman and child were wearing similar blouses, with scarves. They had an intense, dead look.

The two men watched Betsy kiss her daughter on the forehead, then her granddaughter. Steve, at her side, held her as she cried into a uselessly small handkerchief. Grant touched him on the shoulder and turned away. They stood awhile, gazing inwardly, environed with collective memory, death and the life it had been, persons and remembered persons, the tones of personality echoing yet, the stillness, and the cause of it. Lament is an exercise of heart to keep it from breaking fully.

Delicately Grant dispelled the initial mood by gesturing to Steve and having the elderly couple sit down. Once seated, Steve put his head in his hands. Betsy touched his arm and said, "No," quietly and something incommunicable passed between them, a route retraveled. They had lost two children early in their marriage.

In the next hour little was said. The chattiness of the usual wake was unnecessary with just the three of them.

73

Steve paced the room periodically and muttered, "Those bastards," whenever his thoughts went in that direction. Betsy had never really stopped crying. Most of that time Grant stood by the coffins, his face grimly set and immobile, remembering and remembering, his emotions played out, time not meaning anything as the twenty-fourth hour arrived and left as unreal as the prettified room.

Some time past ten-thirty, Betsy in her soft dignified way stood up and went to the coffins. There she touched them both on the hands, turned and looked at the two men. "It *is* the last time," she said with tearful control. "Now." Reed bending, baffling the wind, strong without strength. The men went along with the ritual leave-taking.

The place was deserted and quiet, probably since ten o'clock, the regular closing time. Mr. Doyle appeared from the main corridor as natural as a tree in a forest and after a brief confirmation of tomorrow's schedule he escorted them out the front door and saw them to the car.

There was enough light traffic for Grant not to notice the inquisitive headlights behind him.

At the motel in the Harrisons' unit Grant and Steve had drinks, Betsy abstaining, and they tried to talk of other things, all of which sounded hollow and couldn't really work especially when sudden griefs appeared and when Steve began speculating about what the police might be able to do.

"Catching those men won't change things," said Betsy.

"They may never get them," Grant said.

A knock at the door interrupted them. They stopped short. From being alone to confronting others required adjustment. Grant, thinking it was the manager, swung the door open.

**7 4**

The man stepped inside immediately and let the photographer stand in the doorway. They were still in sport shirts.

"Good evening," he said as if he weren't used to the phrase but had decided to use his idea of a little elegance. "I'm Klidebur of *The Press,* also with Radio News. You're Mr. Joe Grant, is that right?"

Grant still held the door by the edge. He eased it forward.

"Not now, fellas. Sorry."

The photographer stepped back and took a picture in one quick flash. A camera can be intimidating. He got ready to take another.

"We'd like to know what happened. Was there . . . ?"

"You'd better talk to Captain Sparrs."

"He's not cooperating."

"He must have his reasons."

"Sure, but he's not telling us why, maybe you can."

"Sorry."

"The public has a right to know."

Grant looked the man over carefully. Another stranger, a new-style hustler with his foot in the door and an eye on a story he could print or work up dramatically on the air to entertain an imagined society with the thrill of bad news.

"Captain Sparrs," said Grant slowly, "is representing that public right now. Have it out with him."

"What's the matter, you afraid or something? Did he have you under arrest?"

"Out."

"Mister, we're gonna run it anyway, and you're gonna yell distortion, so you might as well give us the straight goods."

"See Sparrs. Good night."

**7 5**

"Look, the press is your best friend. You can't let the cops run everything, all they wanna do is hide things from the public. Come on, open up, a little good press won't hurt you."

Steve couldn't take it any longer. "Goddam it, you're not that dumb," he yelled. "There's nothing doing, so get out!"

"Who are you?" said the man. Get them mad, work them up, they may say something.

Grant took Klidebur by the arm and firmly eased him to the door.

"End of interview," he said.

"Okay, if that's the way you want it."

Grant closed the door before the last few words were out. Steve was still fuming. The episode had taken their minds off things.

"Horseplay," said Grant. "It's even got a funny side."

"I suppose it has," said Steve.

# 9

The next morning Grant hurried through the inevitable routine of washing, shaving, dressing, eating, very aware of them as some sort of obstacles, to what he did not know. He had slept an exhausted sleep and woke rested and fresh, feeling vaguely guilty about it because this was no time to enjoy anything even slightly. He noticed the Harrisons were up.

He delivered the rented car, walked to the repair shop and got his station wagon. They had fixed the driver's window and washed down the car inside and out. He didn't look at the luggage, not even a glance. He got in as if it were an empty sedan. At the motel they settled their bills and waited briefly. On schedule, Mr. Doyle and a driver arrived in a big hearse as solid as the establishment and with formal ease he explained the route, the meeting point if they thought it best to separate, he was going to drive fairly fast, suggested a gas check, and got them moving slowly through the town, lights on, and on to the through-way, where they gradually picked up speed, the hearse leading, Grant following, and then the Harrisons. At seventy they had to leave long distances between them. There was little traffic. It was nine-thirty, another sunny day.

He accepted the images and ideas that necessarily came to mind. He realized by now that there was no way of avoiding that sort of buffeting. It's better to let it happen, fighting it makes it happen all the more. So when he looked at the hearse, he really looked at it. The unused holiday things in the wagon, the salvaged candies the garage people had not thrown out and which he could not throw out, all this and him and the bodies up ahead. Buffeting. The hollowed-out, gouged-out home, the not-needed wagon, the slow growth of family interwoven with good habit and imperceptible links of love and a thousand physical things still there as expressions of all of them, atmospheres, and clothing, and the traces of work, and toys, and junk, and a purpose in life—and zero, and sunshine on a speeding pre-grave limousine. More buffeting. And those aging people behind him, love compounded into generations now abruptly not there, more growth by pain, the refusal to be bitter, no one is too old not to suffer a little more, or too young to begin. Look at it. Let it happen. He saw Sue and Patty in their last sharp terror when they knew that pain and unimaginable death were coming at them in the dark. His soul did everything to put himself there instead of them, like nerves twitching in a dream jumping into nothing. Raw powerless psychic effort. It passed. Back to the sunlit road, to the gleaming black and chrome in the moving distance ahead.

Outwardly the journey was uneventful. Cars came between them, but drivers, noticing the hearse and the head-lights, passed and left the small cortege to itself. One old car, unable to pass, drifted back in the left lane as though frightened. In a little over two hours, with a stop at a rest area, they were on the city's freeways and next on the congested streets and finally at the church where Steve—the Harrisons had been Catholics—had made arrangements by phone for a funeral service to be held. He had also called a few of his friends and some of Grant's, and these and others were now there, perhaps two dozen people who, to be helpful, kept their distance and communicated their sympathy by eyes meeting and small bows and tiny motions of the hand too brief to be a hearty greeting. Professional pallbearers, thanks to Mr. Doyle, did the carrying like culturally invisible prop men. The two coffins and their different sizes conveyed their own message, with ef-fect.

The service was realistic and not sad. To Grant, who had steeled himself for gloom, it came as a small welcome surprise. The priest was in white vestments and he and the whole ritual spoke of them, boldly presuming God, as if they were still in existence and somehow happy, and for the moment this met Grant's feelings and his aching de-sires. He wasn't getting religion, he was acknowledging a gesture that was more than just nice and that was also very seriously intended. The few people who went to the altar at the communion service touched each coffin on their way back to their seats, a personal act, not part of the ritual, and Grant, more buffeting, was his own touch in the dark on the embankment.

When it was over and they were outside and the hearse laden again, people broke out into talk and went to Steve and Betsy, while Grant, who didn't want this, excused himself and sat in the wagon, itself an object of curiosity and some horror. Presently they were moving again, a few friends joining.

Slow now, 25 m.p.h., concentrate on driving that slow, city and traffic distract from anything, even grief, into the winding asphalt paths of the huge cemetery, tall old seemingly eternal trees losing out against polluted air, headstones and mausoleums defying it, the imperceptible arrival at the open graves side by side with lowering devices over them, mats of phony grass hiding the piles of fresh diggings. A spoken prayer to God about them, a blessing, and down into the receiving earth, warm with early summer. You stand, and look and wonder, and can't move. An older man, short and paunchy, with an expressionless face, a friend of Steve's, gently squeezed Grant's upper arm and said, "Come on," and led him to the wagon, passenger side, and got in to drive, holding out his hand for the keys. Another friend was taking care of the politenesses with Mr. Doyle.

"We're going to my place," said the paunchy man.

Yes, yes, of course, that's smart, very wise, I can't take the next step, it leads home.

# 10

"I'll go with you, Joe," Steve said. "You shouldn't go alone."

"I want to go alone."

"Why make it worse for yourself?" said Harry Posser, the paunchy man. "I'll go. I'm the stranger. It'll make things easier."

They were in his apartment. Betsy said nothing. And Harry's wife, a slim woman in her late fifties, full of nervous energy, busied herself in the galley-like kitchen, ready to spring into helpfulness.

"No," said Grant, "thanks, I'm going alone."

He spoke gently, tonelessly. Harry shrugged and nodded his head, "Yes," as though he understood both sides, and Grant left the apartment. He felt grateful to them, they were right, of course, but he didn't want to impose more hurt on them and his own feelings excluded company. He rode the elevator down to the street.

It was mid-afternoon, the sun strong, everything hot. He

went to the still-unpacked station wagon, opened both doors, rolled down the front windows, lowered the back one and waited for some of the heat to blow out. He loosened his tie, took off his jacket and tossed it on the front seat over the package of melting candies. He noticed. There was nothing that was not noticeable anyway. It was like that.

He drove intently toward his own neighborhood, a ten-minute ride, the streets becoming more and more known, their meaning organized by one place, approached by one corner, which he took when he turned slowly into his own block. It was vivid with early summer, trees in May freshness, hedges here and there, and flowers almost everywhere, compact lawns, middle-class trimness, a few cars parked under cooling trees, noisy little boys down the street, the whole sweep of warm afternoon and greenness and shade and hot pavement. Small detached houses, all mortgaged. It was a street of families, mainly young families.

He stopped on his driveway and hesitated. A routine once unconscious now needed a separate act of will for each step: lever in park, keys, unlock the garage door, make sure no kids are in the way, or kids' things. He didn't look around for neighbors. He got the car in the garage and pulled the door down behind him.

It was cool and dim, only one small window on the north side. He set to work. Steadily he unloaded the camping equipment and piled it on large shelves he'd put up in a corner. Piece by piece it went, not with the rhythm of work, slower, or with the care of someone who would be using it again, heavy, dead weight for long storage, there seemed to be a lot of it.

Left was the borrowed equipment—the long lens in its carrying case and the children's tent—and three canvas suitcase-like bags and the large tote bag for the camera. These last he placed side by side as a porter would near the door that led inside the house. Time to go in, no more work to delay the moment.

He unlocked the door and propped it open because it was on a spring to close against car fumes. It was a small point. It gave into a wide vestibule almost the size of a small room that led one way to the kitchen and another to the rest of the house. He took two pieces of luggage and edged through the door, noisily it seemed to him, put them down and went back for the other two, this time letting the door swing shut. He put these down, straightened up and went by habit into the kitchen. He was in, under cover of work, and he was home without any cover at all.

Silence and dimness in the kitchen. The window was closed, as were all the others, shades partly drawn, the air not moving, the place clean, tidied, ready for them when they came back. He could hear the electric clock on the wall. The refrigerator came on. He was staying too long, there was nothing to do in the kitchen, it was the busiest place in the house, and his feelings churned, threatening, like the first signs of a sudden wind. Shelter.

He took the three canvas suitcases to the upstairs hall and set them down. He could see partly into four open doorways, the bathroom, two bedrooms, the spare room where he had a drawing board—he was an engineer—and lots of family junk. Don't stand there, keep moving.

The smaller bag he put in his little girl's room. He did it quickly and left quickly. And stopped, was stopped in mid-step. No good, you can't dodge it. He went back into her room and gazed at it. He knew each thing that was there. Let it hurt, Christ, let it hurt. There's more too. "You shouldn't go alone." The winds are up, there won't be any shelter soon.

Slowly he turned away into the hall, picked up the two bags and brought them into the other bedroom. One by one he placed them gently on the bed. He decided against unpacking, he couldn't bring himself to open her bag. Everything about the room indicated her presence, it filled his mind with the sight of her, as clear as a voice heard, response rushing forward. He let it happen, as he felt somehow it should, loyalty like tough roots, love that was all pain, and the sharpness of the moment diminished, ever less, and became something waiting in the background. Then the memory of the road and the dark. His face burned with held-back tears. No groaning to the night sky here. This was city, civilization, you can't be human here, to be human is to break down. Try it on the street and they'll arrest you.

He left the room, glanced through the little girl's doorway as he went by, took the stairs and found himself standing again in the kitchen, vaguely wondering what to do. But there was nothing to do, nothing that could be done. They were there in every way except actually. At every move he could hear them, at every turn he thought he'd see them, reminders at his elbow, presences just over his shoulder, the haunting patterns of his brain, the involving fullness of family that could never be undone, it could only be left to be, left in part behind.

A decision was taking recognizable shape, going against all his feelings, mocking every desire, the rational intruding—I can't stay, can't live here any more—guilt engulfing him as though he were abandoning them, collaborating with the hated event.

He was leaning with his forearms on the refrigerator by then. He opened it, more reminders, enough for a snack when they got back, took out a pint of beer, a glass from the cupboard, the opener, he wanted to stay, this was his home, he also wanted a gesture, an impossibly difficult act, a leave-taking. He poured the beer, took glass and bottle to the table and sat down, not relaxed, as they often had, talking, planning, conspiring for Patty's happiness. He was fully exposed now, the winds all around, no shelter. "Sue . . ." he said, actually addressing her, "Sue . . . I . . ." His eyes blurred with tears, he couldn't get his throat to work, he could only let his grief pour out.

And it did, for an uncontrollably long time, until exhausted, actually tired, he got up feeling not better but less bad, put the pile of tissues into the garbage can, and went upstairs and threw water on his face.

After that he got two suitcases from the workroom, went into the bedroom and filled them with suits and shirts and anything he could spot for immediate use. He took it all downstairs, phoned for a cab, and got his tie and jacket from the station wagon.

Then he waited inside the front door so that he wouldn't meet the neighbors and have to give them the news.

# 11

---

He went back to Harry Posser's apartment. They'd been waiting for him to return, but no one said anything at first, just looking at him and the suitcases was enough.

"I'm not going back," he said simply.

"Yes," said Harry, nodding his head heavily, "yes."

"It was too soon, Joe," Steve said.

"I couldn't stay anyway, now or later, it's . . ." He didn't complete the idea. He turned to Harry.

"Will you do me a favor, Harry?"

"Sure, what?"

"I borrowed two things for the . . . trip. They're in the car, at home."

"I'll get 'em back, just give me the addresses."

"The neighbors. They're good neighbors. They don't know yet."

"That's all right. I'll take care of it."

Silence for a while.

Grant's feelings were still raw. His eyes were glassy and he shuddered slightly from his recent weeping. He didn't try to hide it. Small talk was hard to make and other subjects of conversation seemed out of place. He saw the sense of having noisy wakes, with lots of people and chatter, and food and drink, and emotional eruptions, and even jokes.

He said as much with a half-tearful short laugh, and that was Harry's cue to start putting a little distracting action into the scene. He did it subtly, a round of drinks, comment on Irish, French, Polish, Jewish customs, kept the drinks coming, the talk alive, put the radio on FM not to get a pile of bad news, and didn't try to entertain Grant or cheer him up.

Around six-thirty, as though it were pre-arranged, and it was, they went out to supper. Harry picked a downtown hotel, where the dining room was busy, expensively quiet, where sounds weren't noises and you could talk normally over the background music. Grant said little. But he listened, or tried to. The alcohol wasn't having much effect. He was hyper-aware of things, the smoothly engineered eating place, the put-on refinement, the bought-and-sold social occasion, not festive, the wall of pleasantness around the workers, it was the closest that society could come to being community, strangers surrounded by strangers. He wasn't bitter, he was just seeing things as they are, or thought he was. Your taxes buy you a highway phone and cops in the night, your income buys you a hotel dining room for an hour or so.

They got through the meal, slowly, not eating all that had been served, and idled over coffee. They let the talk touch on the tragedy, but didn't allow it to be discussed at length. Betsy said once, "So young, so young," and wiped

**8 7**

her eyes with sad dignity. "Don't worry," growled Harry, "the cops'll find those guys." And then on to other things. And Steve remarked, "It seems impossible, doesn't it?"

Eventually Grant said, "Do you know anybody who could take things off my hands, you know, the house and all the rest of it?"

"Yeah, I know a few men who . . ."

"I'll do all that," said Harry, "one way or the other. We'll fix it up later."

"Whoever you get, put it on a business basis," said Grant, "fast and clean."

It was final with him, he was now nowhere, adrift, but he had made a decision, and that was better than being helplessly tossed about by the circumstances. They closed the subject, and Harry's wife began a short lecture on how many chemicals they had just eaten with their supper. She was serious, or seemed to be, and it drew laughs and gave them a chance to break it up. They went back to Harry's for Steve's car and the suitcases.

By the time the Harrisons arrived home with Grant, it was well after nine o'clock. It was a bad time, forty-eight hours had passed, and this was no public place full of distractions.

"Let's watch the goddam ball game," said Steve.

They did that for the rest of the evening, the men drinking Scotch and cursing the commercials and not once giving voice to their thoughts about Sue and Patty.

Grant stayed the night, only that night.

The following day he cashed his remaining traveler's checks, drew out more money, rented a big car, a blue sedan the man said was smooth at any speed, and drove around looking at apartments. He kept an appointment with Harry, gave him all his keys, the registration for the wagon, instructions about where to find legal papers, signed a pile of authorizations, and went back to keeping busy with his search. It was deliberate make-work. In late afternoon he found a furnished apartment about two miles from the Harrisons', far enough to be alone, close enough to be in touch easily.

It was on the tenth floor of a fifteen-story building overlooking a grown-over suburb. The view was a main artery with gas stations and shopping centers, a railroad line that snaked under roads and made earth-shaking noises, rows of repeated houses, small factories, traffic at peak hours, and filthy oily air that had blackened the aluminum window frames and made the screens look like old filters. The apartment was a workable kitchen, a small dining area that angled into a large living room, two bedrooms, and furniture in some sort of consistent "taste" that looked as if someone wanted to leave it behind. For the present he bought all their services and bribed his way into a month-to-month lease payable in advance. Everything the busy bachelor could want. It promised a new emptiness. Home is where you hang your self.

He settled into it as if it were a hotel room, by showering and standing around and putting clothes in the closet.

He ate a sandwich at the ground-floor lunch counter. It had a lot of teenagers but it wasn't a hangout, they kept the prices too high and there were enough citizens in the building to keep business brisk.

Later he called Steve to let him know where he was. Then he direct-dialed Captain Sparrs. He wasn't in. But Lieutenant Ketner was.

"Joe Grant, Lieutenant."

**89**

"Hello, Joe. How are you making out?" He spoke slowly and meant what he said.

"Not too bad. I moved."

"Yeah."

"Any news?"

"Not real news. We've questioned a lot of people. Nothing promising."

"Oh."

"Don't worry, you'll be told fast enough. What's your new address and phone number?"

Grant called them out, reading from the dial and from a card the manager had given him.

"The captain managed to keep it out of the papers. What about your end?"

"Nothing. I didn't talk to anybody. We'll be putting in an obituary to let our friends know. Those punks don't know where I'm from, and they don't read newspapers."

"Yeah, but they might now. We'll be in touch."

He hung up slowly as if he didn't want the contact to slip away. He resented the ease of phoning, on and off so suddenly, he would rather have driven for two hours to see Sparrs, that way he'd be doing something or at least have the illusion that he was. All of it was still with him, a fixed conscious knowing, always present, and charged with feeling like an obsession. He sensed vaguely that he might be in some sort of shock, but he couldn't see past it to diagnose it right. The facts were there, the feelings were there, both real, it all fit together in a tight bind, one giving energy to the other.

He turned on the TV set, low, barely audible. He didn't watch it, he only wanted something to hear besides his own thinking. He stretched out on the sofa and tried to

**9 0**

lose some of his alertness. The attempt only made him un-comfortable. He put his hands behind his head and stared at the top of the opposite wall. The ceiling looked dirty and he realized it wasn't his job to paint it. Canned laughter from the TV. The dialogue wasn't funny, and the laughter was having too good a time. He turned to see it. It was like looking at nothing. Orange faces. The big comic book. He went back to the ceiling.

Gradually he felt his fatigue, let himself sink into the sofa a little, and put his arms down. That big car can proba-bly move, I could be down there in less than two hours, with nobody on the road, later when it's really late, then what? get Sparrs out of bed? what for, just to tell him I'm there? don't be crazy—no, it's not crazy, you could drive around, looking, those guys come out at night, and a fast car's not a slow car, no vibration, no tail wag, no cargo, no passengers, no passengers to defend, oh, God, again. The fast car became a shimmying wagon and he became alert and his eyes gaped at the ceiling.

But the ceiling had gone and the TV wasn't there. He was staring inwardly at something he knew. His hands were gripping hair and his knee was striking teeth and his fingers were tearing into somebody's flesh.

He sat up. He was calm. But he felt very cold. He re-membered it all, even the chain, the curses, his own thoughts.

He wondered now if he would ever sleep.

# 12

At first light he was on the road. By not trying to sleep he had dozed on and off through the night, on the sofa and in an armchair and once at the dining-room table resting his head on his arms. In waking moments he kept his mind clear by making plans, reviewing what he knew, second-guessing police procedure, anything to relieve the pressure of his sorrow, to snap out of the chaotic dreams that came with partial sleep. He showered for a long time, ending with cold, and left the apartment without eating because he had neglected to stock up on food.

He appreciated the almost deserted highway without being able to enjoy it, and felt easy with the darkened peaceful countryside that emerged green and bright as time and pavement moved under him. In a deliberate test he brought the car to 100 m.p.h. and carefully noted its performance. After that he cruised at 70 and tried to watch the greening scenery.

He was too early at Sparrs' headquarters. A different officer was on duty behind the counter in the lobby, no rank on his sleeves, but the same gun barrel peered from over the metal cabinets. The man said Sparrs got to work early, but this was too early. It was not yet seven. Grant asked about a diner and went there to eat, came back and stayed in the car in the police parking lot. With the night and the drive behind him, he felt easier, dozed and finally fell asleep.

He was awakened by Sparrs.

"Hello, Joe."

It was hot. The sun was in full day. Grant looked at his watch. Nine-fifteen.

"You're late for work, Captain."

"No. I let you sleep."

"Oh." Realizing it was a good idea, he added, "Thanks."

"One of the men thought you might be a drunk."

"Fine place to sleep off a drunk."

"Yeah, but it's been done. Safest place in the world, some people think."

Grant thought of the shotgun leaning on the cabinet.

"It used to be," he said.

"It never was," said Sparrs, "not in this country. Let's go in."

The regular man was behind the counter, he didn't look at them. They got coffee from a machine on the way and went to Sparrs' office.

When they were settled, Sparrs said, "What's on your mind, Joe?"

"I got to remembering."

"The fight?"

"Yeah."

Grant gave him the details in careful chronological

**9 3**

order in case that might be of some importance. Sparrs listened until Grant was finished.

"Did you see his face?"

"Not very well. There wasn't enough light where we were."

"Anything about him?"

"No. I ran at him, and that's all I was thinking of doing."

"Nothing that can identify him?"

"I hurt him, he's marked."

"You hurt somebody," said Sparrs, mulling over another point of view. "It confirms that drugstore lead. The guy was bleeding, he bought bandages, or his buddy did. All we have on that is the fact of the purchase, nothing about the purchaser except that he was a bike rider."

"A guy with missing teeth and a gouged neck, that's enough to identify him. Hell, it's narrowed right down. Proof, right there."

"Yeah, it's proof, in a way. For you. But it's not evidence for a court."

"I was there, I had the guy in these hands."

"He'll deny it. Even if you could recognize him, same thing. You say he did, he says he didn't. It's no good."

"It shows he was there."

"Yeah, it might stretch that far, if they believe you instead of him. But it proves he got hurt, probably in a fight. It doesn't prove he killed anybody."

"Well," said Grant, disappointed, "at least it'll help you find him."

"We already have."

"You got him?! And the others?"

"*Had* them, Joe, had them. Don't get worked up. We brought them in for questioning, along with a lot of others."

"But what happened?"

"There was nothing to hold them on."

"But you know it's them."

"Sure, we think it's them. You can say we're almost personally certain it is. But there's no physical evidence to clinch it. The only thing that worked was that we didn't scare them away. At least that much."

Grant drank his coffee in silent frustration.

"Who are they?" he said almost casually.

Sparrs paused before answering, "Three guys. Late twenties. They seem to belong to some sort of loosely organized gang, but these three seem to travel together most of the time. Each one has a history, arrests, no convictions. No permanent addresses. No means of support. They use grass, booze, they're not choosy, whatever they can get. They're not just the ordinary sub-culture types, they run crazier than that. The gang, whenever it's together, they call the Shit Stokers. To them it has a variety of meanings. Very poetic."

Grant's face was drained of expression.

"I shouldn't be telling you this," said Sparrs. "Why not let it rest?"

"No. It happened. I want the whole picture."

"Why bother? There's no point to it."

"There's no point to anything else."

"Leave it behind, Joe. Go back to your job."

"I'm on vacation."

Sparrs sighed and sat back as if there was nothing more to say.

"Couldn't you get anything out of these guys? Did they have names?"

"Yeah, they had names."

"What are they?"

"Just names. It's not gonna mean a thing. One is called Leonard Stitte. He's the one with the bandages. They call him Len's Tit, or the Iron Tit, they get a big charge out of that. Nick Wafton, calls himself the Vike, short for Viking, right out of the comic books, or maybe the movies. Alex Oguire, O-g-u-i-r-e, they call him the Ax. That's it."

"Where do they live?"

"Here and there, they're always moving around."

"What did they have to say?"

"Nothing."

"Didn't they say where they were that night?"

"No."

"What about the milk bar and the gas station and the . . . ?"

"Nothing. You've got to understand. They're not going to do any talking. They don't have to. And there's no way to make them."

"They just said nothing, didn't talk at all?"

"They jabbered a lot, nothing came of it."

"But you had them! Right here!"

Sparrs didn't reply.

"I'm sorry," Grant said, "I want so damn badly to . . . I'm sorry."

Sparrs got up and went to a filing cabinet. He took out a crumbling audio tape container and from it a reel of tape. Without a word he threaded the tape into the machine on his desk, consulted a log sheet, set the counter and sped the tape to where he wanted it.

His voice came on, low-key, almost bored: "— . . . clear it up by telling us where you were two nights ago, Monday night.

**9 6**

—Roadin' around, like I told ya, exercisin' the old pis-
ton."

The voice was inarticulate, high-pitched, distant as if the
owner weren't quite sure it was his. He spoke with a mor-
bid guffaw, seeing hidden jokes. The words were mushed
as if his teeth were missing.

"—Where?

—Up and down, it's gotta be up and down.

—Yeah, but where?

—Anywhere you go, it's everywhere.

—Name a road.

—Fifty-five, thirty-two maybe. Some dirt.

—You weren't on a dirt road, your bike's clean.

—I washed it. (Guffaw and giggles.) I always wash it
after a little action.

—How'd you cut your neck?

—She assed up on me and I fell off—man, that was a
spill, hair to shoes, we-e-e-e-e! Br-ruph! Like that. Had me
shakin' like a big red rod. (More guffaws.)

—Where was this?

—Can't say—on the black somewhere.

—You wouldn't fall off a bike on a paved road, you're
too good.

—On the dirt, rocks maybe.

—You've got no scratches, no burns, so it wasn't gravel.
Tell it straight.

—I hit it, man, I didn't rub it.

—Traveling?

—I'm always goin'—or comin'.

—You weren't standing still when you fell off the bike.
You were moving. If you were moving, the marks would
show. They don't. So you're lying.

**9 7**

—Like ya say, I'm lyin'.

—How about the stuff you bought at the drugstore that night?

—Me? Stuff? Hell, they don't sell stuff there, you oughta know that.

—Bandages and aspirin.

—Not me. I never bandage it, I like it free, free and flappin'.

—Your neck's bandaged.

—So I fell off her, I told ya that, she assed up on me and I flew, he-ey did I fly.

—So you got a bandage.

—So I *had* a bandage, first aid, ready, ready, ya never know.

—Ready for the bike to rear up on a level road, eh?

—Man, I was fuckin' the saddle too hard and she cunted up on me, I told ya that. Ya like to hear it, eh?

—The man in the drugstore will know you.

—So let him know me, it might be kicks.

—Where were you when you fell off the bike?

—On it.

—Come on.

—Can't say like I say—got no idea where I am till I get there—a road's a road, long and black and ready to take you.

—You like milk?

—Wassat?

—You like milk.

—Depends whose.

—You stopped near Howard Johnson's that night and got milk in cartons.

—I did?

—That's right.

—Shit that's good, man, good—shows what I can do, milk out of a carton—a carton of what?

—Then you got oil at the filling station across the way.

—Oil? (A rattle of giggles.) I get oil all the time, I keep changin' it, man, that's nature.

—What happened to your knife?

—What knife? I don't need one, man, pussy's always open.

—Nothing to defend yourself with?

—Doneedit, I got karate.

—Stand up.

—What for?

—A little karate.

—I donwanna hurt ya.

—Up!

—Hell, fuck that, I'm a pacifist.

—With chains?

—What chains? Those're beads, ya know, pussy beads.

—Yeah. What do you do with them?

—Love pussy, like around your neck, it's smoothcool, downwards—yah-ah, that'll roll your rocks wild in the ole mammoloos down there—e-e-e-ee, that's when ya got her lookin' at your ass.

—What if she don't want?

—Everybody wants.

—Not everybody, some don't. What then?

—Then they want.

—If you can't get your rocks off, what do you do then?

—They want!

—They don't.

—They always want! Only they don't know it, sometimes.

—Why not?

—They dunno what's good for 'em, they're out of it.

—How?

—Out of it.

—How?

—Whattaya tryin'a do?

—You don't always get your rocks off, do you?

—I do, all the time!

—Not when they don't want.

—All the time!

—How do they do it for you?

—They lie quiet.

—How quiet?

—Quiet—just quiet—but I like 'em wigglin', so I always pick me somethin' I can roll with."

Sparrs turned off the machine.

"Three hours of it," he said, "that's as close as I got. The bastard almost wore me out."

Grant shook his head, shrugging in dismay, not finding any words to speak with. Sparrs rewound the tape and put it away.

"What," Grant said, "are you going to do now?"

"Wait for a break."

"What kind of break, against that?" he gestured to the tape recorder.

"I don't know. I really don't know. If I knew, it wouldn't be a break. A weapon might turn up, a witness who can pinpoint their whereabouts, a spiteful girlfriend, they might have a falling out, we might pick them up on another charge and one of them might want to deal, anything like that. You never can tell. We keep working on it, and waiting, that's basic to police work."

He spoke like a man trying to keep a faith.

Grant nodded as he got up, waved a weak goodbye, and left the office mutely as if he were going out to be sick.

# 13

He drove around the town noting landmarks and taking bearings mentally. At ten o'clock daylight-saving time the sun was really at nine o'clock, roughly in the southeast. The throughway ran north-south, he was somewhere west of it. The town had a university with a scattered campus, most of it seemed to be in an older section with spacious three-story houses and wide terraced lawns, still residential, now probably boarding houses for the students. The rest of it was new and four-square and looked hot without trees, and past it was a newer part of town which ate up old farm land and looked the way suburbs look everywhere, right off the drawing board, and as flat, with newly planted trees that couldn't interfere with the rigid driveways. Not far was a shopping center, farther away a cluster of light industries, a road to an airport, a sign that said an army base was in that direction.

Closer to the center of town were more shopping centers, better restaurants and bars, bigger gas stations, motels that looked like apartment buildings. Downtown was old and commercial and thriving and tapered off into a section of run-down houses and onto a highway with unkempt motels and dry dusty country. To the east, past the throughway, was a big lake, unbridgeable, that could be crossed by ferry at certain points. This he noted as an unlikely route for motorcycles in a hurry.

He went back to one of the bigger shopping centers and at a bookstore he bought a map of the town and its surrounding areas and topographic maps of the countryside. With these he went to a restaurant that had booths, ordered coffee, and busied himself with the maps, marking the areas he had just seen and trying to visualize the ones he could ignore. The topographic maps were not up to date and didn't have the throughway marked, but the old highway was there and that was enough to go by. He ordered lunch early, left as the noon customers were crowding in, and took the road again.

He began at the Howard Johnson's and got on the throughway going south. He tried to keep his mind on his work, such as it was, but he could picture the night and the three toughs and the attack, and he could hear the psychotic tone of Sparrs' tape. At the place where they had been killed he slowed down to thirty, looked at it as he passed, and picked up speed again.

He got off at the Hayestown exit. The ramp ended at a crossroad directing him left or right. Left would eventually get to the lake and probably the old highway, right led to Hayestown. He made a note of his mileage and turned toward Hayestown.

In less than five miles he was there. It was small, barely

two city blocks long, and had the usual store, a diner for quick lunches, a filling station, a mechanic's shop that had probably once been a blacksmith's, a few houses with vegetable gardens, an antique shop that was simply an old shed filled with discards. It seemed to symbolize the town. Just past it another road went to the right, more or less going north. Grant took it.

It was patched and rough, narrower than the other road, and it twisted as if they had built it over an old trail. Tangled and overgrown bush alternated with fields, in places fences were unrepaired and the land uncultivated, houses sagged and rotted. The working farms stood out, cut grass around a house, a mailbox that was accessible, a gravel driveway that wasn't overgrown, plowed sections with new growth, hayfields, and in two places children on bikes who looked at Grant and waved when he did. He wondered what forced people to abandon their farms.

Twenty-two miles later the road ended at a better highway and forked into it at a diagonal. Along this road were large tracts of farm land with huge barns and massive machinery and the general air of commercial enterprise and prosperity. Soon there were high chain-link fences topped with barbed wire and a big sign that announced the army base and explained its policy about unauthorized personnel. Past this was an open-air theater, a series of cheap motels competing for the army trade, and finally houses and stores and a drugstore with the sign, "Open 24 hrs." Grant had completed the circuit. He wasn't sure it meant anything.

He pulled in at a motel bar and ordered a beer. He sat with it at a table where he was left alone and thought about what he'd do next. The light was dim, but as his eyes grew accustomed to it he was able to read the maps. There was another circuit to be made east of the through-way along the old highway and again along a route that followed the lakeside. That section would be populated, it would hold tourists and campers and people with cottages and boating clubs. It would also have its share of lean-to hamburger stands and cheap hangouts. A transient popula-tion, good to get lost in. But not if you wore a load of war-like junk and rode a big motorbike. Unless there were lots of others like you, and unless you thought it was a good idea to stay in the open as if nothing had happened. That was all right now, but three nights ago you'd want to stay out of sight. And the easiest way to do that would be to disappear into the countryside, like guerrillas. It was an idea worth testing. He finished his drink.

He drove back the way he had come, past the twenty-four-hour drugstore, the outskirts, the army base, the lush farm land, and into the rough road that bounced through the desolate country. He looked carefully at every aban-doned farm. It was hard to see. High grass and massive weeds blocked his view and overran the gravel driveways. For over eighteen miles at these places he saw no vehicles and no people. Then on this side of Hayestown as he was cresting an incline that turned left he saw sunlight glisten-ing in the tall grass near a house and a fallen barn. He stopped the car to take a better look.

It was perhaps a mile away, or more, and seemed to be off the main road. He checked the map. From where he was, the road would go slightly downhill and he'd lose sight of the reflections, but it would also bend in the direc-tion of the house. Broken lines indicated either a private or a disused road. He drove to it.

It was an ill-kept private road. A piece of a sign, illegible, clung to a fence post. He turned in, going slowly, trying not to make dust on the dry dirt. Finally, to his right, behind weeds and bushes he saw the crooked skeleton of the barn, then a broken mailbox, and a driveway that was little more than a wide path. The mailbox had the faded and eroded word, "Brenan." He backed into the driveway and pulled out onto the road, ready for an exit. He took the map and got out. As he walked up the driveway the house, badly disrepaired, and the barn came into view, then, upright in the tall grass, motorcycles, five of them, their handlebars gleaming in the sun. He felt his heart go faster. He took deep breaths to keep his hands from trembling.

He looked at the house as though he were appraising it. No one seemed to be around, but he assumed they were there and watching him.

"Anybody home?"

He tried to sound casual, like a country neighbor.

Nobody replied. He thought he heard noises from inside the house, like suppressed spluttering laughter. It was hard to tell from outside. Birds in nearby trees were protesting his invasion of their territory. Still under the guise of appraising the place, he noted the licenses on the bikes one by one and at intervals, not to betray a special interest in them. He stepped up on the porch.

It was sagged and rotting, boards were missing and burdock and grass grew through the gaps and between planks. The windows were broken. Rough screens had been put up from inside the house. The screen door was patched and repatched with different weights of screening, the hinges were twisted, the bottom sill was missing. A heavy buzzing indicated a nest somewhere. The porch shook under Grant's weight. He knocked on the doorframe and called out immediately. "Anybody home?"

With that he pulled open the screen door and walked in.

They were there, five of them, sitting and lounging on the floor. Four of them had leather vests studded with metal shapes, no undershirts. The fifth had a denim vest with a sheath knife sewn into it where a shoulder holster would hang. Jeans that looked tarred or resined, elaborate boots like cowboy storm troopers, one with spurs facing front. Denim Vest had his boots off, no socks. Four had plentiful hair, not hippie-style, matted, without form. The fifth had shaved his head a short time ago and still looked bald. No beards, only stubbles. Necks visible, no bandages, no wounds. Three wore big sunglasses, probably what Sparrs had called shooting glasses. Two were sitting cross-legged, hunched forward, arms on knees; one was leaning against the wall with his legs spread out; another was sitting on a legless chair looking uncomfortable; the fifth was kneeling, resting against the stove. The stove and the broken chair were the only furniture in the place. In one corner was a pile of garbage and what looked like all the flies in the county. In the other room through an archway helmets were visible.

The five gazed at Grant in silence. No one moved.

"Is any of you Mr. Brenan by any chance?" said Grant. He was in a regular shirt, no tie, sleeves partly rolled, holding a folded map, trying to look four-square, semi-official, asking a conservative business question.

"No," somebody said.

**107**

"A relative maybe? I'd like to find Mr. Brenan."

"No."

"Do you rent the place from him?"

"No."

"Do you know where I can find him?"

"No."

"That's funny," said Grant as if he had something on them.

"What's so fuckin' funny?" asked Bald Head.

"A guy said somebody here would know."

"Who here?"

"Guy said a Mr. Stitte would know. Is one of you Mr. Len Stitte?"

That brought giggles and spitting bursts of chuckling. "Len's Tit, eh? Who told you that?"

"Guy up the road. He had a big bike."

"*Mister* Len's Tit, is that it?"

"Yeah."

"Did he say Iron Tit?" said Denim Vest.

"Or Iron Cunt?" said another.

"Mr. Tit is called Iron Cunt now. You ask for an Iron Cunt," said a voice.

"How's that?" said Grant.

"Dunno, guess he did a little cunting with some iron."

That drew the house down again. Grant was tiring fast of their special rhetoric. He didn't really know what he wanted to find out, and he knew he was in danger of some sort of irrational outburst. He shrugged in feigned disappointment and took a step for the door.

"You buyin', man?" a voice said.

"In a way. I'm with a company, real estate."

"Like for cash, for the place?"

"No cash, no cash at all."

"Maybe," it was Denim Vest picking up the theme, "ya know, maybe for finding your Mr. Tit, could be worth something, only he don't own the place, don't ever come here."

"All I want is the owner, and it seems this man Stitte can locate him for me."

"That's a goody, though, ain't it? Here now Len's Tit's in business, is he goin' square balls?"

"I wouldn't know."

"How much you payin'?"

"For what?"

"For where Len is."

"Hell," said Grant with fake good humor, "*I'm* not buying *him*, the company wants to deal with Mr. Brenan."

"But you need Len."

"I don't need Len, all I need's Brenan. Post office, the county clerk, relatives, somebody must know."

"Lotta sweat and work for nothin', Len can tell you in two shakes, save you tires, money, mileage, good biz, man, good biz."

"How do you know Len can tell me?"

"You said that, and the other guy said that, now I say like you said and he said. I can front wheel you to Len, okay? Five bucks."

It was a probe and a threat. If he was too interested in Stitte, they might make trouble. If he really wanted Brenan, they might as well extort a little safe-passage money. Grant stayed in his role.

"Hell, no, too much," he said in a wouldn't-hear-of-it tone of voice, "he might not be able to help me. And I'm gonna have a hard time explaining to the company that I paid five bucks to talk to a guy called Len who maybe knew where a guy called Brenan was. Forget it."

"Four bucks."

"It's not worth four cents to me personally. It may be worth something to the company, I don't know."

"Shit, man, that's tough. I could sure use the paper. Three bucks."

"What are you so hard up about?"

"Gas, man, gas. Without that, I'm grounded."

As if by signal, or as if the mention of gas stirred them, they got up and collected their gear. Denim Vest was putting on his boots.

"Well," said Grant, "tell you what. I can buy you some gas and I can claim that for expenses. Let's go find some gas."

"Can I bring a can?"

"Bring a toilet if you want."

"A toil—?"

Denim Vest laughed and ordered somebody to bring the toilet, and as they made their remarks and giggled Grant went out the door, not fast, and strolled to his car, inspecting the property as he went. Stomping feet and motors banged behind him. He started the car quickly and made dust getting to the paved road. He drove to Hayestown with the five bikes following in line and pulled up at the one filling station. Bikes surrounded Grant's car. He got out. Nobody spoke.

A man appeared in the entrance of the garage, saw the group around Grant, went back in immediately but not quickly, and presently came out to the pumps. He was tall and toughened, with a grooved face that could have been sixty years old, a man used to heavy work, dressed in work clothes that seemed to be part of his large frame. He looked at everyone with appraising blue eyes, and held on Grant as if asking if there was trouble afoot.

"I'm going to buy gas for these fellows," Grant said. "We have a deal going."

The tall man didn't move. Grant addressed Denim Vest.

"Okay, let's have it. Where's this man, Len?"

"Put in the gas first."

"Tell me first."

Grant almost burst out laughing as he heard his own words, like a tit-for-tat kid's quarrel which made the costumed toughness look even more absurd.

"It's a stand-off, man. And you owe us for comin' here."

"Just you."

"Us."

Grant was tempted to push the point, to press the right psychological nerve, but there was nothing to be gained that way.

"Let's organize," he said. "I'll give the man here the price. You tell me. Then I go. Then you get your gas."

"Okay. But you stay. We get gas, we go, then you go."

"Why's that?"

"Just feels right."

"Okay by me. One small point: what if your information's no good?"

"Tough tit, man. Len moves around a lot."

Grant gave the tall man a five-dollar bill. He put it in his pants pocket, took the gas hose from the pump and waited, looking at Denim Vest. The action seemed to commit him on Grant's side, as if they had planned it. Suspicion for a moment, two against five, another piece of psychology, who was top dog? Denim Vest held out his arm

111

and one of the toughs put the gasoline can in his hand. He put it down at the tall man's feet.

"Len's around the beach."

They all giggled, top-dogging. It was like saying Len was in North America. Grant suppressed the follow-up questions he wanted to ask. The tall man filled the can and the five tanks as they came by one by one, roaring their motors to dispel the self-conscious silence of the line-up. They grouped smartly near the road, at pains to make the maneuvers look effortless, and burst away in the direction of the abandoned farm.

"I'll get your change."

"Don't bother," said Grant. "It's close to five anyway."

"It's less than that. We marked up the price to keep fellas like that away, they go around looking for cheap gas."

He went inside and came back with the change. Tips didn't mean anything to him.

"Did those fellas gang up on you?"

"No, not really."

"It looked that way when you pulled up. I got ready before I came out. Like my grandfather and his Indian stories. Jesus, I'd hate to have to shoot anybody. How'd they happen to get you?"

"I walked in on them. About five miles that way on an old farm, Brenan's, I saw their bikes shining and went in to look. Said I was interested in talking to Mr. Brenan."

"George Brenan's been dead five years. Children are all in the city and the place is rotting to hell."

"They didn't know anything about Brenan."

"You with the police?"

"No. Just a citizen. Why?"

"Troopers've been by. There was trouble a few nights ago."

"Yeah, I heard."

"You're looking for one of them, the guy at the beach?"

"Yeah."

"It's none of my business, but it's a big beach, lake goes for miles."

"I know. They really didn't tell me anything."

"The part you want is south of the town."

"Thanks, I'll look it up."

Following the map he drove east, passing under the throughway, and got on the beach road curving north. For miles it wound in front of cottages and homes, a few walled villas, landscaped mansions in what seemed to be a highly segregated section, boathouses and docks near the lake, camping sites full of trailers, collections of diners and stores and amusement joints, and cabins for rent that hadn't been repaired for years. As he got closer to the town, motels appeared and the sort of restaurant that specializes in dining you out. Then empty untended lots as if the owners were still speculating, and finally, beachside, a tavern and diner and some sort of dancing pavilion, old and unpainted, the kind that was popular with summer colonists a generation ago. A flaky sign called it "Jake's Palace." Next to it was a big gravel parking lot with picnic tables on two sides under trees, next to that two rows of cabins looking like barracks, a few separate bigger cabins, a sign that called them a motel, and past all this, lakeside, a string of dressing rooms like outhouses glued together to keep them from falling down. Scattered and partly out of sight near and behind buildings and tables were some dozen motorcycles.

Grant pulled up in front of the tavern and diner. Three second-hand cars were in the parking lot, and an old half-ton truck. Business looked bad, but it was daytime, close to five, it probably picked up at night. Grant's car stood out like the prize in a raffle, and he knew he'd be equally conspicuous inside. He went in.

The place had everything except sawdust on the floor and spittoons in the corners. The floor was wooden, patched with plywood, the walls were old tongue-and-groove painted over and over years ago and then left, the ceilings were like a barn floor with old beams, an interior decorator's delight, and some walls had been torn down to make room, leaving upright beams in the middle of the floor. The furnishings were mainly wooden chairs and round porcelain-top tables, all chipped and disfigured. The bar was a counter made of planks worn smooth and full of gaps from years of washing. Tall wooden stools lined up in front of it. A few fluorescent fixtures gave a sparse harsh light and killed any atmosphere the place might have had. The customers would have killed it anyway.

Grant sat on a stool at the bar. Two men in their late twenties, dressed in work denims, sat morosely awkward and muttered to each other over quarts of beer. Farther off, unseen, what must have been teenagers were making music from a machine. A man ducked into a low doorway behind the bar, stopped when he saw Grant and went to the cash register to punch up some business, probably from the teenagers. He was bulky, not tall, sweaty, with a puffy face, eyes that had once been blue but now looked yellow, and tough wiry black hair that couldn't be combed. He looked fifty and could have been sixty with dyed hair. He wore a spotless short-sleeved white shirt, crisp and business-like, as though it were the only way he could assert a professional pride. He looked at Grant and the map.

"You lost?" he asked.

114

"No. Just looking around. I'll have a beer."

"What kind?"

"Any kind. Cold."

"They're all cold."

He served it and stayed. "Looking around for what?" he said.

"Nothing special."

"You don't look like a cop."

"I'm not."

"Then don't talk like one. If you're looking around, maybe I can help you." He turned on a radio under the counter and that gave them a little privacy. "What's on your mind?"

"Lots of motorcycles around."

"Oh, jeez, you better know it. They come down on me like hail. Over a week ago. At night. Noise, I thought the war had started. They sleep down by the beach, pay me just enough to keep the cops from tossing them out. They scare away the trade, give my place a bad name. They'll go away though, they like to swarm, goddam locusts. Then the cops slammed in here a few nights ago and dragged them off and I figured that's that, but the buggers were back, laughing like hell and shitting all over the beach, and I said I'd call the cops on them for that, littering, and they made fun of that, but they stopped. They use the toilet now, and maybe that's worse, 'cause I gotta clean it. You don't want to buy the place, eh?"

"No."

"It's a good place. Jeez, it was nice when I first got it. Real country. Barn-dancing and regular dancing. Now it's a goddam raceway and that lake's becoming a sewer. Sorry I'm talking so much, it's all I've got." He poured himself a

**115**

drink, about half a glass of Scotch, and drank most of it in one gulp. He brightened a little. "What about the motorcycles?"

"A guy, maybe with two buddies. But one guy with a bandage on his neck and some teeth missing."

"Yeah. The cops were keen on him too. He's around, off and on. Why?"

"Is he here now?"

"I dunno. I try to keep out of their way. Why do you want him?"

Nothing could have induced Grant to talk about it, not to anyone, and especially not to a man who was working up to a self-pitying drunk. He tried to appear unconcerned.

"He skipped his payments, and he may have been in an accident. So we've got an interest in it."

"Oh, is that it? Well, I'm not surprised."

"I think I'll look around."

"I'd be careful if I were you. I wouldn't tangle with those guys, not without lotsa help."

"Yeah, you're right," said Grant, not to disagree with a drinker. But before he could get off the stool, bikes roared in from the highway and raised dust in the parking lot and settled down in the back of the place.

"That's at least four more," said the man. "Jeez, jeez, I wish I could do something about it."

A form passed by the window, outside, near Grant's car, and he came in. It was Denim Vest, all excited and trying to appear loose.

"You find Titty?" he said to Grant.

"No," said Grant casually, "he's not around."

"He's in back."

"Well, I don't think it's important. The man at the gas station said Mr. Brenan moved away, nobody knows where."

"Big fire out there." He was ready to explode.

"Where? Brenan's?"

"Ass right. It's burnin' now, right into the ground."

"How come?"

"Lightnin'." He almost sputtered the word, then burst out laughing.

"On a sunny day?"

"Best time." More laughter, and abrupt seriousness. "How come you knew for Len?"

"Guy told me."

"Guy on a bike, you said, eh?"

"Yeah."

"No guy on no bike names names."

As inarticulate as it was, Grant got the message, he had aroused their curiosity.

"Well, this guy did."

"You're shittin' me."

It was a call-out, third-rate movie style, lost in fantasy. Grant looked at him innocently, stroked his chin in deep thought, making no move that could be interpreted as getting ready for a fight, and spoke slowly. Gary Cooper to the surrounding Indians.

"Well," he said, "that guy probably thought it'd be a helluva good joke to send me in there."

Denim Vest had to adjust. He wasn't used to thinking. Grant sat still, he was too tense to move casually, and he kept silent, to over-explain would be to ruin it. He was

**117**

counting on the tough's ego, too big to want to be taken in by another tough's joke. A long half minute went on forever as the radio tried to dramatize the town's traffic.

"Yeah," the tough finally said, "only reason he would. Man, we coulda ground you to pieces and left you roastin'." He was still excited by the fire.

He laughed, not quite convincingly, and went out through the back.

It was time to leave. Grant went straight to his car and drove away. Another five minutes and Denim Vest would stumble on the fact that it was Grant who had taken him in.

He felt tired, exhausted by the role-playing, the lying, the tension of danger. It wasn't like the private-eye stories he'd read, he knew it wouldn't be. But something had been accomplished, he had located Stitte, though he hadn't actually seen him. He would. There was going to have to be a next phase, with help.

# 14

By eleven he was stretched out on the bed in the motel room, the lights out, listening to the traffic on the road a few hundred yards away. It surged periodically and diminished, like a drunken ocean, the cycles growing less as the night deepened. The windows were open for a cross breeze. With lights on, he hadn't been able to see outside and could be seen inside. It made him feel watched, hunted in some way, liable to detection. In the dark, all was reversed and he felt more at ease. He'd come a long way from the secure casual life of less than a week ago. Porch lights, hung in lanterns under the motel canopy, enabled him to make out everything in the room. He was still dressed, in the cotton pants and sport shirt he'd bought to be less noticeable. He felt too vulnerable undressed, too unready for a vaguely hostile universe. It was paranoid. He was aware of it, he just couldn't shake it off.

The dim room made memory vivid. The toughs. The

image of Sue and Patty in their hands. It was too much. Mercifully he was interrupted.

A car poked around outside and pulled up next to his. Someone knocked. He got up, put on a table lamp and opened the door. It was Sparrs and Ketner. They weren't happy. Grant went back to the bed and sat on it.

"We'll come to the point," said Sparrs. "You've been getting around, Hayestown, the burnt-out Brenan farm, Jake's Palace—what for?"

"I just have to."

"It won't do any good."

"It might."

"How?"

"I don't know."

"Look, Joe, I understand how you feel, but use your head. All you're gonna do is get those guys to gang up on you. Then you've had it. Nothing's gonna happen except more trouble for you."

"Maybe that's the answer."

"The answer to *what?*"

"They're *there,* Captain, right there, and the law can't touch them, and you can't touch them. But I can touch them. Let 'em gang up. Maybe you'll get them for killing me. That'd be something, wouldn't it? Damn sight more than you've got now."

Grant spoke with animal ferocity, emotions that took self-sacrifice for granted, deeper than self, raw with basic love, dangerous. The two policemen sensed his level. It was an answer, all right, it answered Grant's feelings. No argument could reach it.

"Sure," said Sparrs, "that's the way I'd feel too. But don't get yourself killed, Joe. It might not pay off."

"Yeah," said Grant, "yeah. I'll think about it."

"We'll be on our way. Keep in touch, will you?"

"Maybe."

"Be better if you did."

"We'll see."

They left.

Grant bolted the door, put out the lamp, stood by the window awhile looking at the distant traffic, and finally lay down again. The exchange with Sparrs had cleared his mind, clarified his feelings. His thoughts took shape without words and he wasn't haunted by images for the moment.

The day was taking on a meaning for him. It was showing him his own remorse, a guilt that was the other side of love. With bitter clarity he was saying inside himself, I was the only one who could have saved them, and I didn't, no one else, me. It seemed like an immense truth, and it was strangely calming. He gazed at it. Traffic sounds became more infrequent. Gradually and imperceptibly he fell asleep.

He slept deeply. So deeply that when he came to he wondered why he was waking up.

He knew he wasn't dreaming. He was completely awake, tired and heavy, and he hadn't moved, he had only opened his eyes. He could hear traffic in a close muffled way. He was about to dismiss it as a cause for his waking when he realized the sound wasn't going away. It was steady, an idling motor, idling motors, more than one, and they were close. Motorcycles.

He slipped out of bed, crouching low, and went to the window. The light outside seemed brighter, and since it was shining on the screen he counted on it to hide his movements. He peered out.

There were three bikes. They were about ten feet from his car in a scattered formation facing left on the driveway. They were looking at the car. It seemed to have them puzzled. They looked at each other from time to time and out at the highway. The one in line with Grant had a bandage on his neck. The same three.

Grant studied them carefully. He couldn't see plates at that angle or read them in that light. He was surprised at his own calmness. He wondered if there was a patrol car in the area. There was a phone in the room, it'd be of some use if anything started. But the toughs didn't seem sure, and Grant's car was parked ambiguously. They'd have to try both units to be sure, and that would be noisy, but they counted on terror to cow people. Grant surveyed the possibilities. He didn't move.

An inaudible conference took place. A light came on from Grant's right where the office was, a floodlight that didn't reach the toughs directly. One by one they eased along the driveway to minimize the noise and disappeared with a roar when they reached the highway.

It was a little after two by Grant's watch. He sat by the window, not really watching the road, but looking at alternatives, possible moves. He couldn't be sure that they wouldn't be back. He hadn't even thought, when he bought gas for the five, that they'd use it to burn down the Brenan place. They were spur of the moment, darting from behind a wall of terror, they needed that to function by. In their eyes the real-estate salesman wasn't local, he was at a motel, he should have left town. They wouldn't live with mystery too long. But they might live with it till tomorrow.

Grant undressed and got into bed, under the covers this time. He felt certain he was reading them right, and he was past being afraid.

He awoke early as he knew he would, there was no sleeping in for him. By six-thirty he was cleaned up,

dressed in his suit, complete with tie, and out on the traf-
fic-free roads, moving fast. Two hours later he was well
into another state and into a thriving big small-town
where he had breakfast and waited for nine o'clock to be
sure the stores were open. It was raining. He had just
missed it on the road. Somehow he felt relieved by the
rain, everything had been happening on brilliant days and
clear nights. He noticed it was Saturday. Meaningless. Another system, like the law. For a flashing moment he remembered the bright star he'd seen that night, and suddenly felt alone on earth. Funny. He shrugged it off. But it
wouldn't stay off. He paid for his breakfast and left the
restaurant. He ducked into the nearest likely place and
bought a plastic raincoat. Then he went to a prosperous
sporting-goods store. He was in a state that had few re-
strictions on firearms.

A huge, jovial man greeted him. He had a tanned face,
crew-cut gray hair, and mirthful eyes behind heavy-framed
glasses. Years of selling seemed to have made him happy.

"Hi, hi. How's it going? It'll be a nice day when it stops
raining."

"Oh, I don't mind it the way it is."

"That's the spirit." He was old enough to have been
Grant's father. He talked like a coach. "What can we do
for you?"

"I'd like a handgun."

"There's all kinds for all purposes. They hunt with them
around here."

"I've been going to a shooting club with a friend, I've
been borrowing his."

"Range shooting. You got the bug, eh? That's the spirit."

"Yeah, and I can't keep borrowing them."

"You better believe it. People are touchy about their

**1 2 3**

guns. Takes a lotta work to get them just right. Sighting's different for each user. Big or small?"

"Small calibers are out, they think they're corny."

"A .45 is too much gun to learn by. Maybe a .38 would do you."

"That sounds all right."

"Come on over here, I'll show you a few."

He led Grant to a long glass showcase and unlocked it. It held a bewildering variety of revolvers and automatic pistols.

"These," said the man, as he put three guns on the counter, "are about the best you can buy."

"I don't know enough about it to make a good choice. I want something that's very accurate."

"Well, the experts argue over that. Course they modify their own guns. This one," he placed a Luger-like pistol in front of Grant, "is an auto-loader, the sights and the receiver are all one, just this bolt goes back, just like a rifle. It'll group all the time for you."

"That sounds okay, I'll take it."

He also bought a clip-on holster, ammunition, a spare magazine, a cleaning kit, and books on the subject. It came to a little under two hundred dollars.

"You'll have to sign the register."

"Sure."

Grant gave his name, the address of his apartment, and signed the book as the man put everything in a stout bag.

"It's not law, you know," the man said. "It's only for our own records."

"That's fine."

"I hope you get a lot of pleasure out of that gun."

"Yeah, thanks."

# 15

It was a place few people would want. It was isolated, away from any fun, in country that was unfarmable, bush-land where new evergreens were growing wild and tan-gled, inhospitable as if it knew it would be razed again when it matured. The front part of the house was a centu-ry-old one-room affair made of logs, the rest was more re-cent, also made of logs, but they hadn't been able to match the back-breaking appearance of the original. Electricity had tamed it with light and heat and a ready water sup-ply. Around the house were three big gnarled old pines whose knotted shapes had saved them from the chain saws. Grant knew the place well. It belonged to a friend and be-fore that to the friend's father. It was an elaborate camp. From there they went fishing in the neighboring lakes and hunting in the forlorn forests. It was 150 miles north from Grant's home city, crisp and chilly in the mountains, still too rugged for people who wanted everything the city had except its dirty air.

It was peaceful in an innocent, rough way, and demanding, you couldn't earn a living here, you could only survive. Jagged hills rolled away into black clouds, making it impossible to tell the horizon. It might rain, and it might not. Weather was tricky here. Grant took time to look at all of it. It had good memories. And the men didn't bring their families here. He didn't have to be vigilant about his feelings. They might even heal here. But he wasn't going to stay that long.

In the house on a handmade plank table he laid out the pistol and the equipment and the literature. The manufacturer's box contained diagrams, instructions, take-down exploded drawings, the ten commandments of safety, and subscription cards to hairy-chested gun magazines. He studied the diagrams carefully against the pistol and worked every operating part. He didn't strip it, he wanted it intact. He removed and replaced the magazine, cocked the gun, sighted it, dry-fired it, made the safety catch work, and repeated the process until he was sure he knew what he was doing.

He loaded the magazine with the nine bullets it would hold, placed it in the handle, made certain it had caught, and laid the gun on the table. It was a nice piece of machinery, black, efficient, designed for death. He admitted to himself that he had a fear of it. He also had a use for it.

Outside, on a decaying lifeless tree he nailed a folded-down cardboard box. He went into the house and got the pistol. He stood some twenty-five yards away from the box, cocked the gun and held it pointing to the ground. Then he raised it to aim at the target. But before he was ever in line with it, the gun went off. The report was deafening. The gun jumped and jarred his hand, enough to cause pain, and almost fell out of his grip. It had all happened at once with sudden and unintended explosiveness. He went cold, and he began to tremble. Then he realized that the gun was still cocked, ready to explode again, an auto-loader the man had called it, what they call an automatic. Gingerly he set the safety and put the gun on the ground pointing away from him. Lesson number one.

Silence came back to him, and the countryside, and his muscles went back to normal. He picked up the gun, not touching the trigger but keeping his finger around the guard, and removed the safety.

He pointed it at the target, looked along the sights, and with great deliberation and care he put his forefinger on the trigger and squeezed. It fired and jumped. The noise seemed less loud, the recoil less strong. Slowly he shot the remaining seven bullets. He made doubly sure the gun was empty and harmless. He put it down and went to the card-board box. There wasn't a single hole in it, he had missed completely. Lesson number two.

He went back inside with the pistol. He feared it openly now, and mistrusted it. If this had been a game with friends, plinking on a Sunday afternoon, he would have abandoned the whole thing. But he had to master it, and something was wrong, with the weapon or with him. He had to discover which one.

He opened a can of beer and started going through the three books. From the table of contents he marked off what might be pertinent, skipping historical run-downs, editorializing on gun laws, the joys of the sport, and con-centrated on ballistics, sighting in, and gripping. He came across a chapter called "The First Burning," and found that the author was using a term from the old powder-and-flint days and what he was really talking about was the beginner's first attempts at firing. The romanticism annoyed him, but the information was good.

"There is nothing more disheartening than finding that you have missed the target completely," the page said. "The human organism cannot hold sights absolutely steady on the target." "A bullet crosses the line of sight twice, somewhere near the muzzle and again at an indeterminable point in the distance." It all came down to: start close to the target and then move back. There was no romanticism in the practical parts, the advice was to use a gun rest and two hands. In two hours of reading and note-taking and diagram-making he understood the physics of the thing. He was ready to try again.

This time he brought a small table outside and upon it placed the pistol, unloaded magazine, and a box of bullets. He saw the sense of going about it professionally.

With the gun ready he paced off fifteen feet from the box on the tree. He supported his right hand in his left, watched the sights sway a little, and fired. His tight grip held on to the recoil, the sights swayed again into line, he fired again. The noise made him uncomfortable. Echoes snapped through the quiet hills. He couldn't stay unexcited, couldn't quite stop the tremors in his arms. He fired systematically until the gun was empty. He went to the box. He counted nine holes in the radius of a foot. But good shooting called for a radius of two inches, and at fifteen yards, not fifteen feet. The book even spoke of fifty yards. He repaired the target with tape and marked off a center.

He tried again and did better, and once more and did worse. He was tired, it was exhausting work. He put the table at fifteen feet, used it as a gun rest, and shot slowly, pausing to rest between shots. The grouping was less than two inches, he could rely on the weapon. But it was firing low, which meant according to his calculations that he was too close.

He rested by making targets with available material, the sides of cardboard boxes, a marker, freezer tape for straight lines, he didn't try to make circles, a big center cross would do. He noticed that the sun was starting to get low. It was close to six. He opened another can of beer and went outside to look at the country. He felt the tragedy of what he was doing, a line was being crossed, and everything looked less human on the other side of it. Not to cross it, though, seemed worse. Perhaps an answer dwelt somewhere. Perhaps. He went back to work.

In the next hour, with slow, careful progress, he extended his range to twenty-five yards and was shooting well, with one hand, placing bullets virtually where he wanted them to go. It was grim discipline. He saved one of the paper targets for later, and as a last test he placed his beer tins, two empty and four full, on a disused crude platform that once held an oil tank. In nine shots he struck five tins, three full ones exploding into foam. He cleaned up his debris, removed the ripped pile of targets from the tree. He was appalled at the damage the bullets had done to the wood. He put up a fresh target and left it. The rest of the equipment and material he brought inside.

He cleaned the pistol, put a frozen dinner in the oven, and drank the surviving can of beer as he waited for the food to cook. The line that was being crossed tugged at his attention. He had no myths to give glory to the crossing, only the knowledge of his wife and daughter, his own made-empty life. He should have been here last summer or even earlier, learning the cold skills that now disturbed him. Would it have been different? The pistol had nothing to say.

He ate the dinner without will, and when it was dark he put the lights on in the side room facing the dead tree outside. He went out with the gun.

He walked away from the house, turned, barely able to see the target, and fired nine times at it from different positions. He tore it down and brought it into the house. He had not missed. But this was like sport, and the line was still there.

Around ten, after reading to pass the time, he went to bed, glad for the silence of the hills and the real fatigue that would drain away by morning. But he was glad too soon. He dreamed. And it seemed the night had not been. Perhaps it was being in a place he liked, or perhaps it was because he felt he had done something, or even going to do something. It was his first such dream. He was home, really home, from a trip weirdly filled with obstacles, and they were all glad to be together, the three of them, delighting, joy in their faces, oh, it was so good to be there at last, but Sue and Patty looked strange somehow and vague, and he couldn't make them come clearer and couldn't hold them as they finally faded away. He awoke to the sounds of birds, his face wet, realizing all.

# 16

Sunday evening he returned to the same motel, and since there were vacancies he got the same room. He thought he was lucky. He waited there until it was really dark, waited in a positive way, letting time go by as if its passage had a meaning. At ten o'clock he got in the car and drove away slowly. He saw no one, wondered if anyone had seen him.

He started with Jake's Palace. He sat in the gravel parking lot among the second-hand cars and waited again. There were no bikes around, and in a half hour none came. A few customers went in and out, looking as if they had decided to go some place else. Grant got out of the car, locked it, and walked behind the place. A dim bare bulb over a crooked door lit the debris and the garbage. It was deserted. He went around to the front entrance.

Jake was behind the bar looking at a small TV set. His shirt was still very white, his eyes still yellow. He seemed not to recognize Grant.

"Bikes are all gone," said Grant.

"For now, anyway," Jake said. "Too much to hope it's for good." He spoke to the television set.

"Any way of telling?"

He shook his head, no, to the set, and finally looked at Grant. He shook his head again.

"No way. They don't clean up, or anything, they just go."

"When?"

"Little while ago. They made a big noise and they were gone. They were cutting up some."

"High?"

"Something like that."

He turned back to the TV set. Grant went outside.

They hadn't all gone. One was on the other side of the highway, sitting on his bike at the side of a closed-up vegetable stand. He was barely visible, faraway lights over the doors of a small factory on his side, the general glow of a gas station on the other. He was like a nightmare traffic cop waiting for a speeder. Grant kept walking, he only caught a glimpse of him, and from the parking lot he couldn't see him.

Grant drove toward the town watching his mirrors. He was coiled, tense. He told himself it was too early for that. The gun pressed heavily at the pit of his stomach. It was clipped unnaturally on the inside of his waistband, it had been the only way to reduce the bulge it made. Nobody seemed to be following him. A few miles later, still nobody. It wouldn't do to drive around aimlessly. They could avoid him more easily than he could avoid them. If it was cat-and-mouse, right now it was all mouse and no cat.

He slowed down for a big blue neon sign that spelled

"The Iron Bars" and ran vertical lines of light across the entire length of a long low building. The parking lot in front was floodlit and filled with cars, a place with business. He parked near the road, more or less in line with the long window of the bar, and went in through what looked like permanently open heavy wrought-iron gates, probably made of plastic. They weren't kidding about the iron bars, they looked like heavy board bolted to an iron frame. There was one in a music and entertainment section, one in what doubled as a dining room, and one in the bar for drinkers. There were lots of customers, lots of music, no cuisine at this hour, and the tone seemed to be a little tired, boozy in the dim plastic environment. Grant went to the drinker's bar, it was less noisy, had fewer people, and he found a seat near the window after casually spotting his car outside. The barman gave him a funny look that had Grant wondering for a moment, a man alone, serious, sport shirt worn outside and a jacket, the bulge maybe, a stranger, a cop, a tough guy, a man with a problem. When the waitress came over, he tried to look like a guy out for a little female fun.

She was big and shapely, not young, panty-hosed with some sort of briefs, breasts uncovered for just enough inspection, her face theatrically made up and producing a good role-playing smile, an old pro. He was being assessed. He gave her a chummy smile.

"Hi," he said.

"Hi, dear," she said, like a telephone operator being nice. "What can I get you?"

"Oh," said Grant, in phony thought, "I'll start with a beer. I'm going slow."

"It's slow when you're alone, dearie." The theatrical face

smiled, her eyes under false lashes glistened in the light and said nothing at all.

"Not for long, the pace'll pick up."

She chuckled in a modulated way with her head thrown back a little, a good neck. "I'd better get you started then."

"You already have."

More chuckles and she left. There was a run in her panty hose. He wondered if she knew about it.

He watched the parking lot, and the road, but not steadily, glanced around the bar and beyond, stopping on the women who were mainly young and seemed to be trying to hang on to a good time. It was a waiter who brought the beer and he stuck around to be paid.

"I'll settle up later."

"Sorry, chief, house rules."

Grant took his wallet out from his left-hand breast pocket, the folded-over kind thick with cards, junk, and money, an equalizing bulge. He let the waiter go away with the whole dollar. Big tipper. And any bulging was accounted for. He felt overcareful, but they seemed to lose interest in him after that. He tried to drink with satisfaction as he gazed out the window, just another guy on the loose, girl-watching.

Time waited with him. It lulled him into a more casual vigilance as he concentrated on the idly passing traffic. There were no motorbikes. It puzzled him a little, made him vaguely suspicious, uneasy. He noticed that glass and bottle were empty, and that a woman had taken the neighboring table.

At a glance she was legs, a red mini, a wig with varying shades of blond. Then she was a symmetrical face with dull eyes, a little drawn, and she was wearing a mini with large oval cutouts showing waist and back and seeming to be held up by the firmness of her breasts. Her fidgety hands flicked at a small handbag for cigarettes. Her sexiness was stagy, what she had come to believe the audience wanted. Youth and prettiness overcame the dullness in her eyes.

"You waiting for company?" she said to Grant.

His mood was elsewhere, but it was smarter to play out the role.

"Not any more," he said. "Would you like a drink?"

"Sure, that's the idea, isn't it?" Grant stood up as she did and signaled the waiter, it covered his sense of protocol. "In a bar, I mean," she added.

Close up, her eyes were deep blue, wide, she looked like a comedienne doing a dumb role. She was just into her twenties.

"Where else?" said Grant.

"People have been known to drink at home."

She ordered vodka and orange juice, Grant nodded when the waiter held up the empty bottle inquiringly. It was that kind of place.

"Yeah, but it's better here," he said, just to keep the thing going.

"Oh, yes. I like bars, don't you?"

"Love them."

"Do you come here very often?" Her tone was stilted, like someone practicing enunciation.

"No."

"It figures. 'Cause I do, and I would've seen you." The enunciation was gone, she was up and down.

"You came alone tonight?"

"Well, I just got back. I mean I just got here, you know."

It was all a mistake, and Grant looked outside, wondering how to end it. Take her home, pay her off, save face all around. He was out of his depth. But what he saw next to his car made him drop the problem. Peering from the driver's side of a battered car was a face like the faces he'd seen at Brenan's farm, the bare shoulder where the jacket sleeve was cut off, the shooting glasses, the tangled hair. There were two more in the old car, possibly three. No wonder he hadn't seen bikes. The cat was real. An abrupt, brief tingling of the nerves tried to tell him something: about fear perhaps, or about folly. He wasn't listening. The old car drove off.

The drinks arrived.

"Will you bring me another, please?" she said.

Grant looked at her hard, still preoccupied with the parking lot.

"Don't you want me to have another?"

"Have all you want."

"I thought maybe something was the matter."

"No."

The game was real, he was thinking, and he had no specific plans for playing it. But they probably had. When he left here they could bide time and choose place. It would be better the other way around.

"'Cause I don't have to have another, you know. Most guys want you to drink, they wanna think they're fooling you, or something."

"How's that?"

"Like they think you wouldn't do it sober."

"Maybe it's them."

She sipped a long sip that was the equivalent of a gulp.

"Maybe it's them, what?" she said.

"Maybe it's them who wouldn't do it sober."

She gave a short laugh, like a cough, as if the idea was nonsense, then she laughed until it was a giggle.

"I never thought of that," she said. She kept laughing, a sexually hesitant male was hilarious, it undermined all the machismo.

"You're funny," she said, with a few less giggles. "I like you."

It was infectious. Grant grinned despite himself. "You're pretty funny yourself," he said, trying to keep irony out of his voice.

The second drink came. Grant hadn't touched the beer.

"Look," she said, after a silence she couldn't explain, "are you doing business, or are we just talking?"

It was right on the point. In the instant he made up his mind.

"It's business." Then, not wanting to deceive her fully, he added, "Not maybe all the business you think it is, but business."

"Like what?"

"Oh, I'd like to drive around a bit."

"Fresh-air stuff, eh? I don't like that, too many bugs, that's for acid heads."

"Just driving." On a sudden inspiration, he produced his motel key. "I've got a place."

"All right," she said in a let's-not-argue-about-it tone.

"Let's go," he said. "We don't have to finish this stuff."

"Business first." She was frankly suspicious.

"Not here. Outside, okay?"

"All right."

Grant looked around the parking lot casually but carefully, keeping his head turned in the girl's direction so that

**137**

it would seem he was interested only in her. A half walk around the car gave him a view of the road and across it. Nothing. He opened her side first, a gentleman, she liked that, and she seemed to like cars, she was virtually posing next to it. She was wearing short tiny boots with high heels, also red and also with oval cutouts, that played up thin ankles and long legs. Very effective. But Grant was reacting with the admiration of a eunuch.

In the car, he said, "You hungry?"

"Hmm-m-m! Come to think of it, yes."

"We could pick up something. What'd you like?"

"Subs."

"Subs it is."

"And wine. It's right next to the submarine place, over there." She indicated the direction to town.

"Okay."

He started the car. She put her hand on his arm. She seemed all legs.

"Business," she said. "Fifty." It had a sad sound.

"Right," he said, and took some money out. "Here's double that."

He drove off, intent on the mirrors, the sides of the road.

She put the bills in the small handbag. She did it slowly, thoughtfully.

"What do I do for *this?*"

"Nothing extra."

"What am I doing in the first place?"

"Just riding in the car with me."

"Oh?"

They arrived at the submarine stand. He pulled in quickly. They went to the counter, and while she ordered,

**1 3 8**

Grant looked past her along the road they had come. They hadn't gone far, and anyone attempting to follow from a distance might go right through. No one did.

They drove a short way to a liquor store. Same routine. And this time the battered car drove by, U-turned as soon as it could, and was going by in the opposite direction when Grant and the girl were going back to the car. Faces turned and held for her.

Grant waited and let her fuss with the big sandwich, napkins, and the two small bottles of wine. They had no glasses, and she said paper cups were no good, so why not drink it right from the neck? She opened her own. Grant got the car moving.

"Good," she said, after the first bite. She was very careful about crumbs and drips, she had napkins all over.

"Glad you like it."

"All you're gonna do is ride around, is that it?"

"Yeah, that's all." He watched behind.

"That's a new twist. You get a thrill doing that?"

"Not really."

"What's the angle?"

"No angle."

"There's something, I know it."

She attacked the sandwich and munched for a while. She was meticulous about wiping her lips before drinking from the wine bottle. Grant was going through the town, toward the road that would go past the army base.

"Where we going?"

"Just around."

"I don't like it." It sounded as if she meant she'd prefer having a clear destination.

"Look," he said, "it's not the usual thing. I just need somebody to ride with me. That's all there is to it. If you're scared, we can call it off."

"I'm not scared. You lonely or something?"

"In a way."

"Whatta you trying to do, work up the nerve?"

"The nerve to what?"

"To lay me."

"Stop kidding."

"I'm not kidding. I had this guy once who was scared out of his hair of going with a girl. Took him hours to get around to putting a hand on me. Christ, I was fit to be tied. Some guys are pretty funny in the head, you know."

"Yeah, that's true. I'm not one of those guys."

"Then what are you working up to?"

"You always talk this much?"

"No!"

They fell silent. They passed the army base. There wasn't much traffic on the highway. No lights behind him.

"You'd like it better if I didn't talk, eh?" she said quietly.

"No, no. Go right ahead. I like it." He paused and added, "It makes you real."

She thought that over.

"You *are* funny," she said, and blurted, "*and* I'm not scared of you. So there."

"Good girl."

"What does *that* mean?"

"Nothing. I kinda like you."

"Oh, so now it starts, after all that."

"Start, nothing. What's got into you, anyway?"

"Oh, mister, if I told all that's happened to me."

"Sure."

**140**

"You think I'm shitting you."

"Don't talk like that."

"Why not? You think like that."

"No, but I guess you're right in assuming it."

"Assuming? Do you always talk like that? *Assuming!*"

"Sorry, that sort of slipped out."

"Ha!"

They were coming to the turn-off that had led Grant to the Brenan farm. It was a dangerous "Y" intersection and they had put up big yellow streetlights which Grant could see in the distance and hadn't noticed in the daytime. He wasn't going to turn, he intended to go straight and he didn't slow down. It made him notice that there was a car up ahead, that it had slowed down, and that it was traveling without lights. When he didn't take the turn-off, the lightless car sped away. He was being followed from the front.

The knowledge almost unnerved him, it made him the amateur he was, and he felt fear for the girl. He fought back visions of the other night. He would have to pick a place and wait for the time. He regretted using the girl to attract attention. It would have been better alone, he could have used the car as a weapon and he could have disregarded his own safety. But he couldn't disregard hers.

She felt his mood shift like a change in direction.

"What's the matter?"

"Nothing."

"I'm scared . . . What's your name, anyway?"

"Joe."

"I'm scared, Joe! For chrissake, I'm scared!"

"Yeah. It'll be all right."

"That car?"

"That's part of it."

A mile farther he saw a sign for a picnic area. He pulled into it when they got there, going as far in as he could, and faced the car toward the highway. He estimated he was about thirty yards from the road. He turned off the lights, the motor, and sat back.

"What's going on?" she asked.

"There may be some trouble."

"What kind of trouble?"

"A fight, I guess."

"What are we doing, sitting here? Let's get out of here!"

"It's no good. There may be a lot of them, and they can move fast, they have bikes, motorbikes. We're better off here, they have to come to us."

"Oh, no," she groaned, sounding as if an old despair had caught up with her.

"What's *your* name?" he asked.

"Reeny, Irene that is."

"Look, Reeny, nothing is going to happen to you," he said with a controlled, hard fierceness. "Nothing."

He got out of the car and stood inside the open door. The dome light felt too bright. He unclipped the holster and pistol from inside his waistband. He took the gun out, threw the holster in the back seat, flicked the safety off, then on, and, sitting with the door open, reached past her into the dash and took out the loaded, spare magazine, which he put in his jacket pocket. He left the dash open, there was a box of bullets there.

She watched with horror at first, then with some relief.

"You knew they were coming," she said.

"Not fully. I thought it was possible."

"Why did you pick me up, Joe?"

**142**

"I don't know."

"Did you want a witness, or something, to scare them off?"

"I just don't know."

It was as if he were re-creating what had been into what should have been. But the past was the past. The present was very different. He was committed, he'd have to cross the line.

"Can you put that light out?" she asked.

He reached up to the dome light. There was no switch on it, he'd have to shut the door. It was too late anyway. He heard the sound of motors. He got out and closed the door. He gave the girl the car keys.

They came in from the right, away from the town. Grant wondered how they had managed that. They turned into the picnic area and stopped at the edge of it, headlights glaring. Three bikes, three headlights. He hadn't thought of that, the lights made it impossible to see anybody. Calmly he walked toward them into sure range, leveled the pistol in two hands and began shooting.

The first light crinkled out loudly under the report of the shot, and somebody yelled something, then the second light, and in two shots the third light. The yelling grew louder. Feet scraped on gravel as they scurried away from their bikes. Grant backed off toward his car, his eyes not used to the dark, holding down panic and useless action. He shot once at the sounds. More scurrying. Five shots gone. If they charged him now, they could disarm him.

He crouched near the back of the car and removed the magazine from the pistol. It left one round in the chamber. He put in the fresh magazine. He now had ten bullets in the gun, three in the old magazine. But he had no targets.

Then he had. One of the toughs struck a match, which made something flare up in a bigger flame, a gasoline bomb. Grant shot at the flaming light and it tumbled forward as somebody yelled, this time in pain. The burning gas came bouncing toward the car and exploded. The girl put the headlights on, and started the car.

In this fresh light, he could see figures dashing for cover. Sirens took shape in the distance. He shot steadily at the moving forms as the girl tried to maneuver the car away from the flames of the bomb. One tough was trying to get back to his bike, and Grant held on the moving target, seeing him clearly, and somehow unable to pull the trigger. A patrol car pulled up in screeches. A spotlight fixed on Grant. Another patrol car was arriving.

"Drop it!"

He put the gun down on the nearest picnic table and despite commands from the police he went over to the girl and held her as she cried hysterically, her wig askew. He straightened it and looked into flashlights and gun muzzles.

"I'm all right, Joe," she said almost inaudibly.

But his thoughts were elsewhere, nowhere.

# 17

They put handcuffs on Grant and put him in the back of a patrol car. The girl was in another, her hands free. She had stopped crying. There were no bodies this time, only wounded, and they were on their feet yelling for a doctor as they were pushed into yet another car. The troopers put the fire out with extinguishers and by shoveling earth over it. A truck came for the motorbikes. A reporter and a photographer darted around asking questions and taking pictures, especially of the girl. There must have been at least eight patrol cars. Grant didn't count them, it didn't matter much. His arms hurt, they were behind him, the handcuffs tight, painful, and it was difficult to sit properly. He was powerless, the huge machinery of society had taken over. He felt cold, and his arms trembled and shook his shoulders. He was glad the girl was safe.

One by one the cars moved out at scattered intervals. Grant's two were silent with him, busy with the radio. He wanted to ask them to loosen the handcuffs, but he didn't, it was that kind of atmosphere.

"Looks like a new gun," the one on the right said to his partner.

"I got it yesterday," said Grant.

"Look, mister, you heard your rights. So keep it quiet. The less you say, the less they can make us out as liars later. We saw you, we got the gun. That's all there is to it for us."

"Will Captain Sparrs be there?"

"I guess so. He's always there. You know the captain?"

"Yeah. From Monday night."

"You the Grant guy?"

"Yes."

The trooper weighed the pistol, thinking. "Holy Jesus," he said, sighing. He made it sound like a prayer. He turned to Grant.

"How you feeling?"

"Okay. The cuffs hurt."

After a pause, he nudged his partner and nodded to the side of the road. They pulled over, had Grant come out and cuffed his hands in front of him loosely. Regulations. They drove the rest of the way without a word.

At headquarters there were more reporters and a man with a strong light and a movie camera. They had cooperated once, they were collecting now. The troopers moved casually and steadily through them, stolid and unspeaking, and took Grant through the lobby's swing doors, along a corridor and into a small room, a cubicle, where they simply left him. The door locked as it closed.

The room had a table in the middle, bolted to the floor, and four swivel stools with backs, two on either side of the

**146**

table's length, also bolted to the floor. There was a window in the door and along the corridor wall, the glass thick and reinforced with wire, vents on the upper walls, a light recessed into the ceiling, no light switch and a wide-angle mirror about the size of a dinner plate near the ceiling in one corner. There was nothing else.

Grant sat down where he could see the windows and put his handcuffed arms on the table. He noticed his watch next to the metal. He didn't look at the time. He wasn't waiting, he was just there. He felt empty, almost bodiless except for the fading pain in his arms. The blank room was telling him something, but he couldn't sort it out. Something about a loss of some sort, of hope perhaps, of feeling, something. He felt detached, clear-minded, his emotions inoperative as if they had disgorged themselves in the picnic area. The blank room was very solid and very empty. Something.

A long untold time went by and Sparrs came in with a trooper. He waved impatiently at the handcuffs. The trooper removed them and left. Sparrs sat down opposite Grant. He looked haggard, grim, which made Grant check his watch. It was past one-thirty, the small hours again.

"In a minute," Sparrs said as if he were resting, "we're gonna have to hear some of your story, off the record at least, so we can decide a few things."

"You can hear it all, I'm not hiding anything."

"That's not the way I want to play this."

"Decide what things?"

"That'll depend on what comes out of the story."

"You make it sound complicated."

"It's getting that way."

"Oh? Did one of them die?"

"Hell, no." He sounded as if he wished they all had. "You hit one in the arm, clean, right through, the other got nicked in the testicles, a scratch, nothing that's gonna cause any chastity."

"The same three?"

"Yeah, the same three. Don't tell me you didn't know."

"I knew. But I couldn't be sure. You're holding them this time?"

"That's one of the things we have to decide."

Grant was aware of the room again, a locked-in space, with a locked-in meaning. It seemed to have Sparrs locked in too. A trooper tapped on the window for Sparrs, opened the door and left.

They went to the interrogation room, the same one as last Monday night. Ketner was there, a thin cigar in his sad, jovial face. He nodded to Grant and blew smoke with a hissing sigh. He seemed embarrassed or disappointed. The foil plate from a frozen dinner served as an ashtray. He finished threading a tape on the recorder and said, "Sit here." Grant sat down in front of the microphone. It was like being in a dirty clinic.

"No tape," Sparrs said.

He sat on the edge of a chair and faced Grant across the corner of the table.

"The gun," he said. "You didn't have it Friday night when we warned you off. We were looking for things like that."

"No. I got it Saturday morning. I've got the sales slip."

"Skip that, skip that. After you got the gun, what?"

"I went to a friend's place, up north, and learned how to use it."

"Did the friend teach you?"

"No, I was alone."

"Then?"

"I came back here this evening."

"To find *them*."

"To let them find me."

"How did you know they were looking for you?"

"They were around the motel Friday night looking at my car, the same three, I could see them."

"You didn't call us."

"There was no use. They weren't doing anything."

"It would have been nice to know. We had a general surveillance on them. Where did you go tonight?"

"Jake's Palace first. They were all gone, but there was a guy across the road watching the place. So I pulled in at a bar to see if they'd come looking. They did, but not the way I expected, they were using an old car."

"That's where you picked up the girl?"

"Yes. In a way she picked me up."

"But you decided to take her along."

"Yes."

"Why?"

"I thought it would look more casual that way, as if I wasn't too interested in them."

"But they might be interested in her, is that it?"

"That too."

"You used her as bait."

"In a way."

"Why that picnic spot?"

"Just before that I saw they were following me from in front. The picnic area was the first place I could find to wait for them. I didn't want to get jumped on the road again."

"So you waited for them?"

"Yes."

"With the gun."

"Yes.

"Now the way those three monkeys tell it, they turned into that picnic area and you started shooting, just like that."

"That's right. They were attacking, and they had that gasoline bomb."

"You didn't know that just then."

"I knew they were attacking."

"They say they were turning in there for a barbecue. That explains the gas."

"It was a gas bomb."

"Until you use it, it's just gas. But a gun is always a gun."

"They used it."

"After. After you started shooting. Self-defense."

"They would have used it anyway. That's what they came for."

"The *event*, what *did* happen, can make it look otherwise. And the girl's story has you there waiting for them, gun and all. Those three monkeys, the girl, the first officer on the scene, do you know what the hell that all adds up to?"

"If you ask it that way, I guess I don't. What are you getting at?"

"There's too much here to walk away from. We have to make a case, for the prosecutor. And right now the case is against *you*."

"Me? Not them, eh?"

"No, not them, you. Illegal possession, carrying a concealed weapon, assault with intent to kill. That's bad enough. If you tell the whole goddam truth, it'll come out as attempted murder, premeditated. The whole bag. Why the hell didn't you leave it alone?"

Silence for a while, the locked-in message getting clearer.

"You know why," said Grant in a low voice.

"Yeah, I suppose I do. All this is off the record. Get a lawyer, Joe, and keep your mouth shut."

"I should've had one on my holidays."

He wasn't making a wisecrack, he was expressing a sort of moral shock, a feeling that somehow the human couldn't count, it was outside the law.

"It's an idea," grunted Ketner.

"We can do this in the morning," said Sparrs, indicating the tape recorder. "It'll give you time to think it over."

"There's nothing to think over," Grant said. "It's fresh now."

"All right."

Ketner started recording and Sparrs formalized things by reciting the ritual about rights, Grant responding, and establishing time, place and who was present.

Grant told the machine what he had done and what had happened. He spoke in a faraway voice like a man remembering his boyhood, and the others listened with unmoving faces and the conscious noiselessness imposed by the microphone. They didn't ask questions, it would only have been more damaging. When it was over, and the recorder off, the detectives felt a little freer. On the record they were professionals, off the record they were themselves.

"You want to phone somebody?" asked Sparrs.

"In the morning."

"Okay. Let's get some sleep."

"I'm staying here, eh?"

"Afraid so. You'll be arraigned tomorrow, it's too late now, you can arrange bail then. We have to book you."

"Weapons?" asked Ketner innocently.

"Yeah," said Sparrs, "it's the least serious."

He left without saying another word.

Ketner took Grant to a room across the hall where an officer filled out forms and photographed Grant and took his fingerprints. From there by elevator they went to the third floor into an office-like lobby with heavy metal doors where the corridors would be. Each door had a square foot of unbreakable glass. An officer sat behind a thick glass partition and looked carefully and questioningly at Grant's free hands. Ketner handed him a form and motioned toward one of the doors.

"The far end free? I want him to be alone."

The officer nodded, pressing something, and the metal door swung open. The corridor was two rows of cells, mainly bars with periodic sections of wall, light dimmed for the night, at the end of which two enclosed cells faced each other. Ketner opened the one on the right and let Grant go in. It was eight by ten with a high ceiling, surgical green, smelling of strong cleanser, supplied with a metal bed affixed to the wall, a sink, a seatless toilet with no tank, a tiny window that louvered open a few inches from the top, a recessed light and no light switch. Its own message was unmistakable, it was a place to keep a live body, no more, no less.

"We don't supply pajamas," said Ketner seriously. "You can fold your clothes over the end of the cot."

"Yeah."

At the door, Ketner paused.

"You should've done it alone," he said, "with a shotgun, a repeater—no ballistics—and with that car you could've been long gone. Nobody woulda got ulcers working on the case."

"I couldn't do that then. Earlier maybe."

"Yeah. We know."

"Or later."

The door closed and caught and became part of the wall.

# 18

Grant awoke from a half sleep at a quarter past six and wound his watch. The plumbing was making noises with increasing loudness as men somewhere in the building flushed toilets and ran sinks. There seemed to be no reason for it, no bell had rung, no siren screamed. Daylight, not direct sunlight, came from somewhere and through his cell window. His side of the building faced east. The discovery seemed important even though he knew it wasn't. It was something from outside, and that gave it significance: the day was unstoppable, at least they hadn't tried to stop it.

He tossed aside the thin army blanket and put on pants, socks, and shoes, not wanting to walk barefoot on the concrete floor, and added to the plumbing noises. He couldn't shave, and there were no towels to wash with. He drank water from cupped hands and wiped them on the blanket. After that there was nothing to do. He sat on the bunk. He thought of toothpaste, deodorant, and the kind of towels he used to like at home, a change of clothing, the choice of something for breakfast, a shower, a look out the window, very small things, things you could really do without, except that you'd stink in no time and you'd have to get used to another way of life. No, they hadn't stopped the daylight, but they had stopped nearly everything else, they—whoever they were—could tell you if and when to wash, eat, and even go to the bathroom if it was that kind of jail. A place to keep a body, a corpus, habeas corpus, you can have the body, and you go with it of course. He wondered about that.

Noises grew in the corridor and progressed until his cell was opened. An officer stood in the doorway, a pad in his hand.

"Breakfast," he said. "It comes from outside."

"I'm not hungry."

"Take my advice and eat, you'll need it."

"All right, all right, what've they got?"

"Regular stuff. Better get something that it don't matter if it's cold."

"Boiled eggs, hard, two, bread, butter, coffee. Can the coffee be kept hot?"

"Yeah, he brings a tank, we all take some. You pay now, minimum three bucks, any change'll be on your tray."

"That's nice." Grant gave him a five-dollar bill.

"Don't knock it. Nobody has to run grub for you, so it costs."

He gave Grant a receipt and left.

Inner time took over again slower than clock time. In a long while, really fifteen minutes, he was taken out to the fortified lobby to make a phone call. He called Steve Harrison, who, over Grant's protests that he could handle it himself, said he'd be down with a lawyer. An hour later breakfast came on a paper tray with paper plates and utensils and two dollars' change. In another long while, close to two hours, he was provided with shaving gear and told to clean up, which he did in cold water. And time once more became his lone presence and his thoughts.

He couldn't deny what he did. Whatever the law might call it, he couldn't go back on it. It would be the same as denying what those three killers had done. The white bodies under his flashlight, the discovered horror, untouchable by police or law, all this was central, everything derived from it, his feelings, his actions, the desire—perhaps impossible—to set it right. It all came together in him, and only him. It was part of his person. So much living reality, so much good had been destroyed, he had to keep something of it in existence, in himself, he couldn't let it slip, unfought for, into a final nothingness.

At twelve-thirty he was escorted a floor below and into a small conference room windowed and watchable from the corridor. Steve Harrison was there with a lawyer he introduced as Martin Aveley, a big man, well dressed, with lots of brown graying hair, innocent brown eyes in a ridged face, a tan, probably from golf, and a voice that rumbled like a drum. They brought lunch with them: sandwiches and coffee.

Once more Grant told his story and answered questions. With every telling and especially every interrogation it was growing less and less actual and becoming something different from what had happened a week ago. Words tried to be more real than events. Aveley seemed to sense Grant's distance. The lawyer lit a cigarette and studied the smoke.

**156**

Grant ended the narration by saying, "Yes, I'd like a good defense, Mr. Aveley, but I'm more interested in putting those three guys on the spot."

"Call me Martin," Aveley said. Then in a business tone, "The prosecutor will probably go for attempted murder, with revenge as a motive. The facts won't be in dispute. They're all provable and witnessed."

"I'll admit what I did," said Grant rather flatly.

"Some of it you won't admit, or else you won't have much of a defense. You may *think* you got that bunch to come after you, you may have *hoped* they would, but you didn't bring it about and you didn't intend it."

"I wasn't really intending anything. I just wanted to be ready."

It sounded silly and hollow without the experience to give it meaning, but Grant didn't elaborate.

"Now," said Aveley, "did they know who you were?"

"I don't think so. But they must know by now."

"So to all appearances they had no reason for attacking you. But you had every reason for wanting to attack them."

"Look," Grant said, waving aside the argumentation, "they killed Sue and Patty, and they would have killed me and the girl if I hadn't had that gun. That's what I want to bring out."

"Then you'd be putting a first-class motive around your neck."

"I want to put it around theirs."

"You'll be the one on trial, not them."

"I want the law to know about them. Goddam it, there must be something."

Aveley sighed and thumped out his cigarette. "It doesn't

**157**

work that way. We might not be able to go into that—all it shows is that you *believed* they were responsible for what happened to your family."

"It'll also show *why* I believed it. Hell, it's all there!"

"It would probably be ruled inadmissible except to show your state of mind—the shock of bereavement. It won't prove anything about them. And it would be bad if you acted as if you were out to get them. So don't do it. It'll be hard enough to believe the bereavement angle."

"What do you mean?"

"The girl. Grieving husband out with whore isn't going to sit too well with a jury. Unless you want to admit you used her to lure those men, and that shows intent and planning."

Aveley lit another cigarette and studied the new smoke.

"Well," said Steve Harrison, mainly for Grant's sake, "we don't have to argue it out right now."

"Joe," Aveley said, "let's get things clear—my job is to defend you in a court of law. It's not roughhouse and it's not just debate. There are rules and procedures. I'll try for acquittal, or for the lightest penalty. That's one thing, and it's the only thing. I can't at the same time try to prosecute those thugs for something that can't be proved. That's another thing entirely. So let's concentrate on your defense. A lot is going to depend on the kind of testimony you give. You understand?"

"Yeah, I understand."

"What are Joe's chances, in your opinion?" Steve asked.

"Not too good so far," rumbled Aveley. "I'd hate to go to a jury with it unless I had a panel of young fathers, all members of a gun club."

"There must be other routes."

"I'll talk to the prosecutor, find out what he has in mind. Then we'll decide. First we'll get the arraignment over with."

They got up to go. Before leaving, Aveley said, "You're a stranger here, Joe, nobody in the community knows you. You're somebody from outside who took the law in his own hands, committed certain criminal acts, added to the general violence, and wants to persist in that course of action. A panel of citizens won't know about the original case, and isn't going to let you run down its law enforcement. And there's not much of a chance they're fed up with thugs of the sort that attacked you, even if they know about them."

"You're saying that's what I'm up against."

"I'm saying don't get your hopes too high."

"They never were. That's why I'm here."

They left. Grant took a sandwich back to his cell.

The arraignment took place at two-thirty in an old brick courthouse in the center of town. Grant was taken there in handcuffs by the arresting officer and Lieutenant Ketner. Reporters had gathered, it was two stories in one, both big. The formalities were over quickly. The charge was attempted murder. Aveley pleaded Grant not guilty, had him remain silent, and with the cooperation of the prosecutor kept the bail to five thousand dollars. Trial was set two weeks hence. Aveley stayed behind to talk with the reporters.

Grant got his car at headquarters and went to his motel, where he had a thorough wash-down and a change of clothing. He left his whereabouts at the desk for Steve and Aveley and bought newspapers. The woman at the desk checked his name and suddenly looked worried. She was in her fifties, thin, graspy, belligerently nervous.

"There won't be any trouble, will there?" she blurted.

"No trouble at all. You can check with Captain Sparrs at the new headquarters."

"Oh, no, no. It's all right, it's all right," she lilted in appeasement. Income fought with fear. "How long will you be staying?"

"I don't know. Those two may be signing in," he said, referring to his message.

"Oh," she chirped in relief. Income had won.

Grant went to the bar and ordered Scotch. It was his first real lull, he was constrained to doing nothing, and he couldn't enjoy it. It was a vacuum in the wake of unreality. At least he wasn't sitting in jail. He opened the local paper.

The front page was full of it. What first caught the eye was a banner headline SHOOTS THREE IN PICNIC AREA and a blowup of the girl, leg lifted, trying to get into the back of the police car. There were shots of the vehicles with the fire in the background, of the toughs being led by police, and one of Grant in handcuffs going into headquarters. The story by Roy Klidebur began in three columns: THE QUIET OF A PEACEFUL EVENING WAS SHATTERED LAST NIGHT AS AN ARMED MAN, BELIEVED TO HAVE BEEN WAITING IN AMBUSH, OPENED FIRE ON THREE CYCLISTS AS THEY TURNED INTO THE PICNIC AREA ON ROUTE 25. THE VICTIMS WERE UNARMED. POLICE WERE ON THE SCENE IN MINUTES AND ARRESTED JOSEPH GRANT, WHO SURRENDERED WITHOUT FURTHER INCIDENT AND CLAIMED HE WAS BEING ATTACKED.

In the bottom third of the page was another picture and another story: MOTHER AND CHILD BRUTALLY SLAIN, with what looked like a police photograph of the station wagon, officers standing around a lumpy area, and

**160**

an arrow pointing downward in their midst. Klidebur told of the account by Joseph Grant of a hectic chase on the throughway, fighting all the way, being forced off the road, clashing with the attackers, and regaining consciousness to discover the attackers gone and his wife and child murdered. It sounded improbable and ended with: POLICE COULD FIND NO TRACE OF THE ATTACKERS AND HAD TO CONDUCT THEIR INVESTIGATION SOLELY ON THE FACTS AS PRESENTED BY THE SURVIVING JOSEPH GRANT. "WE HOPE HIS MEMORY GETS BETTER," A POLICE SOURCE SAID.

He stared at the paper and felt he was in the blank room again, only the room had grown bigger and its message sharper: the locked-in system was everywhere. If you don't talk to the press, you've got something to hide, and if you've got something to hide, you're guilty of something, you're guilty of not talking to the press, and the press is whatever wise guy happens to be chasing down a story. He was held by the picture of the wagon, three columns wide and four inches deep, it conveyed nothing of what he knew, could make no one else know anything but the barest fact. It recorded the event the way a line on a thermometer records weather. One photo and two minutes' reading was his life, their lives. Klidebur was probably a nice guy, he might even have a wife and a child. Grant mentally raised his glass to him, sipped his drink and dispelled the unavailing bitterness. He wondered if the three toughs read newspapers.

The bar radio gave news muffled by distance, and a heavy editorial about "what guns can do to the otherwise decent citizen" and "being impatient with the slow and civilized processes of law." As it got to calling for "barriers between impulse and access"—a professor moonlighting—

Steve Harrison and Aveley came into the dim light and found Grant.

"You've seen them?" Aveley said about the papers.

"Yeah, and I'm hearing it."

Aveley walked to the bar and looked at the radio. He came back lighting a cigarette.

"FM," he said. "They get people from the university."

"They'd know even less than the reporters."

They ordered drinks and chitchatted until they were served.

"I talked to the prosecutor," Aveley said. "He's willing to deal."

"Can he do that?"

"Yes."

"What kind of deal?"

"He reduces the charge to something like assault with a deadly weapon, and you plead guilty."

"If he's so sure it's attempted murder, why reduce it?"

"He's not really involved, he has to go by the evidence and do his job. The evidence fits any number of charges. A trial takes time and money and it can go either way. If you plead guilty, he gets a conviction, the job is done and the record is clean."

"What happens to me then?"

"Depends on the judge. With luck we might get a suspended sentence."

"And the three guys and what they did?"

"Nothing. Forget about them. They've got more rights than you have right now."

"I'll let you know. I have to think about it."

"Worrying is not thinking," Steve said. "Martin, what's your advice?"

"A jury trial is all or nothing, conviction or acquittal,

and we're weak there. But a judge might understand, and the reduced charge helps us. I'd say make the deal."

"Joe?" Steve said.

"All right." He nodded and reached for his drink. He felt as if something were betraying him. In a few hours the week would be complete.

"Fine," Aveley said. "I'll see Philips again, the prosecutor, take him to dinner. The pressure's on him now, he'll want to clear this up as fast as possible. Joe, you stay inside until the news cools off. We don't want the press making heat about a deal."

"Yeah."

Aveley gathered his briefcase, took a long swallow of his drink, and walked away carrying the case as if it contained events he could create. Grant watched him go, feeling the vacuum get emptier, to be filled with slow waiting.

The next few days brought nothing. The news faded from the papers and reporters gave up trying to see Grant. Steve stayed on, intending to go home for a while in a week's time, and helped Grant by finding quiet eating places, providing distractions like movies and bowling, and trying to make alternate plans for a future that would have to be faced. On the fourth day, as their existence was becoming routine, there was an opening on the court calendar.

They appeared on Friday afternoon before a judge named Frederick Williamson who, according to Aveley, was reputed to be thorough and fair. The three toughs were there without their costumes and looking like students, the girl in an unrevealing dress, Sparrs, a few officers, and reporters. The charge, as elaborated by Philips, was assault with a deadly weapon.

After a brief conference at the bench Aveley pleaded

guilty on Grant's behalf and received permission to outline the background to Grant's actions. He stressed the traumatic nature of the rape and murder, the strength of Grant's belief, however subjective, of the guilt of the three motorcyclists, and the real danger in which he placed himself when he began to look into the matter. Bereavement and shock, he argued, accounted for Grant's momentary lack of judgment and made his actions more human than criminal. Without telling the court what to do, Aveley indicated everything that could justify a suspended sentence.

The judge listened, scribbled a few notes, and looked toward Philips, who said nothing.

"Was there any evidence," the judge asked, "that these three young men were involved in Mr. Grant's tragedy?"

"None at all," Philips said.

"None in the legal sense," Aveley said. "But one of them bears wounds similar to the ones inflicted by the defendant on his assailants."

"I would like to see them."

Len Stitte was asked to come forward. He showed the judge his neck wound and missing teeth.

"Can these be connected with the defendant?" the judge asked.

"No," Aveley said, "it's only a moral certainty."

"Young man," the judge said severely to Stitte, "where did you get these wounds?"

"I fell off my bike." Stitte shuffled and giggled.

"Where is the humor in this?" the judge asked sternly.

"I'm a good rider, ya see. Falling off is kinda stupid."

"You may resume your place."

There was silence as the judge consulted the papers before him.

"Mr. Grant," he said, "you seem to have taken consider-able pains to find your family's assailants. Are you now ready to abandon such an undertaking?"

Aveley couldn't intervene. He looked steadily at Grant, hoping to communicate something.

"I don't know," Grant said.

"I'll put it this way: are you still convinced that these three men are those who set upon you some—" he glanced at his notes—"ten days ago?"

"Yes."

"I see."

The judge consulted his papers again. It was a long time before he pushed them aside.

"It is understandable," he said, "that bereavement could give rise to the desire for personal vengeance. But this is precisely why the law exists: to maintain in society an order whereby such penalties as befit crimes will be im-posed by law and not by individuals, however justifiably angry. It is unthinkable that private persons should ever penalize others, guilty or otherwise, let alone those who are merely suspect.

"In this case such an attempt was clearly made, and the subjective and mitigating circumstances cannot warrant setting the matter aside, though they may serve to reduce the severity of both the crime and its penalty.

"Accordingly, I will sentence you to five years in prison. And I may add that apart from this one matter your own character and personal history would be regarded with favor by a parole board. This court is adjourned."

The judge left the room.

Aveley explained to Grant that a determinate sentence like that meant he could be out in a year, it was the judge's way of giving him a break. Grant said nothing. Steve looked grim and also said nothing. Sparrs came over to them.

"Sorry, Joe," he said. "We'll keep working on it."

A sergeant indicated that Grant should come with him. As he walked by the three toughs, who were grouped behind a polished rail, low words through unmoving lips reached him, meant only for his ears.

"They were sweet tail, man."

And suppressed guffaws.

Grant turned and looked at them one by one, and by the time he saw the third, he exploded. "You bastard!"

He was over the rail flailing and kicking at the three of them, fists, knees, feet in all directions. He threw off the peacemaking policemen, who couldn't maneuver among the benches, and continued in hot silence to vent his fury on his screaming opponents. Two were bleeding about the head, a knife appeared, night sticks. It took over ten minutes to restore order.

They rushed him out and took him in irons to the county jail to await transportation to the penitentiary.

# 19

They chained the men together in leg irons and handcuffs.
They did it in batches of ten for thirty-four men, fourteen
in the last, and had them haul themselves into a big old
bus. Six guards stood three on either side of the line with
pump-action shotguns pointing to the sky, some one-
handed with butts resting on wide gun belts. They were
bored with the routine, alert only for departures from it.
The chains and the guns created an air of danger. For
some reason, perhaps the paperwork or identification, the
process was done alphabetically, and Joe Grant found himself in the first batch sitting on a long bench windowside.
The benches were metal and bolted to the floor. Old hands
had told others to go to the bathroom, it might be over
half a day before you could go again. The driver was behind a thick glass partition covered on the prisoners' side
with a grate of riveted metal laths. A guard sat next to
him, with two shotguns, one presumably for the driver

should trouble arise. A car would follow with four armed guards, one of whom had a battered official briefcase, the basic files on the men and receipts to be signed upon delivery. It was all done in silence except for the commands to go and stop, the dull scraping of the heavy chains, a few muttered conversations among the guards. They allowed the men to smoke, there was no danger of setting fire; even if they did, it would only burn the men.

The prison was in flatlands, miles from the nearest town, surrounded by a horizon of fields on which nothing was allowed to grow tall. The road to it kept making right-angle turns, passed through four check points, unmanned at the moment, and a double row of chain-link fences ten feet high with a two-foot fringe of barbed wire, and stopped completely at a massive wall of stone and concrete, thirty feet high, slightly angled, discolored and forbidding, an inverted fortress. Electrically operated steel doors let the bus and its car into a walled courtyard. At the far end a single steel door stood open and four men in guard's uniforms waited without obvious weapons.

The men clanked out slowly in reverse order and short-stepped their way, under commands, into alphabetic ranks. The guard with the briefcase and a prison official checked the roll and signed papers. The chains were unlocked and left on the ground and the men were ordered inside row by row and keeping ranks.

"Face right. No talking. No smoking."

They stood there for a long time, shuffling, taking in the reception room, coughing, clearing throats, no commands to straighten up and look smart, just face out, don't talk, don't smoke, each man with his thoughts if he had any, trying not to wait. It wasn't discipline, it was simply not being allowed to do anything for yourself.

A guard told them to remove all clothing and pile it in front of them, outer garments on the bottom, then shirt, underwear, socks, shoes on the side. After a long hesitation the men began to undress slowly, dawdling like children at bedtime, some sitting to get their shoes off. There was a certain value in going slow, you didn't leave yourself on the floor with your clothes. Joe was the eighth man in the first row. When he was naked he draped his clothes over his left arm and resumed his standing. Others started to copy him. The guard pointed to the clothes and then to the floor. Joe put his clothes down, as did the others. Discipline. More waiting. No briefings, no explanations, just the heavy standing and the nakedness.

Eventually a command came to pick up their clothes and they went row by row into another room where at a counter they deposited all their clothing and signed an inventory. They had nothing now, chains would have been welcome. Five at a time they were led to showers where again they waited, this time for the water to be turned on from outside. They had three minutes to wash, relatively alone, and some cursed under the cover of the water, some finally urinated.

Once more the ranks, the delay, and an examination of every orifice. It was done by two guards with lab coats over their uniforms, one inspecting the head, the other the privates, rubber gloves, probes, lights, antiseptics. It wasn't medical, it was a search. Ear, nose, mouth, penis, anus, check for false teeth, glass eyes, wigs, bumps, anything, everywhere. They did everything but issue laxatives. They

**169**

had the body. It was the only thing they had to work with. The work was not brutal, nothing personal, it was humane in its own way, but it could never be human. Joe wasn't surprised, it was somehow very logical. The system had penetrated as far as it could.

At the counter, one by one, in literal order, serviced by inmates, they received clothing. It was issued piece by piece and stamped with a number by a man behind the counter. The inmate in charge of the operation, a big man in his forties with little hair and glasses, looked at every man squarely in the eye and spoke a name and a number as if he didn't need the list in front of him. It was like a profession. The guard seemed oblivious. When Joe got to the counter, he was just about to speak—mouth open, air taken in—but the glasses and the eyes behind them said no. A sign high up on the edge of the shelves read, "The biggest Con is 3." Everybody saw it, nobody got it, but it seemed to mean something to the eyes behind the glasses. Joe took his clothes to yet another room where only a guard and an inmate waited. The other seven men had gone, the delivery group was being disbanded into the prison population. He dressed. The clothes were a fairly good fit. Maybe the man with the glasses was a tailor, or had been.

"Go with this man," the guard said. "Give this to the officer on duty." He gave Joe a pale green card with data on it. What officer? he thought. "He'll show you," the guard said without humor.

The man with Joe was short and chubby, also in his forties, with a pink face and darting eyes. He looked so clean he almost smelled of Javel. He got a nod from the guard and walked up to a cream-colored iron door that had a block of glass at eye level. He waited, it opened. Joe followed him through. It closed. They were in a long corridor, vented at the ceiling, with periodic squares of windows at the seven-foot level and no doors at all at the sides.

"You are now an inmate of this penitentiary," the man said. "It is a medium-security institution and affords its population certain privileges . . ."

It was a memorized statement. The man said it slowly in a practiced way, enunciating the words without rhythm. He was serious, at least straight-faced, without a trace of irony, like a kid giving the famous oration.

". . . There are twelve hundred men here besides yourself. There are rules and regulations aimed at allowing the men to serve their sentences beneficially and to make use of the opportunities for self-improvement. There are work and recreation facilities . . ."

He walked slowly, a little ahead of Joe like a tour guide, glancing at the high windows as if they were cue cards.

". . . Your rights as a citizen have been temporarily suspended. Your standing as an inmate is based on the rules of the institution. Good conduct is rewarded by privileges, at parole hearings, and by early releases . . ."

He called off the regulations and began itemizing the daily schedule. They arrived at the end of the corridor and stopped at another door. It opened like the first one. When it closed, the man stopped talking. He glanced over his shoulder and turned left into another corridor.

"They got closed-circuit TV in there, and it's bugged. They like to hear the spiel. Orientation."

"Orientation for what?"

"That's what they call it. They had consultants in here,

psychologists. So they don't have a sergeant talking to thirty, sixty men any more. That made them into a group. Negative cohesion they called it. So now they take them individually, like this. The guards didn't wanna do the spieling, the psychologists said the inmates should do it, it'd give them a sense of responsibility. I feel responsible. How do you feel?"

"Bullshitted."

"That's a nice use of the word, past participle, passive voice. It's not orientation, it's control. Keep moving, they got us timed, station-to-station phones. One of those psychologists, older guy, was in the Hitler camps, an inmate. He kinda got their backs up here, just his attitude, but the cons liked him. He never got to write the report though, the other guy did, he had a relative in the federal government. Cheerful bastard, like this was a hotel. He's an adviser to a few universities too, maybe those students got something. You went to college, eh? Engineer."

"Yeah. How do you know that?"

"That's what the psychologists wanted to know. Drove 'em crazy. Up."

They were out of the corridor and into a vast stairwell of iron steps and landings, all open to view from every side, three stories high and enclosed in concrete walls. They climbed to the second landing and stopped at another iron door.

"Give him the card, call him sir."

A capped face appeared at the small window, drifted away, and the door opened. The guard was a bushy-browed eagle-faced thin man with weathered and creased skin that made his age a puzzle. He said, "Okay," to the

**172**

inmate—who left—took the card, waved it at Joe to follow him.

They walked along a wall of cells. It was about fifty yards long and faced another just like it across a wide concrete floor. Each door had an open square foot of three bars at chin level, no glass, and a stenciled number over it. The lights in the high ceiling were caged between the exposed pipes. The place smelled faintly of men and cleaning fluid and something lost. An architect's nightmare. Nobody would ever build a place like this. Nobody did.

"It's here."

The stencil was 42.

"Open up, Dreye, you got company, he, he," the guard said and unlocked the door.

Joe entered the cell and saw the man, Dreye, sitting on the lower bunk holding a paperback. Their eyes met, parted, Dreye's to the guard, Joe's to nothing. For a moment, silence, the awkwardness of not acknowledging people.

"You're Grant-195," the guard said. "We use the last name'n the last three numbers'a the number. We call you that way, you answer that way."

Joe turned to look at the sharp face.

"Ya hear me?" There was a slight edge to the voice.

"Yes," Joe said, vaguely wondering about omitting the sir, "sir."

"That's a boy."

The door was closed, not hard, tried, locked, and the clinking walk faded away.

"You're new, eh?"

"Yeah."

**173**

"First time ever?"

"Yeah."

Dreye chuckled coldly. He was in his twenties, physically tough, a little arrogant. He had a bony off-center face with close-set eyes and a shag of brown hair that kept falling over his brow.

"What they get ya for?"

"Assault, with a gun."

"What happened?"

"I got mad." To change the subject, he added, "My name's Joe."

"Yeah."

Joe looked at the cell. There was something in Dreye's eyes that shut off contact, a gleam of knowledge, a suspicion, an unfounded certainty of some kind. The cell was nine by nine, with a high ceiling, a barred window with the window far outward from the bars. It had a sink with no stopper, small towels, a topless toilet, no mirror, no shelf, a caged light in the ceiling, two concrete bunks probably supported by two more on the other side of the wall, no chairs or stools, nothing on the concrete floor except paint.

"It's $108\frac{3}{16}$ inches by $107\frac{3}{4}$," Dreye said.

"Small."

"It'll get smaller." He sounded as if he were quoting.

"Depends."

"It'll get smaller!" It was an article of faith.

"Yeah, I bet it will."

Joe looked at the upper bunk.

"I like the top one," Dreye said.

"That's okay with me."

"I like the bottom one too."

The cell was now two by two. Joe sat on the open toilet and hunched forward, arms on knees, the look on his face preventing absurdity.

"You and I, Dreye," he said with quiet conviction, "are going to get along."

"I don't have to take anything from you." Another quote.

"That's right. And I don't have to take anything from you. What's your first name?"

"Willy."

"Willy, which one of those goddam bunks do you want?"

"The top one. I don't want nobody peeking at me."

"Okay."

Joe got off the toilet and walked to the door in four steps.

"Can I have your tobacco?" Dreye said.

"I don't have any."

"They'll give you some."

"Don't you get some too?"

"Yeah. I need more."

"You smoke a lot?"

"No."

"What do you use it for?"

"Things."

"I'll see," Joe said. Commitment to Dreye wasn't a good idea. "I might start smoking in here."

An electric bell rang in sharp bursts in the corridor.

"What's that for?" Joe said.

"Supper."

Dreye washed his hands.

A long time had passed. Joe had pains in his stomach, and he realized it was from not urinating. He relieved himself and washed his hands.

"We eat in the cells," Dreye said. "One man goes gets the stuff."

The cell door buzzed and sprang open a little. Dreye disappeared into the corridor.

Joe looked out and saw men filing toward the end of the corridor and into the stairwell. The cell doors were left wide open and the cells were empty. Joe fell into the line and followed it downstairs into a mess hall that functioned cafeteria-style in two rows. Orientation.

# 20

". . . at me," Willy's voice was saying, "and I can't tell from where."

Joe opened his eyes and saw the concrete underside of Willy's bunk.

"You hear me?" Willy said.

"I hear you now. What do you want?"

"You were trying to peek."

"I was asleep."

"You lay there and look up at me, I can feel it, and then you have to try and take a peek."

"I was asleep. What time is it?"

"The bell's gonna ring. If I was in the lower I'd be able to watch you better and you wouldn't be lying there look-ing up at me, you'd be looking up at the ceiling and I wouldn't have to half get up just to see if the sides are clear. Why do you wanna peek?"

"I was asleep."

"You do it in your sleep too."

"Forget it."

"I want the lower."

"A deal's a deal, it stays the way it is."

"You tricked me."

"No."

Willy climbed down. He was dressed to the waist. He urinated and went to the sink to prepare to shave. Joe slowly put on pants, socks, shoes, and approached the toilet.

"Hold it," Willy said.

"What for?"

"I might have to go."

"You just went."

"I gotta know it's free."

"Yeah. Well, it'll be free in a minute."

Joe urinated. Willy remained immobile and watched the wall above the sink. Then he resumed soaking his face.

Joe went back to the bunk and got out the shaving gear he had been issued in the evening. He had also been given shower slippers, tobacco and cigarette papers. The tobacco was gone.

The big bell sounded for ten seconds. That made it six-thirty.

"I always get up before that thing," Willy said. "I don't have to obey it."

The noise of human activity started echoing in the corridor.

"Willy."

"What?"

"The tobacco."

"It's mine."

"No. Get it and give it back to me."

"What for? You don't smoke."

"Get it."

"So what can you do if I don't?"

"I'll go looking in your stuff."

Willy went to his bunk, reached over and took out the package of tobacco. He handed it to Joe reluctantly.

"Can't I have it?" he said with helpless sincerity. It was convincing.

"All right."

Joe gave it to him. Willy put it back in the bunk and continued soaking his face.

He took so long soaking and shaving that an hour later when the breakfast bell rang Joe hadn't shaved. He now had a two-day growth.

In the mess-hall line-up, he heard "195" called out close by and didn't associate it with himself.

"You! 195!"

He finally got it. He turned and saw a chubby guard with a pleasant face and humorless eyes signal him out of the line.

"What's your name?" The tone was calm, low-key, business-like, authority speaking.

"Grant-195," and remembered, "sir."

"You're not shaved."

"No, sir."

"Why not?"

"I didn't know I had to."

"Well, you've got to. Every day. You're new, eh?"

"Yes, sir."

"Every day. It's good for morale. Back in line."

The guard walked away, he had done his job, a rule was

a rule, it was all for the good of the men, no need to look like bums. For a halting instant Joe felt like a schoolboy.

"Cool," a baritone voice said behind him.

It belonged to a man about Joe's height and age with bloodshot brown eyes and black hair and a long face lined like a drawing.

"What was that?" Joe said.

"Cool," the man said. "You handled him nice."

"It just happened."

"He got handled nice anyway. Cool."

And that was the end of the conversation. Early morning wasn't a good time for chitchat.

After breakfast the men went back to the cells till eight and left in scattered slow-moving groups to go to work. Willy stuffed his pockets with his belongings and rushed out, to the machine shop he said, but his hands were too soft and clean.

Joe was left alone. He stood awhile and paced the small floor, half expecting to be assigned to some sort of work. But nothing happened. The expectation lapsed into waiting. And the waiting finally became nothing. He had only himself and the cell. Willy had taken his paperback with him. With elaborate slowness he shaved in cold water, making it last as long as he could, methodical, meticulous, filling in the non-time. He tried not to think, but that is impossible, and he decided not to try to figure out the time of day.

At lunchtime he joined the line, relieved, almost glad, and he ate his food slowly as if to prolong the relief. Already he was beginning to realize what was going on. By the time he was back in his cell he had predicted to himself that he would again be expecting work and that he would be glad to take it. And in the enforced nothingness he did feel that way, but only for a moment. He understood the total stripping away, the removal of the exercise of his own will, not just his liberty, the being and doing nothing but the will of the institution. Nothing personal. It was a system. And systems take themselves for granted. His awareness would go unnoticed, and perhaps it would help him keep his person intact. He would follow the routine, let the non-time be, make no requests.

But not doing anything was very trying. He didn't want to think about the past, to risk reliving happy moments with hunger or remembering the bad ones with fresh pain. The future couldn't be thought of, it didn't exist, there was no one to give it existence. He could choose some of his thoughts, but only some, not the ideas that snapped into mind, or the flashes of insight, or the vivid and sudden memories and the feelings that flooded past them. These he tried to avoid by thinking consciously of other things, like handling Willy Dreye, but his feelings lagged behind and pulled him back to where he'd been. A seesaw balanced on the self, the self quite evident. He was vulnerable everywhere, naked inside and out. The institution's clothes couldn't cover him, or the cell house him, they were an extension of the probing finger, a tremor of knowing in the bowels. No wonder Willy was afraid of being peeked at.

The following day at lunch he sat next to a fat man in loose clothes who was eating his beans and vegetables without looking at them. The man returned Joe's nod by just looking at him and chewing.

"How are ya doin'?" the fat man said.

"All right. I'm not doing anything."

"They'll find something for ya. It's a problem. There's a lot of unemployment here."

It was straight-faced, said just before a forkful of beans went into his mouth.

"Looks that way."

"Total welfare." More beans. The remark sounded like an old joke, a joke from better moods. "In the war on poverty." Then greens.

Between bites and during chews he learned, as he should have from Willy, of the recreation periods after lunch and supper, what to do about showering, about laundry, and of a small library they called the bookery. "Keep eating." It was made to look like a casual, half-resented encounter.

"Ever play ball, baseball?" the man said.

"Not lately, maybe ten years ago."

"Play some. Good for ya."

"Yeah."

"Yeah is right." It was more than conversation.

"Any red tape for this?"

"No. It's our baby. Just be around."

When Joe was leaving, his back to the fat man, he heard, "How do you like Willy?" and he kept going, it was the sort of remark that didn't need an answer, it just meant that others had also experienced Willy. It lifted his solitude a little.

He followed three men to the exit and into the huge stairwell, then right and along a short corridor and into the yard. The sun surprised him with light and heat. It was unwelcome, it was too normal. The place was a vast square, perhaps two hundred yards to the side, three made up of buildings, cell blocks four stories high, and the fourth a wall that was as high as the buildings. In the middle of each side were the jutting remains of an old wall. Joe guessed that the yard had once been divided into four pens. That would fit with the rest of the design, a guard station in each corner and at each mid-point. Some of the surface was blacktop and hot, the rest was grass. It was hard to see completely. In the unmoving air hundreds of men stood and walked, alone or in small groups. They respected the grass.

In the corner to Joe's right, opposite the big wall, was a baseball diamond of sorts, without backstop or bases or plate. There was a pitcher's mound but no rubber. Four men played catch. Joe lounged and watched them. Nothing happened. They seemed not to notice him.

"Hell with it. It's too hot," one of the men said. He turned to Joe. "You wanna throw?"

Joe held up his hands as though to receive the ball, and the man tossed him his glove and walked away. Joe became the fourth man and the warm-up continued without conversation.

In twenty minutes a bell rang and the men began to go inside. Joe gave his glove to his partner and ventured a question.

"Where can I shower?"

"What's your cell block?"

"That one." He turned his head and was about to gesture.

"Don't point. That's B block. Off the center landing up from the dining hall. There's a count in fifteen minutes, get in your cell by then."

"Thanks."

"Nothing."

It was easy to find. Two men went in ahead of him and three behind him. It was in two sections, one a changing and toweling room, the other the showers, about twenty of them along the perimeter. He put his clothes on the bolted bench and went in to wash. Men who knew the routine and had got in early were finishing up, those who arrived with Joe were hurrying. Soon they were the only ones there.

As Joe was rinsing, eyes closed, arms raised, someone grabbed him from behind by putting an arm around his torso. He couldn't walk away, couldn't turn around.

"You got it wrong," he said.

"Not a chance," an excited voice said.

Joe twisted and brought his right elbow down hard. It struck the man on the side of the neck and made him yell and fall to one knee. When the four others saw the look on Joe's face they kept their distance. The man stood up. He was big, about thirty, with a rough face, brutal with sexual frustration.

"You got it wrong," Joe said again.

"Like hell. Willy says you're paying for it. You're pussy."

"He's wrong."

"Then why are you paying him?" This came from a man to his left, glittering eyes, smiling lips like a permanent rictus, a chubby rump flanked by rounded hips. He wasn't cheerful, despite the smirk, he was scratchy. His words were precise and wet as if he liked the feel of his lips.

"I'm not paying him."

"It's your tobacco."

The wet words were somehow accusatory, as though something had been proved to his delight.

**184**

"You're gonna deliver," said the big man.

Joe looked at him across his weeks of tragedy.

"Get warned," he said, hearing his own words and voice sounding like a stranger's. "One move out of you and I'll tear you out with my bare hands."

Wet lips said something like "E-e-e-ee," but otherwise all was silent.

"Yeah," the big man finally muttered, "yeah." Perspective returning. He stepped aside.

Joe went to the other room, toweled superficially, dressed and put his shoes on without socks and made his way to his cell. He didn't look at Willy as he dried his feet and slowly put on his socks and shoes.

"What'sa matter," Willy said, "get your feet wet?"

The eagle-faced guard came by for the count. Joe stood at the door looking out into the corridor. He didn't trust himself to confront Willy. A talk, threats, a beating wouldn't change anything, it would take years with a psychiatrist. A fight would only make things worse. Making a complaint was out of the question, and so was asking for a transfer.

The bell rang, and the men filed out to go back to work. He took advantage of the movement to lag behind the men, and when they had all gone he stood by the guard's station. The guard was arranging papers, probably tally sheets.

"Can I talk to you?" Joe said.

"Sure."

"I'd like to drop the tobacco."

"All right. Don't like it?"

"I stopped smoking."

"That's fine by me."

**185**

"How do I get to the library? I'd like something to read."

"Sorry, you don't. Not until you're classified."

"Classified?"

"Yep, for security, what kind of security you are. If you're all right, then you can move around some. But till that happens, you're gonna wait."

"How long?"

"I dunno, that's all from the office."

"Well, thanks anyway."

"You close the cell door, eh?"

"Yeah."

He went back to the cell and closed the door upon himself. A symbolic act. It wasn't obedience, it was a sort of understanding. The guard knew Joe wasn't dangerous, but he couldn't grant privileges. He had given an explanation instead of a command. It was a kind of trust, and the action of closing the door acknowledged it. Small, simple, unarticulated. Prison had a way of magnifying things. Like tobacco.

This time the cell was a little less confining, his person strengthened by the human contacts, even by the one negative encounter. He stretched out on his bunk, cautiously playing the game of thinking and not thinking, trying to keep things in the idle present and not remembering that it would last almost five years. He would make more contacts, be given some kind of job, find out more about how things worked, even make a few friends, and . . . And what? Pass the time away? That was the only thing that made any sense. Nothing in here could have meaning. But then nothing out there had any meaning either. Unless he could get to those three men again . . . He stood up to

short-circuit that line of thought, and heard the guard outside the cell.

"Open up, Grant, he, he." It was a kindly ritual.

The guard opened the door and handed Joe a thick paperback.

"Something for ya."

Joe looked at the title, *The Greening of America.*

"What's it about, gardening?"

"I dunno. The educated guys'a been readin' it. Lotsa
pages there, keep you busy, they said."

"Who said?"

"The guys in the library."

"Oh. Thanks."

"That's okay. Man's gotta have something to do."

He closed the door and left.

For all his need, Joe didn't begin reading right away.
Merely having the book and knowing he could read it
whenever he chose lifted his spirits. He held it and read
the covers and the testimonials and enjoyed the anticipa-
tion of being busy with it. A seed catalogue would have
had the same effect. A small thing. Magnified. When he
did begin to read he went slowly, letting every word have
its time, finding pleasure in the rhetoric that predicted a
spiritual revolution, feeling the content as less important
than the mind and voice that could be heard on the page.
It was like listening to a sermon and secretly supplying
your own humor. He took to rereading the paragraphs,
arguing with the arguments, and then looking forward
to going on to the next unread passage. A game. It en-
gaged the consciousness, made time uncalculable. It
didn't make him forget, but it allowed him not to remember.

187

When Willy came back from work, he reacted immediately.

"You got my book!"

"No, it's from the library."

"How did you get it?"

"I got it."

"What's it about?"

"Making a garden."

"In here?"

"No, a place called Eden."

"You're kidding."

"Sure."

"I don't like being kidded."

"I wasn't kidding you."

"The hell you weren't."

"I was kidding this guy." He waved the open book.

"Who is he?"

"Some kind of lawyer."

"Oh."

Joe discovered as he read distractedly that the book was
a way of keeping Willy in hand. Somehow, with Joe en-
gaged in reading, Willy felt less watched, but he had to
keep proving it by trying to get Joe's attention: better to
be sure you're being watched than not to be sure you're
not being watched. It was a strange struggle, it's impossible to prove a negative. It could go either way, and Willy
might try to steal the book. Joe took it with him to supper.

In the yard he watched and then joined an infield practice. He fielded at second base for a while and took his
turn batting grounders and calling out play situations. The
catcher seemed to be in charge, a sort of anchor man, with
overtones of being something more. He was medium

height, chunky, hard, about Joe's age, with a squarish face and gray eyes that never changed expression.

"You want to play regular?" he said.

"Yeah," Joe said, "seems like a good idea."

"We practice the whole team, two teams, outfield and all when there's nobody in the yard. I put you on the list, you get permission."

"I'm not classified yet."

"When you are, lemme know."

"Okay."

Near sundown the bell sent the men back in. The players showered and separated as though they had nothing in common but baseball practice. Joe followed a line into the mess hall, which had been converted to show a movie. The screen was fitted with a large homemade adjustable hood because most of the lights had to stay on, the projector was noisy and spilled light, the sound was tinny and loud, and it was hard to get involved in a story of two submarines trying to outwit each other in World War II. But the men reacted with enthusiastic talk and criticism, the three guards watched without being part of the audience, and for Joe it was better than being in the cell with Willy.

For the next three days he read the book, played ball, made limited contacts, and tried to keep life in the cell at a civilized minimum, but Willy was getting worse. On the fourth day Joe was escorted by an inmate through a televised corridor, from there by a guard to a large room with a big table and ten chairs, one side and the ends occupied by six people, all male, two in uniform: the classification committee.

They weren't identified or introduced. Using papers in front of them, they went into his background and record

189

and asked about his education, aptitudes, experience, and general intentions for self-improvement. One, who sounded like a psychologist, asked tricky questions to find out if he were resentful or hostile. After a while they seemed at a loss, and no decision was reached in Joe's presence. The following day the guard told him he could use the prison facilities like the library and the gym, but couldn't join work teams and couldn't roam about without special permission.

In another two days he was assigned to work in the library. It was make-work, already shared by eleven men, but officially he could be forgotten. The place was three rooms, stacks for twenty thousand books, mainly discards and paperback novels, a workroom for the staff, and a typing room for the few serious readers. A special section of the stacks was reserved for "education," which contained textbooks, and "law," for the men who worked on their own briefs. The classification system was alphabetical and used only to keep order, between them the men knew where every book was. The man in charge, a lifer, took his work seriously but couldn't push the men. Alone, over years, he had catalogued the books according to the Library of Congress system, but the men wouldn't be taught how it worked, and he couldn't get the authority to impose it. Joe's job, at whatever pace he chose, was to inscribe call numbers on the books, and that made him curious to know how the cataloguing system worked. But he didn't work hard or steadily. Ass-busters, as they were called, were not popular.

Willy's fears grew more intricate. He accused Joe of deliberately getting the job in the library so that he could read Willy's books beforehand and then be able to know what was going on in Willy's mind as he in turn read the books. Joe prevailed a little by constantly repeating, "I don't read your kind of junk," and as that fear receded, not fully, Willy revealed that he knew of Joe's plans to have the baseball players beat him with bats because of the tobacco-shower episode. This time the constant repetition of "Forget it, it's not that important" did no good. Willy was not to be lulled into relaxing his vigilance. He could go to the library almost any time and check on Joe, but he couldn't join the team and get permission to practice when the yard was empty. When he tried to become a bat boy and was refused, he became desperate with the certainty of Joe's conspiracy. But why try to be near the teams when he was sure they'd beat him? Joe gave up trying to unravel Willy's fears.

At the next practice Joe mentioned it casually to the catcher. And surprisingly it got a reaction.

"Skip practice till I get word to you."

"Hell, it can't be that serious."

"Do like I say." And he softened it with, "It'll be a favor. That kinda thing's bad for morale. Start now, you got a headache."

Joe play-acted a sudden headache, mentioned it to the men, got permission to go to the infirmary for aspirin, and went to the library to read. Anything to keep morale high, but it did seem a little out of proportion. Maybe the coach-catcher was another nut. Or maybe he just knew Willy.

If he did know Willy, he guessed wrong. To him it was proof that the attack was imminent and that Joe didn't want to be around to take the blame. But when three days went by without incident, his fears subsided. Maybe the catcher knew what he was doing. But no word came to resume practice.

Two days later, during the pre-supper lock-up, the eagle-faced guard announced himself.

"Open up, Grant, he, he." And when he was in, "Get your stuff, you're moving."

"I'm moving?"

It was something Joe had refused to ask for. He had had almost two weeks of Willy.

"That's right." He didn't look at Willy, who was on his bunk pretending to read. "You're a troublemaker, he, he."

Joe gathered his books, three of them, slippers, shaving gear, a pair of spare socks, toiletries. He had acquired a small canvas bag without pulls. The fact of moving resonated through his nothingness, the hollow sound of impermanence, even prison wasn't secure. When he was ready he turned to Willy.

"So long, Willy. No hard feelings, none at all."

Willy kept looking at his book. "Why do you have to go?" he said. It was asking for tobacco again. Somehow he made sense, prison sense.

The guard stopped at his station to get papers and led Joe down the stairs, into a corridor, a turn, into a block just like the old one, and up one flight to the big doors of the cell tier where he stopped.

"I put you back down for makin's, it's like money in here, ya know."

"Thanks."

They went to the guard station, a paper was passed without a word, and the eagle-faced guard left. The new one was tall, spit-and-polish, a face almost stern with duty, a professional air blanketing whatever thoughts and feelings he might have.

"Put in for a transfer, eh?"

An alert pause. What to say? He hadn't applied for it. But to say he hadn't would raise questions. It was probably only small talk.

"Yes, sir."

It was done. Wait for the reaction.

"They usually don't last two days with Dreye. Two weeks. And no ruckus."

It was just talk, the pose of professional musing. A good prisoner gives no trouble, he doesn't assert his existence.

"Did you ask for this block?"

"No, sir."

"Do you know anybody in this block?"

"No, sir."

"Library, baseball." He was checking papers. "Some of your friends might be in this block."

"I don't know. I have no friends."

"How about the guys on the team? What're their names?"

"I don't know their names, I just turned up for a few practices."

"Who asked you to?"

"Well, nobody really. I was watching them play catch and one of the guys said it was too hot and asked me if I wanted to sub for him and I did and then I went back the next day for something to do."

"You're good at ball?"

"I haven't played for a while, but it's coming back."

"How long have you been here?"

"You mean in prison?"

"Sir."

"Sir."

"Yeah, I mean in prison."

"Two weeks, sir."

He looked at the papers. At his level, he probably didn't get a full dossier.

"Oh, shit, you're a new guy. Why didn't you say so?"

"I thought you knew, sir."

"Come on."

Without another word he brought Joe to cell 21, let him in and left.

The man in the cell had been washing up. He turned and finished toweling his face. He was taller than short, a little stout, in his fifties, and managed to seem carefully dressed. He had a cheerful, lined face, like an old salesman, and unreadable brown eyes, intelligent, steady, a little dulled with experience, eyes that would be hard to con.

"You're Joe Grant?" he said.

"Yeah, that's right."

"I'm Ben, Ben Vosh."

They didn't shake hands. Ben put the towel away.

"How about upstairs?" He moved his eyebrows to the upper bunk. "You're younger than I am."

"Yeah, sure."

Joe placed his things on the upper bunk.

"In the morning," Ben said, "I get up early and shave slow. You can sleep, I'll wake you, that okay with you?"

"That's fine."

"Did he ask about the transfer?" The eyebrows indicated outside.

"Yeah, he did."

"How?"

"Just said, put in for a transfer, eh."

"And?"

"And what?"

"And what did you tell him?"

"I said, yes. With the sir. But I didn't apply. Would he know that?"

"No, not unless he tracked it down, and he won't. If you'd told him you hadn't applied, then he'd a been suspicious, he's very suspicious, thinks he has to be in his job."

"He thinks I just had enough of Willy."

"Good reason. Willy's a screening system all by himself, put a guy in there and you can tell what he's made of. A transfer outa there is practically automatic. Did he ask you anything else?" The eyebrows moved again.

"Did I have friends in this block. He really pushed till he asked me how long I'd been in and I said two weeks. Then he dropped it."

"He didn't know you were green?"

"No, he didn't."

Ben laughed and chuckled and didn't explain. But it was good to hear a man laugh. His eyes didn't change much, though.

"Wait till he finds out you're not really a criminal."

It was said so casually that it took a little time for Joe to realize that Ben must know all about his case.

"What will that do?"

"Nothing. He doesn't know how to handle guys like you, he'll be close to being polite, in his own way a very sensitive man."

**195**

"And criminals?"

"That's simple. Criminals are being punished. Oh, by the way, word is you can go back to practice."

The bell rang for another supper.

# 21

Joe played at second base and waited for his turn to bat. He knew it would come up, seemingly at random, because the catcher was well organized. The man had every player work at the plate. It saved the pitchers, who didn't want to work very hard, and it gave the men some kind of batting practice. He had watched the routine for three days. There was no special order to it, but the overall pattern was that every man always got a turn. It was fair and thorough, it was also a perfect cover for making contact.

The sun was bright, mid-afternoon, a few crisp clouds, not too warm. Just a group of men playing baseball, it was as normal as scout camp, except for the wall and the guards in the towers. There was nothing to see below, sports were a good thing, they made you a character.

Joe got to the plate. The catcher set up double-play situations and Joe started hitting.

"I got a transfer," he said.

"Yeah, I heard."

"Did *you* swing it?"

"No."

"Somebody did." He was careful to keep playing and not look at the catcher.

"Is that right? I figured you did it yourself."

"I've been thinking."

"Uh-uh."

"When I first got here I was put in with Willy."

"There's always a free bunk in there. It doesn't have to mean anything."

"Not by itself. It's only one angle."

"There's angles?"

"I think so."

"Like?"

"Like later a guy tipped me to start playing ball."

"*Tipped* you?"

"All right, suggested, any way you want."

"I don't want it any way at all."

He stepped out and yelled, "Try it again, man on second, play for third." When he was back in place, Joe persisted. "Then Willy put the spotlight on the team."

"No kiddin'?"

"Said they were organized against him."

"Willy's cracked, everybody knows that."

"Then you said to lay low."

"I said skip a few practices."

"Then I got the transfer. Just like that. A miracle."

"You oughta be glad."

"I am. Don't get it wrong. But it wasn't done for my welfare, and it was no coincidence."

"What wasn't?"

**198**

"That part, maybe all of it."

"The place is gettin' to ya, cabin fever."

"Maybe."

The catcher stepped forward again. "Okay, we're gettin' it. Let's go around once more." He kept Joe at the plate.

"You got a point, make it."

"Nothing much," Joe said. "I think you got something going."

"So? What's it to you?"

"So I can blow it."

"You do that."

"I mean I can blow it by accident too."

"So?"

"So I can do a lot better if I know what's going on. No accidental slip-ups, get the idea?"

"Yeah. All loud and clear. You won't slip up, you're not a talker."

"I am now."

"You're carrying a lot of eggs, man, and no basket at all."

"They're your eggs."

"Yeah. I shoulda known you weren't a pigeon. Not after the girls."

"What girls?"

"In the shower. Cool it, back to second, you'll hear."

It wasn't long before he heard. It came after yard time that same evening, in the cell, and it came from Ben Vosh. They were playing cards on a big old-fashioned checkerboard, Ben talking about prison as though he were making a speech, and finally: "You braced Carl this afternoon."

"Carl. The coach?"

"Yeah."

"Yeah, I spoke to him."

"You did more than speak."

The game came to a halt. Joe faced Ben's unconnable eyes.

"He said I'd hear."

"You're hearing now. You're hearing advice. It's smarter for you to stay exactly the way you are. So don't push yourself in."

"I got the feeling I was kinda *pulled* in."

"Not *in*."

"No, not in. A pigeon, he said. I want to hear about that."

"It's simple," Ben said disarmingly, "a new guy, a square john, a guy who minds his own business, don't raise hell upstairs when it gets a little rough. Guards, and the cons, wouldn't give you a second thought for trouble. You just wouldn't be in on nothing. Nobody looks at these guys, they're invisible. A nice cover. You can't fake being a pigeon, they're naturals. So you organize them, slow, very remote control."

"Like the baseball teams."

"Yeah, or anything else. So that's all there is to it. What you don't know can't get you into any trouble, can't get others into trouble. So you're not being conned at all, you're being protected."

"Like being transferred to here."

"Well, sure. If you happen to have questions, you'd ask me, right?"

"And I'd get answers, eh?"

"Yeah, like right now."

"And I'd still be a pigeon."

"Not any more. You know all about it now, I told you."

"You told me there's a cover."

"Well, that's it."

"Cover for what?"

"Anything. Information, a little racket here and there, you know, food, a bit of gambling, outside contacts, stuff like that. It's all new to you now, but hell, you'll get to see it all. You'll even get tired of it. But you don't want to be part of that, it's just not you, you don't belong to that level."

It was persuasive. It explained everything. But it had told him nothing.

"Ben, I've got no level. And I've got no me. So let's quit dancing around the pile, it's not working."

Ben's dull eyes got a little duller, the salesman left his face.

"You got the floor," he said.

"Carl's setup can't stand any kind of look-see, not even from a nut like Willy. He overreacted when I told him. He probably thought he was lucky. He should've been glad."

"You're still talking."

"So it's more than a simple cover. It's something he can't afford to have buggered. And I'm going to keep noticing things, nobody can stop that, not even me. It'll be a strain on the structure, all around."

"We're gonna trust you not to bugger it."

"No good. I can get out of line without even knowing it. If the setup is that sensitive, you're gonna have to do more than just trust me."

"We could do a lot more than that."

"That's a chance I'll have to take."

"I can't decide this alone. Let's drop it."

At the count Joe thought the guard looked at them a little longer than usual. After lights out he didn't sleep, and he knew Ben wasn't sleeping. A silent contest of wills. He reviewed the odds, the risks, he couldn't afford to be a dupe, dupes were held in contempt, life could take a bad turn that way, he would have to contend with two systems, the official prison and the inner prison, both coercive. With so much already lost, it wasn't even a gamble, it was a form of work, a living. It was probably also that for the other men. It would be too bad if there was a conflict.

Throughout the next day there was suppressed tension and nothing else, no word, no sign, just functional conversation and the strain, as predicted, of making things look normal. It went to the following night when Ben took out the cards and broke silence. The dull eyes were more confident, the voice low and hard.

"The setup," he said, "is for a breakout."

"Sensitive."

"A fight, tightened security, too many guys sick all at once, a bad mood among the men, a feather could screw it. Make sure you're not that feather. So now you know, you can forget it."

"Are you going?"

Ben looked at him for a long time. "No."

"Is Carl?"

"No."

Eyes locked again, a lot was being said and realized. The setup was permanent, or meant to be. Joe plunged.

"I go too."

"Yeah, we figured that."

"And?"

"You go. You'll be easier to get to on the outside."

"You won't have to."

"We don't know that."

"Okay. How is it going to work?"

"No. No leaks, no giveaways, no jitters, nothing until the time comes. You'll get told. If anything goes wrong, you were forced to go along, last minute, you don't know anything, don't know anybody."

"And if I'm left behind?"

Ben sneered.

"Then you start your little war, eh?"

# 22

The men made two teams out of the baseball trainees. It was done after lunch in the yard with great ceremony and publicity. One of the men rose to the occasion and emceed with cupped hands. A guard by invitation drew names out of a box, one by one alternating for each team, as the players lined up for enthusiastic fans who were already assessing the odds on future bets. The coaches and umpires were elected from a narrowed-down slate of volunteers. Everything was out in the open, generous, cheerful, honest with a randomness that couldn't be rigged. Carl easily became one of the coaches, and another season was under way. Joe was on Carl's team. It was going to be a great year. Lots of rehab.

The first game was played after supper. It was well attended. The pitching was poor, but the fielding was good, and that made for lots of action and plenty of arguments.

During one argument Carl walked away angry and continued grumbling to Joe at the end of the bench.

"The guy playing third. Get to know his face. You're only gonna meet him once."

Joe watched a lean, cocky individual who played the ball with suppressed hatred, swift, hard, in his late twenties, thin nose, blue eyes, wavy brown hair, a slick know-it-all face, a handsomeness made to con certain types of women.

The action had begun.

In the cell just after the count Ben stood near the door and checked outside. Then he turned on a tap and spoke.

"Read the notice that's going up tomorrow. It took a lot a planning."

It was up by noon. The notice board was inside the dining hall where the men could see it as they filed in.

The only new notice was an announcement headed "Concert Nite" for next Thursday. This was Monday. Concert Nite was to have "Spit Davis and the Township Four, songstress April Hanly, comic Nile Jackson, and country rockers The Retribalizers." It was from eight to ten in the Hall, which meant the dining hall: "Bring your friends. Admission Free. Your Entertainment Committee." The men were very interested, it was something from the outside.

"The Retribalizers?" one asked conservatively.

"They're McLuhanites," a man said.

"What the hell is that?"

"It's too wrong to go into."

And the man laughed and the others frowned. Another nut.

From Ben word for the next day to memorize a man in the library asking for a book on astronomy and mentioning the North Star. He came. He was tall, apparently shy, slouchy, in his thirties, with a sweaty face and eyes that seemed ready to explode in anger. "We got a bet, they say it don't move, I say it does." He got the book from the librarian and sat where he could see Joe. He stayed a half hour and left quietly without another word.

On the checkerboard that evening Ben laid out a rectangle of cards.

"Dining hall," he said.

"Yeah."

"Entrance. Your side." He removed a card. "Service on your left as you cross the hall. The big exit on my side." He removed another card. "The wall on your right, across from the service, there's a big door in two halves." Two cards lengthwise an inch apart indicated passage. "Remember it."

"Okay."

"Back to my side. For the show they seal off the big exit." He put the card back. "A little ways in front of it the guys put up the stage." A card. "And a kind of backdrop maybe four five feet high. On my wall here on each side of the big exit there's a door, storage rooms. The stage won't hide them one hundred percent, which is good because nobody's gonna bother about them anyway. The storage on the service side, your left, here, got it?"

"Yeah."

"Remember that one too. The show people are gonna be using the other one. Study the layout."

After a while Ben picked up all the cards, shuffled, and handed them to Joe with a gesture to the board. Joe rebuilt the layout. Ben said, "Fine," and remade the deck.

"Is that all?"

"For now. You got six more meals in there. Take a good look around. Let's do a little reading. I'll get you up early."

They were like students when the guard came counting.

There was a third man to recognize.

A known early riser, he was having breakfast sitting at a place coordinated by Ben as the northwest corner of table 4. Joe sat a table away facing him. He was late thirties, getting fat, a bald crown, narrow brown eyes, small nose, a mouth upturned at the corners, jowly, the accepted image of the big drinker, harmless, but his hands and eyes moved fast as he ate. They took each other in, he left, and Joe scanned the designated doors. There was a clock over the big exit.

The day's next two meals went by. He didn't see anything more of the three men. Photos of the performers appeared on the notice board. There was some activity in the library, requests for books by McLuhan, already out, he was popular with the men, talk about song hits and why, the money to be made, a momentary naïvete anticipating Concert Nite. Prison magnifying again. There was even a vigorous baseball practice and gags in the showers.

The briefing continued that evening. Joe laid out the cards. Ben was calm, icy.

"The storage room, here," he said.

"Left of the clock."

"That's right. You start counting from when the show starts. Every ten minutes, about, a guy goes into that room. You'll be the second guy. You move when a number is just finishing and everybody is clapping and moving and hollering and the lights are changing. You move slow every time and get close to the door. When it's time, you go in, fast and easy on the door. Then you do what the guy in there tells you. He's the guy plays third. He's in charge."

"Okay. And then?"

"You get it from him."

"Why not now?"

"No. You'll know when it's happening, and by that time it'll be over."

"What if something goes wrong?"

"Then it goes wrong at the storage room, not later. So you're caught in there, so you're a bunch of queers chewing rocks, no crime, no intent, nothing, the cover's still on."

"You sure figure the angles."

"I do now."

He didn't explain his remark. It was the end of the conversation. He took the cards and spread out a game of solitaire. No advice, no goodbye, good luck, nothing, he was out of it completely. Joe opened a book to stare at while he went over the plan again, but there was nothing to go over, it was too simple.

A long night passed, fitful and troubled with fears, a last night perhaps. He tried not to think about it, but half-dreamed dreams kept waking him and he fought off the certainty of treachery and the visions of shotguns ready to explode. The returning day made the cell seem like home.

After breakfast a group of men began assembling the stage and laying out heavy wires. Most routines were normal. Time was counted by meals and by the growth and decoration of the stage. Supper was rescheduled early. There was no baseball practice. At ten to eight the bell started the flow of men into the converted dining hall.

It was noisy, full of talk and movement. Joe ambled toward the front. The stage was covered with musical apparatus and stools, two microphones on stands, electric guitars already connected. Three spotlights had been suspended from the overhead pipes, three more were on stands at the back of the hall. They were all fed into a portable dimmer panel operated by an inmate and watched by a guard. The men cheered when the spots came on, and howled when an inmate, off cue, went on stage to place a stool. With that a man in show-biz country clothes came to a microphone, four others went upstage to their instruments and began playing a soft background rhythm. They had lots of hair and wild hats, some had big tinted glasses.

"Hi, everybody!" he declaimed. "Glad you could all make it." Cheers. "Pit-ah! I'm Spit Davis." More cheers. "And this here's the Township Four." The music came up with the noise. He introduced the girl, April Hanly, the comedian Nile Jackson, and the Retribalizers, and as they left the stage the rhythm shifted and Davis began a variation of "Sweet City Woman." Joe checked the clock, in plain view in the spill of light, and began the count.

Davis after two numbers gave way to the Retribalizers. Stools were handed up from the front, which created a lot of movement and let Joe edge closer to the side of the stage. "We usually do this number in rockin' chairs," one of them said, "but they don't have any in this place, nobody has time to rock in here." Affirmative cheers. "Our name number, 'Country rocker.'" It was a long one, with pauses for laughs, and was followed by two more. As the last number ended, nineteen minutes had gone by. Under loud applause the group made an exit to their left, men reached for stools, and Davis came back on. Joe moved casually toward the storage-room door. "Did you know that the O.K. corral was a used-horse lot?"

He opened the heavy door and swung himself in quickly and eased it shut. Darkness inside. Dimmed concert noises from outside.

"Don't move. Here goes a light."

The overhead light came on. The room was large, piled with boxes and junk, in which a clearing had been made out of line with the door. A man appeared out of the clearing and said, "Come on." But Joe didn't move.

The man had long hair not quite to his shoulders, a rich moustache, glasses, a fancy shirt, jeans with shiny seams, and sandals.

"Christ, man, move," he said. "I'm third base."

Joe moved into the clearing.

"Get those clothes off."

Quickly, trying not to hurry, Joe took off his shirt, received a fancy one, put it on, then pants, socks, sandals, a leather vest. He sat on a box while the man adjusted a wig to his head and glued on a moustache. The materials came from two large guitar cases. The guitars were there, a small amplifying unit, wire, sheet music. The prison clothing was dumped into a box. The man inspected Joe carefully, gave him a guitar, and said, "Stand there. Wait." The man put out the light, and outside noises grew stronger. The fear of treachery vanished, there was still the shotguns.

Loud cheers and whistles. It was the girl coming on.

The door opened, closed. "Don't move. Here goes a light." It was North Star. "What the fuck is this?"

"Shut up and get over here. Third base."

The second dressing went a little faster with Joe holding and taking clothes. The new man emerged with a plentiful wig, not too long, lots of sideburns, no moustache, large glasses as good as a mask, and a floppy hat that he was told to carry. Again darkness and the waiting. The third man was nervous, his breathing came in spasms. After a while he calmed down.

Applause, but the door didn't open. They had to wait for another number. It was getting hot in the room.

"Can we go three?" North Star whispered.

"Maybe, I wouldn't like to try it. Shut up."

They could hear the thumping of the music, the indistinct amplified singing, no sign of a letup. Suddenly cheers and doubled cheers. The balding head came through the door.

"You here?" he said.

"Shut up, the light."

It came on, and the man stood there with a wrong-room look on his face.

"It's all right. I'm third base."

They worked fast. The new man was covered with sweat.

"What took you so long?"

"The broad was singing on this side. Too much light. I waited."

"Yeah, that's okay."

The fourth man got a wig, moustache, granny glasses, a kerchief round his neck, a shirt like a windbreaker, jeans, and sandals. The box with the prison clothes was hidden, someone would spirit it away.

Joe and Third Base had guitars, Joe's uncased. North Star had the small amplifier and wires, Early Riser had a guitar case, empty, and music sheets in a bulging clear plastic container. Everything was checked and rechecked.

"We go left, behind the stage, over to the double doors. We don't know our way around, so look gawky. We're on our way to catch a plane, too bad we got an engagement tomorrow, in Vancouver. Let me do all the talking. In the tunnel we bullshit about the wonderful crowd and how we'd like to come back. But don't overdo it. Okay, stick to the order we came in. The last guy shuts the door. We go when they start clapping."

Almost as if on cue the applause began. They left. The comedian was going into his act. It was clear behind the stage. "They tell me the warden here is a great guy, I'm gonna try and get in here if I get a chance." Laughter. They passed under the clock, slowly, and in front of the sealed exit doors. "I hear he gives everybody eight hours off every day—for sleeping." More laughter. A guard stood in the corridor, able to look in through the wired glass. He glanced with distaste at the musicians. The other storage room was open. Most of the troupe were in there, some were at the side of the stage. The four men moved past the door and continued along the wall to the corner. "You think things are tough on the inside—why, on the outside things are so tough people are paying fines just for earnin' money, not stealin' it." A ripple of laughs. They turned the corner and made for the big double doors. The first man went up to the guard. "They're thinking of callin' it out-come tax." A groan. "You're right, it's not a damn bit funny." Roars of laughter.

"Hi, it's us, we're the guys catching a plane."

"Ah, yeah."

"Do you take these?" He put forward slips of paper, passes.

"No, not here. At the last gate." He opened one door. There was another guard outside.

"Right. They're sure havin' a good time."

"Yeah, does 'em good."

"Sure thing. Good night."

"Night."

The second guard led them to the right a short distance and stopped in front of an electric door. There was a camera on the ceiling behind them.

"Right straight through here," he said. "There's a man at the other end, he'll show you out."

"Right. Thanks."

They walked down the televised corridor talking about what a beautiful audience the cons were, they really dug things, coming back would be a pleasure, maybe we could send them some records, and fictitious ramblings about how the man who booked them into Vancouver tried to get them to go to a cheap hotel. It was a long, slow, casual walk in sandals. Finally they gathered at the electric door. It didn't open. They were being scrutinized. But they weren't supposed to know it.

"Do we ring a bell or something?" Joe said.

"No idea," Third Base said. "I can go back and ask the other fellow to open up."

"Naw, he said there'd be a guy here, he should know."

They waited, every man ready with innocent talk. A few seconds later the door opened.

To the left was a security booth, heavy glass with cutouts for speaking through and signing things. It was the shipping and receiving entrance of the prison. The next door would lead outside. The guard seemed amused. Third Base handed him the slips.

"Quite a time in there, eh?" the guard said.

"Yeah, great bunch."

"They are, in here."

Third Base chuckled phonily by way of reply.

"See you," he said and walked to the big door. A buzzer unlocked it. They walked through and closed it. They were outside the walls.

Two mini-buses were parked to the right of the door, the closer one pale green, the other maroon, hardly discernible in the deepening twilight. Third Base went directly to the maroon bus, opened the driver's door and got a key from under the floor mat. He wasted no time, he started it as the others were getting aboard, backed a little, and began driving with slow haste through the right-angled roads.

"Geez, we made it!" North Star said and went to pull his wig off.

"Sit still," the driver said. "They watch all vehicles. Wait till we're clear."

"They can't see us."

"Sit still."

They sat still.

"Let's get our story straight. Four of them guitar players were supposed to leave early to catch a plane. They changed their mind and stayed to make the cons feel good. We heard them talk about it, so we stole their stuff, their bus, and we fucked off, period. We took this guy," he indicated Joe in the seat next to him, " 'cause we had to be four guys. All right? Most breakouts are walkaways and this one's no different."

Ten minutes later they were on a highway and going fast.

"Okay," the driver said, "let's get this crap off. There's work clothes back there and shoes. It's in shopping bags, it's marked. Put the crap back in the bags."

The three men changed in silence, instinctively looking out the windows for cars. The bus pulled over briefly to let the balding man take the wheel, and Third Base kept giving directions as he changed his clothes. When he was dressed he sat beside the driver urging speed. In five minutes they got on to a throughway, in another ten they were pulling into a rest area. A lone car was parked without lights, motor running.

"Take the bags."

They got out. The man from the parked car simply got in the bus and drove off.

"One bag to a trash can, try to get it under the shit."

They hurried and raced back to the car. Once under way and driving within the speed limit, Third Base said, "Relax, we're just working slobs looking for a bowling alley."

Joe was sitting in front, the balding man behind him, and North Star behind the driver. Keeping ranks had seemed important. No one relaxed. Joe spoke to the driver.

"What about the guitar players?" he asked.

"What about them?"

"They must have been in on it."

"Just two of them. No sweat. They all put up a squawk we stole their stuff. They're in the clear."

"How did you get to them?"

"You wanna know a helluva lot."

"Just curious."

**215**

"How do you get to anybody? Money, broads, junk, threats, you name it. Nobody runs to the cops nowadays. They cooperate."

"Yeah, organized."

"You're goddam right, organized. A loner is a loser, ain't you heard?"

"So's a pigeon."

"You ain't lost anything. You're out."

"Yeah, yeah. Just thinking."

"Well, it don't matter now anyway. You got things to do on the outside, ain't ya?"

"Yeah, I do."

"Besides you'll have lots of friends when you get back in." The man thought that was funny. His laughter sounded unnatural.

"What time is it?" Joe asked.

The man put the dome light on to look at his watch.

"Going on twenty to ten."

"They'll start looking for us around ten."

"Yeah. After the count."

They rode in silence, going very fast when they were alone, slowing when there were other cars. The driver announced ten o'clock.

"The bus is gone south," he said. "Just about now it'll be parked and locked at a bus depot. They'll look for us south of there. We're goin' north. It's simple. So relax."

"They'll be stopping everybody," North Star said.

"Not after they find the bus."

"Fuck that, they'll stop anybody any time."

"We go the way it was set up. It looks like a walkaway, so the cops are gonna follow their noses. Open the dash."

Joe opened the compartment and took out two envelopes, one thick, the other flat. The dome light was turned on. He could see cigarettes, a flashlight, the registration, no guns.

"Gimme the fat one."

It felt like money. The man folded it and pushed it into his shirt pocket.

"Open the other one."

"Jesus, there's smokes," said North Star, leaning forward.

Joe gave him the package of cigarettes. The envelope contained four driver's licenses. Joe picked blue eyes born in 1937 for himself and the driver and passed the rest behind him. The three others lit cigarettes. Joe memorized "Lington, David," and the last six digits of a long number, "220837," which told officialdom when he was born.

There was no more talk. They encountered no roadblocks, saw no police cars. Joe noticed from the exit signs that they were headed for his home city. That could make problems, the police would be looking for him there.

In town the driver picked a busy thoroughfare and pulled up at a bus stop outside a shopping center.

"This is it for you," he said to Joe.

"All right."

"Here's some eating money. You don't owe us, we don't owe you." He gave him fifty dollars in tens. "Don't get caught too soon."

Joe got out and the car pulled away.

# 23

He stayed at the bus stop. There was no one around. The sign indicated that two bus lines passed there, just numbers, no names. He knew vaguely where he was, generally south of where home used to be. But he had no plans, no place to go, no person to contact. He'd have to get out of the city, away from some five thousand policemen who would be looking routinely for four descriptions. By now, near eleven o'clock, the police were probably at Steve's apartment and maybe at Harry's if they knew about him. Phones might be tapped. He wasn't that important, but a whole system would be in action, a system with force. He knew Steve would worry, and Betsy. Violence waited only for a target, it already had a cause.

He wasn't frightened. He felt numb, disoriented. He had gotten here too suddenly, with no warning and with no specific moves in mind. The suddenness made him aware of how exposed he was. He had no resources, no identity, no way of getting any, just fifty dollars that couldn't last long, a phony license that couldn't stand up to inspection, and clothes he couldn't change. Even getting to a bathroom might be dangerous. He was completely outside society and he sensed its overwhelming organization. He needed an underground, but he had none.

Traffic was light. There was still activity in the shopping center, quite a few cars in the parking lots, the malls brightly lit to keep burglars away. A security jeep was moving about slowly, its spotlights and flasher off. Possibly ex-cops, and possibly they listened to news bulletins. If a bus came, then another, and he didn't get on he'd become conspicuous. Cabs were out, he had no destination, and cabbies remember. Hitching a ride was worse. He waited till the official-looking jeep disappeared, and he went into the shopping center. He felt better doing something.

At a drugstore he bought a razor and lather, a toothbrush and a small tube of paste, various toiletries, cheap sunglasses, a paperback Western, and a small zippered overnight bag. At the cashier's he added two chocolate bars. It came to $9.11. It cheered him. Small things. The beginning of identity.

"I'll put it all in the bag," Joe said.

"Quick trip?" the man behind the counter asked pleasantly.

He was old, gray and lined, with humor in his face. Joe was ready, unsmiling.

"Yeah, they're doin' it to me all the time, I'm gonna leave this stuff in the truck from now on."

It explained the work clothes in the middle-class setting, the late hour.

"Maybe the boss will pay for it," the man said.

**2 1 9**

"No chance. Overtime's all I get."

"Still, it's something. Some people have nothing at all."
Echoes of concern reached way back, Depression days
maybe.

"Yeah. I'm lucky."

He made his way to the bus stop. The jeep was back,
curious in an idle way. He looked like a man on a night
shift. The jeep left him alone.

When a bus finally came he got on. He put in the right
change, got a transfer. The driver didn't look at him. Six
teenagers were in the back chattering to each other. Two
morose young men sat midway near the side exit unspeaking and looking sleepy. Joe picked a place a few seats behind the driver and pretended to read the paperback. He
didn't know the bus routes, but he knew the city. He was
going east toward the center of town. Past that and south
would be an industrial area with old, low-income houses,
transients, cheap rooms and no questions. In that environment he'd be just another guy on the move.

In a half hour he transferred to a bus going south and fifteen minutes later he was in a dark region of old factories,
foundries, railroad shops and junkyards. The area smelled
of meat packers. Past this would be the outskirts and the
end of the bus line. He decided to get off.

He walked back toward the city and into the slaughter-
house smells. The street lights were dim and far apart. A
few cars passed, and a few trucks. He crossed four or five
sets of railroad tracks and could hear the distant noises of
working engines. There'd be truck traffic around the pack-
ing plants. He turned right onto a road with no sidewalks
and kept going for about a mile, watching the contrasting
bright light of a gas station.

An old truck encased with dirt and dripping with liquid had parked a little away from the pumps. As he approached he couldn't see anyone but he heard voices raised in argument. He edged over casually and saw two men, the attendant in company overalls and a roughly dressed man who looked like a farmer. The attendant was protesting about something. Joe strolled up to them like a gawking bystander.

"I don't want that mess all over the place," the attendant was saying.

"Mister, I ain't got no choice. I wouldn'a come here if I didn't have to."

"Move it off the lot, you can work on it over there."

The attendant pointed into the dark.

"I can't go another foot," the man with the truck said. "Lemme have a big jack and I'll be outa here in no time."

"Yeah, and all that crap'll be all over the drive."

"I don't like it any more'n you do, I gotta work in it."

"That's your problem, not mine."

Through the slatted sides and gate of the truck Joe saw the cattle, some twenty of them. They were hot and stinking and restless, and their urine flowed from openings around the truck and carried loose quantities of dung with it. On the right rear the outside double tire was flat and the inside one was showing signs of strain.

"I can give you a hand," Joe said.

The two men stopped talking and looked at him. They were both older men, dirty with work and independence, inclined to be crabby. The farmer was over six feet, heavy and muscled, with hard hands and a face full of bony ridges and deep lines. His eyes were clear, steady, and watered a little.

"It'd go a lot faster if you did," the farmer said.

"Fast or not, you're still making a mess," the attendant protested.

"You got a hose?" Joe said. "I'll clean up as we go along."

The attendant thought it over.

"All right," he grumbled.

They set to work. Joe threw his bag into the cab. The farmer put blocks under the good tires, explaining that the load was going to shift some, dismantled the spare, put a heavy jack in position and began forcing the wheel nuts loose. The attendant brought out a thick hose, gave it to Joe and went back to turn it on. Joe cleaned up around the truck, trying to avoid the farmer, who didn't complain about the occasional spray. When the nuts were off he went to the jack.

"You might wet the animals down," he said. "They're hot and full of flies and they won't feel so bad when I start tipping."

Joe adjusted the hose to heavy rain and climbed on the side of the truck to spray the cattle from above. The truck's right back end went up gently and they eased together toward the opposite corner. They didn't have much room anyway, but if they fell it would be quite a tangle. When the farmer was back at the tire, Joe directed the hose down and let water gush along the bottom. A lot of mess poured out. When the scourings seemed reasonably clean, he got down and started hosing the asphalt. There was an ocean of filth.

A passing patrol car drove in on the dry side and when the officers saw the problem they didn't approach, they grinned and left.

Finally the spare was in place and the blocks and jack removed.

"I'll pull up now and finish up over there."

He moved the dripping truck about a hundred feet away near the road, came back for the flat tire and shoved it in the rack for the spare. Joe hosed the truck's trail and finally turned off the water.

"What do I owe you?" the farmer said to the attendant.

"Nothing. It evens up. I lend you a jack, you clean the driveway."

"Much obliged."

They walked away from the attendant.

"I left my bag in the truck," Joe said.

"You goin' somewhere?"

"If you don't mind company, I'll ride with you."

The man gave Joe a level look. "Where are you going?"

"Anywhere. I'm looking for work."

Another level look.

"Okay. Get in."

It took almost an hour to deliver the cattle, delays in the line-up, waiting for the receiver to finish with other people, checking the condition of the animals, arguments over discounted weights, and the final pieces of paperwork. The big buyers drove hard bargains. Joe sat in the cab and watched and smelled the operation. It was late, perhaps one-thirty, when they left the place.

Once out of the city the man said: "You know how to drive a truck?"

"Yeah, but I haven't done it for about, oh, ten years."

"You wanna try?"

"Sure."

The man pulled up and they changed places. Joe

checked where everything was, put the clutch down and got the feel of the shift. He started a little jerkily but got into fourth fairly smoothly. The man gave directions and they got on to a throughway going east.

"It'll be easy for the next hour'n a half, just keep going straight. We turn off at the Shrewsdale exit."

After a while he spoke again. "My name's Townley Miller."

"Lington, David Lington."

"What's your line of work?"

"I worked in an engineering shop, general labor, ran the machines sometimes. They had to lay off some people, I was one."

"You married?"

"I was." He didn't feel like inventing a long story, so he added, "My wife died. We had no kids."

"Sorry to hear that." Then later: "I suppose you got no place to sleep."

"That's right. I haven't."

There was a long silence. As it prolonged itself Joe glanced at Miller. He was asleep. His head drooped on his chest and his big frame swayed with the motion of the truck. In contrast to his brusque questions this looked like naïve faith. Or maybe he was too tired to care. Whatever it was, Joe liked him for it, it made him feel he had enough identity to be trusted.

The truck seemed hard to manage at first. The steering was stiff, the brake took all his weight, and the mirrors were adjusted for the bigger man. But it all worked, noisily. The motor sounded like distant thunder and everything else creaked and rattled like a bouncing toolbox. The windshield was dirty and got worse as it collected bugs.

**224**

But the lights were strong and the night air felt good and the work of driving felt like honest labor. He soon fell into the rhythm of it, the noises became reassuring, and he was able to hear his own mind. It had been a long time.

He hungered for home. It was the only positive feeling he had, and the only one about which he could do nothing. The rest was negative, absurd: stay in hiding until the immediate hunt wore off, then get the resources to find the three toughs, a car, money, a cover of some kind, a weapon. And then? Again the huge negative of death? More absurdity? And back to life in prison, for life. But life was not in prison. Life was not anywhere. It had died on a highway six weeks ago. He stared ahead of the lights into the incomprehensible darkness. Hearing his own mind wasn't exactly worth the experience, it was full of pain. But suffering somehow found the person. Another goddam mystery.

He had lost track of time and he had no watch. He concentrated on looking carefully for exit signs. He'd have two chances: when the advance sign appeared and when the exit itself came up. There'd be about a mile between the two. It was a welcome problem. It was solved a while later by his spotting the advance sign, "Shrewsdale, Exit 146." The next sign said only, "Exit 146." He'd had only one chance after all. He turned into the exit and went as far as the stop sign. A right or left choice had to be made.

"Mr. Miller."

The man woke immediately and nodded. "I'll drive," he said.

They got out and stretched. The sky was full of stars and the night full of rhythmic chirps.

"It's close on to three o'clock."

Miller placed his bulk behind the wheel without hurrying and turned right along the black country road. They passed through three little towns, dimly lit like sickrooms, and got on to a gravel road. Dust seeped into the cab. After what seemed a half hour Miller turned into a long driveway that ended under a lone lightbulb above the door to a farmhouse. A big dog greeted him silently.

"We can put you up for the night."

"Thanks, Mr. Miller. I'll sleep in the truck."

"You don't have to."

"It's all right. That way I won't disturb anybody."

"Suit yourself."

He went inside without another word. The dog followed him. Lights came on, the outside light went off. Joe left the passenger's door open and stretched out on the seat. It was uncomfortable, and as he was thinking about it he fell asleep.

# 24

The sun was just over the horizon, filling the cab with red light and not yet warming it. It was coming in the open door where Joe's feet stuck out and when he raised his head he looked right into it. He struggled stiffly to a sitting position and looked out at the open country. He was surprised at the space before him. The early light intensified the greenery and made the trees glow with backlighting, rows of tall maples lining the driveway, apple trees in the adjacent field, other kinds he couldn't identify, and expanses of hay rolling with the gently sloping low hills. The air was noticeably clean and the sound of half a million birds was almost annoying. He got out of the truck and closed the door without slamming it.

No one seemed to be up. The house was big, old, well cared for. It had two stories, a shining metal roof, peaked, with chimneys at each end, and a large veranda along two walls. Flower beds surrounded the veranda and a lawn traveled part way down the driveway and set off the big maples. The lone lightbulb he had seen last night was part of a large shed attached to the house. A short distance away were two outbuildings and still farther a big unpainted barn with a tin gambrel roof. A three-year-old car was parked near the outbuildings.

He walked past the barn looking at the unfolding scenery. A fenced-off cow trail led downhill and stopped at a timber bridge over a noisy brook. On the other side was chewed-down pasture land spotted with animal leavings and tough bushes, its distant ridges looked as smooth as a golf course. Inexplicably it made him remember the city with fear. But he kept looking at the fresh hills and he perceived them as they were, no cars or flagpoles or people, just the warming light on the greenness of the countryside. He followed the rocky brook till it leveled off a little and watched the glistening water slip past him. On impulse he knelt down and drank from his cupped hands. Morning sun and clear water and cold on his face, shirt wet, knees hurting on the rock, he was no place he knew, and yet it was not alien. Something reached within, something welcome. A moment of sheer forgetfulness. But he came to fast and it became a memory. And he told himself that prison was still magnifying things.

All the same he went back to the truck, got his bag, and returned to the brook, where he stripped to the waist and washed and soaked his face and went through a smarting routine of shaving an unsoftened beard by feel. The brook carried away the lather, and he thought of the technology of the whole business, and then of the ecology, and said the hell with it. He rinsed and splashed and made a mental memo to buy a towel. It was all silly. And good.

A female voice that was used to the outdoors filled the spaces like a breeze.

"Mr. Lington, are you still here?"

"Yes, I am," he shouted back.

He dressed, remembering that his underwear had some sort of prison laundry marks, and ran, still wet, up the slope and on to the gravel near the barn.

She was a small woman, in dress and apron, wiry, restless, with a handsome aging face, black hair pulled behind her head, and swift inquisitive eyes that were ready to be skeptical.

The big dog came out of the shed and sniffed at Joe.

"I'm Claire Miller. Where you been?"

"Morning, Mrs. Miller . . ."

"You sound like a salesman, call me Claire." Her eyes darted to the bag.

"Claire it is. Glad to know you. I'm David." But not wanting to extend the deception further than he had to, he said, "But everybody calls me Joe. I was shaving."

"At the brook?"

"Yeah, it was nice down there."

"You coulda shaved inside, you know."

"I didn't want to bother anybody."

"A-ah! That's no attitude. Livin' is bothering *some*body, generally everybody. Towny's still asleep, I'm doing the chores."

"Can I help?"

"You know what to do?"

"No."

"Then you'll be in the way."

"I can shovel like the next man."

"Maybe you can at that, only there's not much to shovel, we only milk two cows. Come on."

Joe threw his bag in the shed and they took the cow trail downhill, the dog running ahead, crossed the timbers

**229**

over the brook, and roamed the pasture until two cows from a grazing herd of around fifty shambled toward them and continued homeward, apparently oblivious to the urging dog. The sun was higher now and warmer.

"Towny tells me you're looking for work."

"That's right."

"You got anything particular in mind?"

"No. Whatever comes along."

"Towny tells me your wife died."

"Yes, she did."

"That's too bad. You're young though, got plenty of time for a new life."

In the barn Joe was of no help. The woman tied the animals in their stalls, cleaned their udders, and attached the cups of a milking machine. It seemed like a lot of equipment for two cows.

"We used to milk the whole lot," she said as though reading his mind, "all sixty-five of them. Too much work. We turned over to beef."

"Just like that?"

"What do you mean?"

"Well, don't cows have to be milked all the time?"

"I don't mean to be rude . . ." she started to say, but the fun got the best of her and she burst out laughing, a little embarrassed at herself. She wiped her eyes and tried to be serious. Joe couldn't help grinning.

"Cows are like women," she finally said. "They get milk when they're pregnant and they dry up if you don't milk them."

"Of course," he said.

And she laughed all the more.

"Ever work on a farm?" she asked.

"No."

"I guessed not."

More laughter.

When the milking was over, she had Joe carry the big container into the milkhouse, pour some into a plastic jug, and put the rest into a cooler.

"You can turn those animals out."

Joe finally managed to unhook the chain around their necks and they stumbled out on their own. Claire Miller was already walking to the house carrying the jug of milk. He followed her in, stopping to pick up his bag.

The kitchen was big, with a linoleum floor, two sides with large windows, a wood-burning cooking stove, an electric range, a refrigerator, a washing machine, all old, a solid table, no two chairs matching. Everything was trim and clean and in good repair as if someone had gone through the place with the passion of a hobbyist. But on top of every surface working things had accumulated, pots of flowers, papers, tools, cans, gloves, clothes, the debris of day-to-day living, making the place look cluttered to someone who didn't live there. An electric clock over the washing machine said it was 7:45. He didn't trust it, he had a different sense of time.

Without asking what he wanted, Claire Miller made and served up a breakfast of eggs, potatoes, honey, bread, milk, and coffee. She didn't talk while she worked. But at table she did.

"Is that everything you own, in there?" She indicated his bag on a chair near the door.

"Yes, it is. Can't lug a big suitcase around. I figured I'd get to buy what I needed."

"Just like a man, wasteful. Do you drink?"

**231**

"You mean liquor? Yeah, not much, and not often. Why do you ask?"

"That's another kind of waste."

"I guess it is at that."

He was having no trouble putting away what to him was a big breakfast. He noticed she had taken much less than she served him.

"Well," she said, "what are your plans?"

"You mean, like right now?"

"Yes, now."

"I don't know. Move on and look for work."

"Where?"

"The nearest town."

"A-ah," she said and didn't go into it.

He wondered how big a town it was and whether it had a detachment of police. A small town would ask a lot of questions, a big town would have a lot of cops. And he couldn't ask her about it, she'd pick up the smallest clue.

"Well," she said, "I have to go in to get a few things, you can come along."

From a drawer in the cupboard she took two sets of keys and gave them to him.

"See if you can get that car started. There's a cable in the trunk."

It didn't start. The ignition clattered a little and couldn't turn the motor. He brought the truck close, uncovered the battery in the cab and hooked up the cable. He tried the ignition again and this time it caught. He swung the truck out of the way and brought the car to the house. He was glad to be of help, but he had no doubt Claire Miller would have known what to do.

She came out carrying a purse and his bag, which she threw in the car.

"I'll drive," she said. "It's less fuss."

She drove slowly to keep down the dust and to give him a chance to see the countryside. She pointed out things, a good place for meat, another for honey, a five-generation farm now dwindling, a few histories so intertwined he couldn't follow her narrative. They covered about seven miles of dirt road, then pavement and a sign saying, "Wareby."

It was a main street, a few side streets that didn't seem to go far, a church and school, and what looked like small factories and warehouses. A little bigger than a village, not a good place to stay.

The woman went to a grocery, a dry-goods store, a feed store, and a welding shop for a piece of machinery. She took long in each place and the day got hotter. While she was at the grocery he went next door and bought two sets of underwear, a change of work clothes and three pairs of socks. It left him with less than thirty dollars. A dollar a day for food, another for a cheap room, and he could last perhaps two weeks. But not in this town. By the time he'd done the rounds looking for work the whole place would be busy asking questions and inventing answers. He'd have to get to a bigger town, one big enough to have dirty jobs and local bums who didn't want them.

"It's a small place," he said when she was back in the car. "It'd be hard to find a job here."

"It would at that. It's none of my business but I asked around and there isn't much."

"Well, thanks for the breakfast and everything. I'll start looking for a ride."

He had the door open ready to leave.

"There's lots of work on the farms," she said, "but you won't get rich doing it."

"I don't want to get rich."

"Well?"

"All right. Do you know of any?"

"Some."

He closed the door. He felt he was taking a chance. He hadn't thought of a farm, a farm is a hard place to find, but it's also a hard place to get away from on foot.

They drove back toward Miller's place and he saw the countryside from another aspect. It was like being on vacation, the idleness, the scenery, the disregard of time, seeing new people and new places. For him it was only an illusion, strong enough to be enjoyable, and it soon passed. Near Miller's she turned left onto another dirt road that curved and rose and fell with the topography and brought them a few miles later to a driveway and a mailbox belonging to a "C. Fraser."

The driveway was at least three hundred yards long. It dipped as though entering a valley and rose to meet a porchless two-story house in an orderly grove of trees that must have been planted two generations ago. The house had a series of steep-roofed one-story additions, one of which showed the outside of a big stone fireplace. Perennials grew in a rock-strewn bed and the grass needed cutting. Away from the house was a storage shed for vehicles and a weathered barn also with additions, and beyond that a fenced pasture, fields, and woods that looked impenetrable in the distance. The whole place seemed deserted.

Claire Miller, satisfied the car would start again, turned the motor off and led Joe around the house and into an enormous garden. To Joe it seemed like half a city block, neat rows of mysterious plants, the lanes covered with old hay and the rest of it looking like a controlled garbage dump.

In the middle of it was a tall old man, as lean as a sapling, with a peaceful face that had aged all it could. He had a white moustache, gray eyes, and white hair that showed under an old railroad cap. His clothes seemed to be organically part of him and he smelled of work. There was an air of dignity and command about him, a face that couldn't be easily referred to by a nickname.

"Morning, Charles," said Claire.

He nodded, his eyes smiling as if he were amused by her.

"You're moving fine today," she said.

"It's been good weather."

That led to a conversation about the relative progress of the vegetables in his garden, how Townley Miller was, how someone called Jeffrey was trying a new kind of corn, and about an offer he'd had to sell his farm. Finally Claire introduced Joe to Mr. Fraser.

"You're not a farmer."

"No, I'm not," Joe said, "just a worker."

The old man appreciated the distinction and chuckled.

"Came in from the city last night with Towny. Had his first experience hosing down a cattle truck."

"On the road, eh?"

"In a way, yeah. I'm looking for work."

"I hear times are tough in the city, the way they tell it on the radio."

"They are."

The mention of radio made Joe alert, he wondered if they got newspapers and watched television.

"Lost his wife a little while ago," Claire said gently.

"Them all your belongings?" the old man asked.

"That's all of it."

"New start, eh? Well, it happens."

**235**

"I figured," Claire said, "that if you didn't mind a little company, I'd bring Joe round to see you."

"You can stay here if you want," he said to Joe. "You can earn your keep, but there's not much to do. You'd have to work out at other places to get any solid pay."

"That'd be fine. Just show me what you want done."

The old man chuckled again. "That'd kill you. I'll show you what you do for your keep."

There was more conversation about local matters and eventually Claire said she had better be going.

"Drop in and see us," she said to Joe.

"I will. Thanks."

She had no trouble with the car. Joe watched it go down the driveway and along the dirt road making dust. It was a good view of the roads.

"I don't suppose you know anything about gardening," Fraser said.

"Six tomato plants in my back yard, in the city, and two four-foot rows of carrots, my wife and I did it for . . . the fun of it."

"A child's garden. I keep a few patches for my grand-children."

"Yeah."

"I'll show you around the place. It's getting too hot to garden."

# 25

At seven o'clock in the morning Charles Fraser explained that he wanted to extend his garden to almost twice its size. He directed Joe accordingly and gave him a hat for the sun. He showed him how to use a tractor and a mower, how to lift the blades to avoid rocks and woodchuck mounds, how to turn at the corners. It was about half an acre of weeds grown tall and hiding all sorts of obstacles. Joe practiced with the machinery and finally had to do the job twice, once cutting high enough to expose the rocks, removing them, and next time cutting low. The cuttings were raked into a pile and kept.

A few visitors came, ostensibly to do business with Fraser, but they took a good look at the "new man." Word had got around, Fraser would be getting more crops. Joe waved at them and kept on working.

With breakdowns and repairs and delays and his own inexperience, it was a day's work. It was also exhausting.

The first night he skipped supper and fell on a couch near the kitchen and slept, clothes and all, until awakened early next morning by the amused old man. There was no letup. With tractor and plow and an aching body he turned the earth and buried the sod, and with a rotary tiller and repeated passes he pulverized it until it was eight to ten inches of fine soil that made him think of the moon's surface. Another day's work. But he had supper this time and went to bed in his assigned upstairs bedroom. He still wasn't finished.

With spade, fork and wheelbarrow he dug up and spread old manure over the entire surface, and did the same with what looked like a big garbage heap of black silt, which strangely enough didn't stink. More visitors watched, more waving, he was a hard worker. Finally old hay and straw and cuttings were piled to a depth of six inches and the thing was done. It'd be ready next spring, Fraser said, to grow anything he planted. The double handling was tedious and the spreading had taken three days, five days in all for the new bed. At the end of it he had stopped aching and could tolerate a day's hard labor. But he was having second thoughts about earning his keep. The price seemed high.

He didn't mention it. The old man in his own way was working as hard as he. And it was still a good place to hide out despite the visitors. Fraser received no newspapers, hadn't turned on the radio, and didn't watch television in the summer. There was simply no time for that. They lived mainly in the outdoors, getting up at first light and going to bed when it was too dark to do anything. The outdoors wasn't merely scenery, it meant blistering work. It was alive, it changed daily, and it grew constantly, unheedful of Joe or Fraser or anybody else, and it would grow wild in one season if left untended. But the old man tended it, and made it tame, as it had him, and it delivered for him.

There was another job, a big maple in front of the house. Fraser mentioned it casually at breakfast. It was dying and had split and would crash through the roof in a high wind. It would have to be cut down. He watched for Joe's reaction.

"With axes?" Joe said.

Fraser seemed to enjoy the more-hard-work look on Joe's face.

"No, a chain saw. It's easier to do in the winter when it's froze up, but you probably won't be here by then."

"You never can tell. I might get to like it."

The old man laughed. "I was just fooling a little. The tree can wait. You already earned a fair amount of keep."

"A deal's a deal."

"I don't want to take advantage. That garden you dug will grow more food than you can eat. It'll do it for years."

"I bet it will, for you."

"It just will, if you care for it." He gave Joe an ignition key. "You can use the pickup. You want to go looking for a paying job. Just put back the gas you use."

"That's very kind of you. Thanks."

"It's too soon to thank me. People are starting to bring in their hay, ought to be lots of work."

"I'll soon find out."

It was raining, not heavily but steadily. It cleaned the countryside and made everything look greener and fresher and left mud patches on the roads. The pickup was a half-ton, old and battered and running well. He felt freer riding

**239**

it, and stronger, a callused hand on the wheel, hardened muscles making him sit up straight, the general feeling of being able to do things. He was mobile. And plans were taking shape. A second-hand pickup for a few hundred dollars would give him all the mobility he needed. It was simple. Perhaps because it was so unreal.

The first farm was less than a mile away. The man was around, preparing to go to town while the rain kept him off the fields. He was stocky, about forty, reserved, unhurried. He recognized the pickup and Joe explained where he was living. They stood in the rain and talked about Fraser's health, his garden, the times, and the weather. There was no rushing it. He was simply there and the talk acknowledged his presence. Fast business-like conversations were impossible, they wouldn't communicate anything. At length Joe revealed the purpose of his visit.

"I'm sorta free to work if anybody needs help. Mr. Fraser says it gets pretty busy at haying time."

"It sure does, especially if you're trying to beat the rain."

"Well, I'll be available, at least till somebody hires me."

"Have you baled hay before?"

"No, I haven't."

"I figured not. It's not for me to mind your business, but usually people want the whole job done, mowed, baled, and stored, or delivered if they've sold it."

"All I can do now is drive a tractor. And maybe mow a little."

"Meaning no offense, but so can every boy in the county."

"No offense." Joe grinned a little. "I can heave a bale higher, that should count."

"It should. Anyway I'll remember what you said."

At the next farm it was much the same except that the man's wife came out and the conversation lasted longer and had more questions. At the third the man had sold his hay standing and didn't have to worry about it any more. But he liked company and showed Joe around. The next two places brought nothing and he began to realize that the first round was just visiting and that he'd have to follow it all up. At the sixth place he was invited to stay for lunch and that told him the morning had gone by. He refused politely and drove back to Fraser's.

He was uneasy about showing himself so much. All the houses had television antennas, some must get newspapers, all must have radios. He didn't know what measures the police were taking, but they would have put out pictures by now. And he hadn't expected the chatty visits, the intense personal scrutiny, the openness of the people. You can't stay hidden in a community, maybe it was just as well he was getting around, he'd be less noticeable that way. The Millers and Fraser might be a good cover, just enough to prevent a closer look.

He told the old man of the morning's failure.

"They haven't turned you down," Fraser said. "You gotta let things develop. It's too early for them to know."

"Don't they plan these things?"

"You bet they do."

They were eating sausages, eggs, potatoes, and bread, which was what they had for breakfast.

"But there's too much to plan," the old man continued. "With a warm spring you might cut early, if you've had enough rain. It's never the same two years running. It's been good but a little dry this year. This rain'll help some."

"I'll go back when they start mowing."

"Even then. If the weather's right you can take in all your own hay and help with your neighbor's, so you don't hire anybody. If the weather's bad you're gonna lose part of your crop anyway and have to buy some for the winter, and you don't wanna go paying out wages on top of that. So you don't hire. You try to plan for in between as it comes along. Farming's a gamble."

"So's a lot of other things."

He continued his rounds in the afternoon. It was still raining. Knowing the routine and expecting less, he became unhurried and all but abandoned his business purposes. At one place they were churning butter and he stayed awhile to watch the older technology. At another he spoke to a man repairing a huge vehicle full of chutes and belts, which turned out to be a threshing machine. The man knew its intricacies the way a child knows its toys. One farm had work horses as well as a tractor and that led to talk about the old days and the muscle it took and god knows how they managed to live. Elsewhere it was coffee and homemade bread, which was for sale, and he bought a loaf to take to the old man. An afternoon of public relations. And he had to admit it was a pleasant change.

He was miles from Fraser's by then and the roads were muddier. The rain had washed the dirt from the old pickup and it glistened like a younger truck. He drove slowly, barely 20 m.p.h., to be able to look at the passing country. Away from others he lost whatever social good humor he had and went back to dwelling on possible next moves. Things seemed more natural that way. But no new ideas came to him. He wasn't really thinking, he was acting from feelings that had become habit.

As he braked slightly to go down a long incline he noticed someone moving on the road ahead of him. When he got closer he saw a hooded yellow raincoat, black rubber boots, a kid walking a bike. Nothing unusual in that, and he was going to go right by. But this wasn't the city. There were miles of dirt road and you didn't walk with a bike, not down an incline. He stopped and backed a little and got out.

He waved, and the child hurried toward him.

"You wanna ride?" he asked over the noise of the rain.

"Okay. My bike broke."

She was about seven years old, looking small in the raincoat, blue eyes full of trust in a tanned face.

He put the bike in the back of the pickup and opened the cab door for her. She climbed in next to the loaf of bread, wet boots dangling on the tools and junk on the floor. He felt big and noisy as he got behind the wheel and slammed his door shut. She threw the rain hood back and pushed wet hair away from her cheeks. Her face was oval, fine-featured but undefined in the soft contours of childhood, and she had lots of light brown hair that looked recently washed. She sat completely self-possessed and watched the road.

He didn't, he watched her.

"Well," he made himself say, "you're gonna have to tell me where to go, eh?"

"It's over there. You go by Mallory's."

And that seemed to be that.

"Do you know Mr. Fraser?" he said.

**243**

"Old Mr. Fraser?"

"That's him."

"Oh, yes."

"That's where I'm working, at Mr. Fraser's. But I haven't been there very long. And I don't know these roads the way you do."

"You know where Mallory's is?"

"No."

"It's that way," she pointed right. "I'll show you."

"That's fine. My name's Joe, what's yours?"

"Henrietta." Then: "My big brother calls me Hank."

"Do you like that?"

"Hank is nice. But Bert calls me Hankie and I don't like *that*."

"Who's Bert?"

"He's my brother."

"Your other brother?"

She giggled at the rhyme.

"Tim's my *big* brother and Bert's just my brother."

"Is he smaller than you?"

"No. I'm the smallest."

He fell silent with his thoughts. A crossroad sign appeared and she said, "Here," and he turned right.

"Where's Mallory's?" he said.

"This is Mallory's, Mallory's road."

"Is there a farm by that name?"

"No. Just the road."

"What's your farm called?"

She giggled again. "It's not called anything, it's home."

"What's the name on the mailbox?"

"Oh. Shefford's our name."

"So you're Hank Shefford," he said in his best TV manner.

She twisted in the seat and grinned. "I guess I am."

He fell silent again. Talking to the girl was like summoning spirits, who came. And stayed to haunt. His face felt tight.

"There it is," she said and pointed.

He turned left at the mailbox "R. Shefford" into a few hundred feet of muddy driveway and pulled up at the house. It was two stories with a veranda on one side and it needed paint. A big police-like dog came out from somewhere and sniffed at the pickup. Trees marked off a lawn, which was cut, and an old car was parked facing him alongside the house shed. The girl's manner said she was home, and he was very aware of it. He took the bike down and wheeled it over to her.

A woman appeared on the veranda and stayed there out of the rain.

"Is something wrong?" she said.

She was in her thirties, slender and muscled, looking tall in jeans and a green shirt and her hair tied back for work, brown like the girl's. She had a good face, not pretty, with even features, a little shiny without makeup, and glinting blue eyes. The eyes were worried, perhaps suspicious, searching things out.

"Oh no," the little girl said with a quite-the-contrary emphasis. She took the bike inside.

"Mrs. Shefford?" Joe said.

She nodded.

"I gave your daugher a lift, her bike had broken."

"That was very kind of you."

It was only a polite phrase, well meant but vague. Her eyes went to the pickup, then to him and his clothes. He was a stranger, and she probably knew everybody for miles around. A neighbor bringing the girl home would have been only natural, but this was different. He didn't want her to start inquiring.

"Nothing at all. People have been kind to me all day. I'm staying with Mr. Fraser, working there part-time." Eyes back to the truck, to him, she relaxed a little. "And today I've been driving around seeing people, asking if they're looking for somebody to hire. That's how I came across your girl on the road."

"I thought something might have happened."

"No. Everything's fine."

"Are you related to Charles Fraser?"

She was still defensive, protective of the girl, he could understand how she felt, but there seemed to be no need for that now.

"No, I'm from the city. Work is scarce there, so I decided to move on. I met Townley Miller one night when he was shipping cattle and he brought me out here. Then Claire Miller put me in touch with Mr. Fraser."

"They're good people," she said.

"Very good. I was lucky to meet them."

"What kind of work do you do?"

"Right now, anything. And that's almost the same as nothing. I'm not a farmer."

A faint smile crossed her face.

"You can laugh if you want to," he said. "It *is* funny, in its own way."

"Well," she said with a wider smile, indicating she wasn't responsible for the joke, "I suppose it is."

He was aware of her as a woman, but that was a closed-off route in his life. The light rain was finally making him wet.

"I'll be running along," he said. "Say goodbye to Hank for me. Nice meeting you."

"Yes," she said. "And thank you."

He drove back to Fraser's aching with the normality of it all.

# 26

It was too early to follow up his visits, and with the return of the sun the next day he couldn't be idle. He decided to fell and cut the big maple in front of the house. What he really wanted to do was go back to Shefford's and see Hank. But he had no pretext for that, only reasons, and he couldn't just go there, like a child seeing a friend, as an adult he'd be suspect. Instead, under the old man's tutelage he concentrated on learning the chain saw. It was heavy and cumbersome, as noisy as an outboard motor, and used at arm's length it kept him off balance until he got the hang of it. He was shown how to aim the fall with a wedge cut on the falling side and a normal cut on the other. And in noise and fumes the big maple crashed down as if nature had come to an end.

He began the long job of trimming limbs, cutting up the huge trunk, and moving the wood from the front of the house to behind the outbuildings where it would dry and wait for winter. The old man said he'd split it at that time and Joe thought that seemed impossible, the ax only got stuck in the hard ringed blocks.

By the evening of the fourth day the work was done, and following instructions he raked the sawdust into the grass. The only thing left was a huge stump over a yard wide. The old man hinted at its removal, by now Joe was wise to his teasing, and went on to recall the days before tractors when men used horses to clear fields. Today it was bulldozers, but it would ruin the lawn. The phone rang inside, Fraser's two short rings on the party line, and the old man went in to answer it.

He was gone about fifteen minutes and when he returned he took a while to mention the call.

"That was a neighbor," he said finally, "asking what kind of worker you are. Looks like a job for you, if you want it."

"Sure. What doing?"

"Didn't get on to that. Haying, I imagine."

"Where?"

"Ellen Shefford's. She said you met them the other day."

"Yeah, I did. I met her, I didn't meet him."

"There's no him. He died about three years ago."

"Oh."

That would explain the woman's attitude, the alert worry in her eyes, the partly let-go state of the house.

"Does she work that place alone?"

"She tries to. Doesn't always get help."

"That must be hard, for everybody."

"She manages. She's a good worker. Bring your hat, it'll be hot tomorrow."

The morning brought more sun and the promise of more July heat. He drove off early while the light was still soft

**249**

and the dew hadn't lifted. The roads weren't yet dusty and the clear air let him see the surrounding hills, he watched them as he drove. They were always an unfolding discovery, they had lost their vacation look and he regarded them with hard-earned respect.

The road climbed and rolled toward Shefford's, something he hadn't noticed in the rain, and brought new series of hills into view. From the farm the horizon opened on all sides. He parked near the house and got out and waited.

The children were in the garden some distance away, weeding he imagined, and they waved at him, Hank energetically as if he might not recognize her, but they didn't come to see, which was unusual. They had probably been told to stay put, it was going to be a private conversation.

Ellen Shefford emerged from the side door.

"Morning," she said, "you're early."

She was in tan jeans, a work shirt, hair again tied back. It seemed to be an awkward moment for her.

"Good morning, Mrs. Shefford."

The formality felt wrong and doing business felt just as wrong.

"Ellen," she said in a correcting tone.

"I'm Joe."

"Henrietta told me."

"I kinda like to think of her as Hank."

"We all do. But pretty soon she'll want to be called Henrietta and I call her that now so it won't sound too strange later."

She seemed organized, she'd have to be. He looked at the countryside and changed the subject.

"It's a great view. I missed it the other day in the rain. How big's your farm?"

"It's about two hundred acres, about fifty of it is bush."

"Bush. You mean wasted?"

"Not exactly." She smiled at his urban ignorance. "It's woods, a maple bush, a cedar bush. I get offers for them, people want to cut them down."

"Mr. Fraser mentioned that you're alone to work the farm."

"I am. But I'm not really working it, it's too big for that." Her eyes changed with the thought of things. "I rent part of it to neighbors. I'd sell it, but I don't want the children growing up in the city, and I'd . . . well, a lot of things." She drew a deep breath and continued, "What I have to do now, though, is the haying, and that's why I called Mr. Fraser about you."

She looked as if she'd finally plunged. The awkwardness of the moment had reached its peak. He broke through it.

"Well, I'm here. Let's get started."

"I can't pay you. I mean right away."

"That's all right."

"No, it's not all right. You should know before you agree. I can't pay you till I sell the hay."

"You'll owe me. It's still all right."

"By the bale. We'll ask Mr. Fraser to set a fair price."

"You set it."

"It varies every year. Mine's been low because they wait till I can't do anything about it but sell cheap. This time it might be different."

It was a glimpse into her life, a complex pastoral survival, it was no holiday, to hell with the scenery. He took in the hills, then Hank and her two brothers.

"Look," he said, forgetting himself for an instant, "we'll have Fraser set a scale, x percent per bale, with variations

**251**

if you want, minus something for my lack of experience. That'll settle it."

"Yes, it will."

She was going to ask him something and quite evidently stopped herself. He realized he hadn't sounded like a man confined to manual labor. His turn to be awkward, hers to ease it. She began walking toward the outbuildings.

"I teach school," she said, "part-time. I was a teacher before I was married."

It said a lot of things. It told him how she survived, and more subtly that she had caught his minor giveaway. It invited him to say what he was or had been. He was sure Fraser had told her about him and he hoped the hard-luck story would stand up. No reason it shouldn't, except that chances were good that she read the newspapers.

As if their walking had been a signal, the children dropped their work and discipline and came over to see the visitor. Hank was first. He resisted the impulse to lift her and hug her. Tim, the eldest, was ten or eleven, a little shy, with thick brown curly hair, dark blue eyes full of curiosity, a sturdy body. Bert was about eight, short, chubby, with sun-bleached hair, brown eyes and a manner that was all pushiness and go-ahead.

"It was just the chain on my bike," Hank said. "Tim fixed it."

"Are you the worker?" Bert exclaimed.

"Great," to Hank and Tim. "Yes, I am," to Bert.

"That means I won't have to shovel out the barn any more."

"Well, you'll have to ask your mother about that."

"Don't be a ding-ding." It was Tim's turn. "He's gonna do big work, not cleanup. Aren't you, mister?"

"You can call me Joe."

"*Mr.* Joe," said Ellen Shefford. "And we all have work to do."

"Can I help Mr. Joe?" Tim said.

"Later if he needs you."

The children reluctantly went back to the garden. She led him to a big shed, whose doors slid open on an overhead track, and showed him the machinery. He recognized the mower and nothing else.

"I can run that," he said. "I did it at Fraser's."

"It'll need fixing, it wasn't used last summer."

"I'll fix it."

She pointed out where the tools were, the spare parts, and said he could call Tim for anything he needed. She went back to the house.

He spent the rest of the morning dismantling the mower, oiling the working parts and sharpening the long line of blades with a flat file. The children came over to watch for a while. Tim helped with the oiling, and they all had questions, most of which he enjoyed, some of which he had to evade. The questions continued at lunch, but Ellen put a stop to them and he was able to ask them about their farm life and school and what things they found the most fun. Tim was anxious to use his father's guns to go after woodchucks but he'd have to wait till he was older and bullets cost a lot of money. They all liked TV, especially Bugs Bunny, Tim Westerns and cops-and-robbers, and they never watched the news, it was just people talking. He felt bad about exploiting the innocent talk, but it would be ironical to have a child turn him in through his own carelessness. He felt Ellen was searching his face. He couldn't be sure.

After lunch Ellen rode with him, standing on the back of the tractor, to a wide expanse of hayfield and explained its boundaries, the road, a brook, dry at this time of the year, that separated two properties, the distant bush, a single wire electric fence, and over the noise of the tractor she demonstrated with gestures that he was to mow along the outer edges, working his way toward the middle. He got started, cautiously did a practice piece, and gradually picked up speed to a comfortable rhythm. When he looked back, she was gone, and he was surprised at how far he'd come.

He worked under the glaring sun, which bounced off the hood of the tractor and hurt his eyes. He kept his head turned and watched the path of the blades, ready to lift them free of any obstruction. The only result that showed was behind him. When he turned a corner, all he could see was the standing hay. He rode the long perimeters trying each time to estimate the distance and how long it would all take. But it couldn't be done that way, he'd need a watch and accurate measurements of distance and speed, any two of those factors would do. Do what? Tell him when the job would be over? The job was in the present, it would be over in its own present. Knowing when didn't matter. That future "when" was being created now by the rattling blades and the falling stalks and the rows settling like waves behind him. Time, speed, and distance, and the neat interrelated formulas they could make, all abstract, had nothing to do with anything. Distance was the blazing field before him and speed the roll of the big wheels and the snipping of a billion stalks, no two ever alike, ever, and time was what he was doing and knowing now under the hot sky that was so enveloping it felt low.

He gave himself to the present and the long perimeters became shorter and shorter. His skill grew with every go-around and he didn't have to watch the paths so closely, his eyes did the seeing for him, and he allowed himself to think unguardedly and dwell on things freely, daydreaming like a man without a care. He was alone in the open, wrapped in the engine's noise and the heat and his streaming sweat. And he dwelled on Sue and Patty, and spoke out loud about them, and to them, factually, without breaking, his pain undiminished, but somewhat at peace, for they too were present, a part of him always, and they were a sort of benediction to the place where he was, as though all he did was for them. And in a way it was true. Then his plans came back to him and he became grim for a while, but that was soon lost in the effort of work and his awareness of the living fields.

At the turns now he could see rows of mown hay bringing out the contours of the land, and the shrinking center made the mowing seem faster. The sun was lower, still hot, but promising to be less harsh. When he swung into the side facing the house he saw a small tractor pulling a flat trailer, Ellen driving, the kids on the trailer. He turned off his motor and waited. They stopped alongside. On the trailer were big milk cans, a funnel, a jug of some kind, plastic cups.

"You're doing fine," she said.

"Bit by bit."

"You'll need gas."

The kids didn't say anything, they were used to this. She tugged down a milk can, handed him the funnel, and then heaved up the can. He poured the gas in. It took most of what she'd brought.

"It's too clumsy with a full can," she said, "so I half filled a few of them."

From the jug she poured him a cup of water. On his third he took off his hat and dribbled the water over his head. The children laughed, Bert uproariously.

"We were gonna bring Kool-Aid," he spluttered, "sticky."

Joe swatted him with his hat and that set him off again. Hank looked pleased at his symbolic comeuppance, and Tim wasn't interested in his brother's antics, he wanted to work. Ellen left the gas and the water in the field and drove off, the kids scrambling to get aboard the trailer.

He returned to work. Imperceptible hours went by and the fields took on shadows that sculpted the hillocks and the oceans of hay. And at length he saw Tim waving both arms from the entrance to the field as though he were guiding a jet. Suppertime. He waved back, stopped the tractor, and walked toward the house carrying the jug of water.

Ellen was more at ease at supper. She talked more with the children and did less supervising. Joe was no longer a stranger to be assessed, he worked hard and minded his own business and got on with the children. They watched the weather on the TV news, it promised fair for a few days. There was no mention of escapees, it was old news by now, and nothing about recaptures.

As he went to go outside, Ellen said: "If there's no dew, you can start around ten tomorrow."

"I'm gonna do some now, there's still a few hours of light."

"Think you should? You're not used to it."

"It doesn't matter."

Outside, Tim caught up with him. "Can I go with you?"

"Sure."

The sun was getting low and red, colors changing over miles of country, shadows stretching to become darkness. As they walked he noticed the boy was trying to keep step and he shortened his pace. There was something elemental about it all, easy to miss, lost to sophisticates, something, like unsought joy. They saw woodchucks alert and safe in the distance, and Tim watched them with disciplined frustration.

"Can you drive a tractor?" Joe asked.

"Yeah, I can!"

They poured in gas and Joe let Tim drive. The boy was too short to reach the levers of the mower and Joe stood behind him and worked them. They didn't talk over the noise of the tractor. The sun dropped noticeably at every circuit they made and they stopped to watch the last red arch slip below the hills. Joe took over the driving and the boy leaned on the fender, careful not to let the big tire catch his fingers. Gradually the darkness thickened around them and the sky dimmed to reveal two bright stars.

"It's got lights," Tim said and pointed to a switch.

Joe turned them on.

"Not bad," he said. But it was difficult to see properly. He turned them off, stopped the tractor.

"Let's call it a day, eh?"

"Can I do it tomorrow?"

"Sure. If you've got nothing else to do."

"Oh. Yeah."

The fields were still visible but their color was gone into the grays of late twilight. The coolness was welcome, and the tiredness that made thinking impossible. Ellen was outside sitting on the grass. Tim said good night and went in to wash up for bed.

"You've put in a long day," she said.

"A good day," he said, "good." And fell silent to knowledge that couldn't be expressed. Unembarrassed time passed.

"Mr. Fraser says you're not planning to stay long."

"No. Not much longer."

"He also mentioned about your wife."

He nodded. More silence. Then he said: "There was also my little girl. And I'm only saying it to you. Because she was six, like Hank."

The fresh night absorbed the statement, and their presence to each other was almost tangible. He could see the gathering stars.

"Reminders," she said, "everywhere."

"That bright star is south," he said, holding memories back.

She turned to look.

"That's Jupiter."

"Good night, Ellen, I'll see you tomorrow."

On the way to Fraser's he stopped to look at the planet and let his emotions drain away from him. He hoped he hadn't been careless. He was easier to identify as a man who had lost both wife and child.

But the next day Ellen didn't say anything about it and didn't ask for details. And they made no reference to their momentary closeness. Knowing seemed to be enough, and they felt freer in each other's presence. Talking about it would have falsified it. The work continued. It lasted that day and another. By that time he had done close to fifty acres. He was going to do more, but the forecasts said the weather would change. And the gamble against the rain began.

Ellen showed him how to use the baling machine. It was pulled and powered by the tractor, it scooped up the rows of hay, pressed them into bales, tied them with two cords along their length and pushed them out on the field behind the machine. It was easy to operate, but it was complicated to adjust and repair. Once more he began riding over the now familiar fields, leaving the tied bundles strewn in his wake. The baler pounded and thudded as he tried to go fast, but hurry was impossible. He found the right pace, a little faster than mowing, and watched the sky for signs of growing clouds.

In late afternoon Hank came running out to him and rode on the back of the baler where it was safe. Then he noticed that Ellen had taken the smaller tractor and the trailer and was beginning to load the bales. Bert guided the tractor as it moved slowly along the rows, Tim was on the trailer stacking the bales, and Ellen, wearing gloves, was lifting them up to him. It was work that got heavier and harder as it went on. They could take only small loads, two layers at most, because Tim wasn't big enough for the work and Ellen couldn't throw the bales very high. They brought each trailerful to the barn, unloaded it and stacked it and went out again to the fields. They managed four trips before supper, and were going to continue after, but he insisted they stop and went out and baled alone until dark.

He was at it again by mid-morning, and this time things went wrong. After two circuits he looked back and saw that the bales behind him had burst open. The cords weren't knotting properly. He stopped everything and examined the mechanism, but he couldn't tell what was wrong just by looking at it. He scooped up some burst hay, piled it in front of the machine and made it go. He fed hay into it until a bale was formed and tried to watch the tying process, but the bale itself obscured his view.

He brought it off the field and toward the house, explained to Ellen, who had come out, that he was going to the neighbor's for help and drove the cumbersome machinery down the driveway. Better to take it along than try to explain the problem.

The closest was about half a mile away, the name "Peters" on the mailbox. He saw movement in the kitchen windows as he approached, but no one came out. He parked the rig to one side not to block the way and went up on a small porch and knocked. A woman came to the door.

She was middle-aged, stocky, in dress and apron, with sharp blue eyes, no smile. She didn't say anything.

"I'm working on the next farm," he explained, "and the baler's not tying right. I wondered if anyone here could help me fix it."

"Oh, you are. Come in."

He went into a kitchen cluttered with laundry and cooking and furniture and junk piled on top of everything. A man in his thirties was sitting at the table. He had a big-boned wide face with careful eyes and no expression.

"The man's workin' over there," she said and nodded generally toward Ellen's.

The man at the table gave him a slight nod. Joe explained his problem.

"Them things are pretty tricky," the man said, "especially if you're not used to them. I'd like to help but I can't go now."

"I brought the baler with me." He was sure they'd seen him outside.

"Like I say, it'd take time to fix."

"Maybe if you just took a look at it, it might be a simple thing."

"You're new in these parts?"

"Yeah."

"You known Ellen Shefford long?" the woman asked.

"No. I don't know her at all, I'm just hired help."

"Help's hard to get these days," she said.

"Yeah."

"Farm work's not easy," she kept at it. "You mighta took on more than you can handle."

"That's right." To the man: "I'd appreciate it if you could take a look."

"Well, you could leave it here. But I can't promise I'll have time. Hate to say yes and then not be able to do it."

"When would you know?"

"Can't say. Few days maybe. I'm pretty busy."

"Yeah, I know how it is. So am I."

"Well . . ." the man droned as if he'd exhausted the pos-sibilities.

Joe looked into the two pairs of sharp eyes.

"It's been nice talking to you."

He left.

He dragged the rig back to Ellen's, phoned Fraser, who said he could fix it, and went to get the old man. Someone had been listening on the party line. He felt he was every-body's business.

The old man cleared the machine of hay, rethreaded the

cord so that Joe could see where it went, and by trial and error, which took over an hour, he adjusted the knotting mechanism. He told Joe to call him if things went wrong again and he took the pickup home.

It was clouding over by then, well past lunchtime, and Joe ate sandwiches as he continued baling. He pushed the machine to its limits on straight runs, slowing for turns and uneven ground, but he knew he couldn't go fast enough to gather the present crop. In a few hours he stopped, disconnected the tractor and took it back to the yard, where he hitched it to a long trailer.

There were hundreds and hundreds of bales in the field, perhaps a thousand or more, strewn at all angles and in all positions, stretching so far the distant ones looked tiny. Tim guided the tractor between the crooked rows and Joe walked to every bale and carried it by the cords to the trailer and heaved it aboard to Ellen, who placed it on the growing layers. When the load was too high for her to reach, they took the creaking trailer to the barn, unloaded each bale and placed it in new stacks.

A round trip took almost two hours. They rested going to and from the barn and during a quick supper, barely ten minutes, with Hank and Bert charged with cleaning up. Apart from that there was no stopping and the work grew into aching labor. For the third unloading they used a conveyor, called an elevator by Ellen, which fed the bales into an opening near the roof of the barn. It took longer this way because someone had to be inside to place the bales and Joe went from trailer to loft to keep things moving. In the cloudy sky there was no sunset, it simply got dark. Hank and Bert were told to go to bed.

They began a fourth load, more slowly than before, fumbling in the darkness behind the headlights and urged to go faster by the lightning and the unheard thunder. Tim slumped on the wheel, it was past being fun. Ellen wasn't lifting the bales any more, she was pushing them up into position, and Joe took more and more time heaving them. They managed to load three tiers.

"You better stop," he said.

She shook her head, unspeaking.

They continued onto a fourth tier. But before it was finished, it began to rain lightly, then too heavily to ignore, and Joe signaled Tim to climb on the load.

He drove in as quickly as he could and when Ellen and Tim got off he backed the partly filled trailer into the vehicle shed and left it there out of the rain. He'd unload it when the sun came out. Tim went straight inside without a word. They put out the yard lights and hurried to the veranda as the rain suddenly poured. In the near dark they stood looking out at the unseen fields and waiting for normal breathing to return.

They were wet and overheated, covered with the debris of work, and tired past speaking. Ellen cleared children's things from a bench and sat on it exhausted, her back slumped against the wall. The rain pounded the veranda roof and seemed to hiss through the grass. She put her hands to her face and tried not to show she was crying.

"We'll lose a good third of it," she said.

"Yeah, but we took in a lot too. And there's more still growing."

"How many bales? Did you count them?"

"No."

"There's a counter on the baler."

"I didn't know."

"I forgot to set it. I'm sorry. I'll estimate it from what's . . ."

"It's not important."

"Well, I have to figure it out anyway."

"Those people," he said, indicating the neighbors, "aren't very helpful."

"No, they're not." And after a pause she said, "It seemed like such nice weather." She covered her face again.

He sat beside her this time and took one of her hands in both of his.

"Look," he said, "it's not all that bad."

The words meant nothing, but his gesture did, and his tone. It was all familiar, domestic, impelling with memory and experience, touch and response subtle with understanding.

"I know, I'm just tired."

She squeezed his hand by way of thanks and stood up.

"I don't feel up to driving you to Fraser's," she said.

"Don't bother. I can take your car."

"No, I wouldn't feel right without it. The children. I mean . . ."

"It's all right."

"You can stay. You can sleep downstairs, there's a cot in that small room near the TV."

"This'll get on the community grapevine."

"It's already there. Good night."

"Night."

# 27

It was still raining, off and on, the next morning. Ellen took him to Fraser's, again with no reference to their growing intimacy, and chatted with the old man before leaving. He said he could use the spoiled hay for mulch. Joe heated shaving water in an old electric kettle and last night's thoughts came back to him for light-of-day assessment. He had sat a long time on the porch listening to the rain and slowly forming a decision. He'd been here over two weeks, close to three, too long, he was becoming known, gossiped about. He knew he wouldn't take wages from Ellen, the money was needed for the family. And the longer he stayed the harder it would be for everybody when he left. It was time for other and better plans.

He changed to clean clothes and washed the others in cold water, an almost daily routine now, and asked Fraser for the use of the pickup to go to town. He always asked, and the old man, pleased at not being taken for granted, always said yes.

Going to town was step one, and easy enough. The rest was all risk. He had pushed out of his mind the memory of his own home, it had stopped existing for him, physically, and continued only as suppressed pain. But being at Ellen's had allowed him to remember it as a fact, created and sustained by years of work. He had resources there, the leftovers, cash, till now unreachable and maybe still, but it would be a suitable irony to use them for his present purpose.

Wareby was too small a town to have telephone-company offices. He got gas, five dollars' worth, which left him with $21.89 to work with, couldn't get a map, but got directions to the nearest sizable town, a place called South Hillsbury, thirty-five miles away.

He drove carefully in the rain, under 50, and was at the phone company in an hour. He got the book for his home city, borrowed pen and paper from one of the girls and copied out Steve Harrison's business number and the one for the Drummond Plaza Hotel, where he knew Steve often went for lunch. At a bank he changed five dollars to silver, looked around until he found a phone booth near a busy garage, double-checked the parking signs and left the truck on the street near the garage. He went into the booth and his heart began to pound. He'd be leaving traces at this end.

He got the operator and gave her Steve's number. The name on the garage was Mitchell. When she had Steve, Joe dropped the coins.

"Mr. Harrison?" he said.

"Yes," on an up-note, cheerful, a quick hesitation as if a name was not said.

"You may remember me, Mr. Harrison, I'm Cliff Mitchell, with Industrial Plastics. We met about six months ago over our marketing program." He talked on to give Steve a chance to be sure of his voice.

"Yes, of course, Cliff. I heard you got promoted."

"I most certainly did. I have a whole team on the road now."

"Keep you busy, eh?"

"You wouldn't believe. In fact, I'm a bit rushed even at this minute. The reason for the call, eh, is that one of our V-P's is in town right now and I recall your saying you'd like to meet him."

"Great."

"I sorta jumped the gun on you, Mr. Harrison. I told him I'd arrange an early lunch at your place. I hope you don't mind."

"No, no, not at all. My place. He knows where it is?"

"Oh, yes, he'll be in touch with you there."

"Fine."

"I'd like to talk some more, but I have to run. Goodbye, Mr. Harrison, and many thanks."

"A pleasure."

It was done. He was sweating with the effort. He hurried to the pickup, to get out of the rain, and drove as purposefully as he could while searching for a place to wait. A clock on an old building put the time at 11:15. He had become unused to time, and going by it now made him uncomfortable. He pulled in at a hamburger stand, ordered the usual things not to be conspicuous, and brought

**2 6 7**

them to the truck. He sat eating some of it, a legitimate idleness for men in work clothes.

When he felt enough time had passed he looked for another outdoor booth. Somehow he dreaded going inside a building, not being able to see the truck, who was around. He found one just off the driveway of a farm-equipment firm and he parked on their property.

The operator got him the Drummond Plaza and the hotel girl got him the lunchroom. They paged Mr. Harrison.

"Steve?"

"Joe."

"Is your office bugged?"

"I don't know. But they've been as thick as flies. Are you all right?"

"I'm fine. How's Betsy?"

"Worried, you know. Let's get to it, Joe, they may have figured this one out."

"Yeah. I need money. Cash. Did Harry sell my place?"

"Yes."

"Okay. Highway 21, going east, the first rest area after, *after* exit 116."

"Got it. How much do you want?"

"A thousand. Two if you can get it up without attracting attention."

"It'll be two. When?"

"The next rainy day, after supper, leave just after sunset, we meet as it gets dark."

"Say nine-thirty."

"That's too close. I haven't got a watch."

"Oh. It's raining now. Why not this evening?"

"All right. Tonight."

"How will I spot you?"

"Never mind. I'll spot you."

"Need anything else?"

"Just money. Goodbye, Steve."

He was on the alert again. As he hung up he took in the passing cars, the ones parked, the uncrowded wide street, the seemingly idle businesses, a few people who stood talking, a motel up the road with big clean cars outside, the local status eating place. He felt that his caution was unnecessary and tried to regain his earlier composure, the sense of inner being that had come to him in the last weeks. It was only now that he realized that it had been there at all. To hell with it, he couldn't get careless now.

He recognized the name of the farm-equipment company, it was on Ellen's machinery. He went in and chatted with the clerk, a knowledgeable older man with a shirt and tie emphasizing clean work and his sleeves rolled up past the elbows. Joe limited his vocabulary and whatever know-how he had and came away with a detailed handbook on the balers of some five years ago. From that he could learn, and shopping for it would explain his morning's traveling.

In South Hillsbury he got a map and in Wareby he got more gas to keep the tank full. He thought, too late, that this might appear unusual to the attendant, but a boy served him and Joe covered with "Is that all? I thought I needed more," and made a mental note to carry spare gas. On the way back he threw out the uneaten food, the birds and animals would get it, no pollution. He kept the containers for burning.

He dropped by Ellen's, sensitive that his absence might raise questions, however innocent, but he didn't stay long.

He couldn't bring himself to play-act, and she would feel his tension eventually, so he joked about going to Fraser's to earn some of his keep.

The old man wasn't curious, young men got skittish over women, and that was that. He was amused by the handbook. They spent the afternoon servicing a big snow blower that went on the back of a tractor. Joe thought it was make-work in the middle of the summer, but the old man was serious about it, he had his own inner time made up of short years. They ate early and Joe lied, with regret, about having made new contacts and needing the truck for the evening. He'd fill some gas cans while he was at it. Fraser merely nodded, eyes not hiding their humor, women again. Joe wished it were true.

The timing would be difficult. Fraser's clock was stopped half the time and ill-set. Joe studied the map and calculated the distances. It wouldn't do for either of them to have to wait too long. Steve would probably check the newspapers for the sunrise-sunset times and take it slowly from there. He looked it up in the almanac and turned on the radio for the time. At 7:40 he put two five-gallon cans in the back of the truck and left. It was still raining.

He followed the route Townley Miller had taken, not recognizing it, stopped for the gas, and in what felt like a half hour he was at the Shrewsdale access and on to the throughway. He was hurrying despite his planning and had to watch the speedometer to keep the pace at 50. He was excited, nervous, not grim and cold as he was two months before, and he resented it somehow, it was like re-entering an oppressive climate.

On his left he saw the rest area. There were no cars,

only one trailer truck. He kept going past the next two exits, turned off at the third and circled back onto the throughway, now going east. This time the rest area was empty. Two exits away he doubled back again. Still no one. He went slowly when there were no cars on the road. He narrowed his circuit to the closest exits. This time there was a car parked without lights.

He swung into the area, lights on, braking, looking intently past the wipers. It wasn't Steve's car. And there were two men in it. He decided to play out the role and stop. He edged over well in front of the car and put out his lights. He got out, made business with one of the gas cans, and casually walked over to the car. It was Steve all right, and Harry Posser, in Harry's car.

He got in the back seat and they all shook hands awkwardly.

"First, business," Harry said, and handed Joe an old wallet folded thickly. "Fifty twenties and a hundred tens."

"Thanks."

"What are you going to do, Joe?" Steve asked, very worried.

"I can't tell you that."

"Too much time has passed, it'd be murder now, and they'd kill you on the streets."

"Yeah."

"Betsy doesn't know about this, I just told her you were fine."

"Maybe you'd like to see this," Harry said.

He opened the door to get light and gave Joe some newspaper clippings. GROOVING CONS GO WAY OUT, one said and described a "daring bid for freedom," the musicians' account, "They stole all our stuff, passes and all," and an official "all four men have records of violence and are to be considered dangerous." Another had pictures, stiff, sinister police photos, follow-up stories, background, more quotes. Joe gave them back.

"I can't carry that around. Close the door."

"Think," said Harry. "You can't even carry yourself around. So why not let it go?"

"I'm in too far now. I might as well go back for something I did do. Was this," he flicked a hand at the clippings, "on TV?"

"Two, three days, then it died down. But the cops haven't died down, you can count on that."

"Look, Joe," Steve said, "we're on your side, we'll even come back with more money. Turn yourself in, eh?"

"I better go."

He squeezed both of them by the shoulders and thanked them. Harry started the car and pulled away as soon as Joe got out. He sat in the truck and waited five, then ten minutes. It wasn't caution, it was indecision. He was going to cause pain to the people he loved. At last he got started and drove hurriedly to the Shrewsdale exit. Once into the countryside he felt easier and freer, time and place once more within him, as if his soul were his own. There were messages from this, but he wasn't listening.

He arrived quietly at Fraser's, not to wake the old man. He made a cup of coffee and sat at the kitchen table, the map before him, and stared at it and thought of everything and everyone. He had resources now, an advantage of sorts, he could move out fast, he was equipped to decide, free to act. He could stay in hiding awhile, two weeks, three, fake a job to account for the things he bought, work with Ellen a little longer, and then a time would come, as it had to. In the small hours of the morning he stretched out on the downstairs couch and finally fell asleep. Nothing had really changed, except perhaps him.

# 28

The late afternoon sun made the fields a deepening gold and spotted the green hills with shadows. In two days it had dried everything and Joe had resumed the mowing. From where he worked he could see the house, small in the distance, the neighboring farms, the road, the rolling horizon merging with the sky. Alternately he faced the sun, still high enough to be hidden by a pulled-down brim, the fields swept with low light before him, then the side-lit country, rich in contrast, then a turn into his own shadow and the still hot scenery ahead of him. It was good to be in the living fields again. He worked slowly, somehow trying to make it last.

When he faced the house again he noticed a dust trail on the road from Wareby, made, he assumed, by a truck. He watched it crest and disappear and turn up again among the apparently small trees. It would pass the house in about two miles. He followed it intermittently as he worked in that direction and when he came to the end of the row he didn't turn.

It was a car, not a truck, and the dust showed that it was going fairly fast. He kept watching. It didn't go right by. It stopped at the driveway, backed a little, drove in, and stopped at the house. A man got out and was lost to view as he went on the veranda. Presently he appeared and was walking up the slope toward Joe.

He lifted the blades and began driving the tractor back down. Little by little the man became defined, a sport shirt outside the belt, a white cap with a peak, like a golfer's, sunglasses, a slow pace.

He felt he knew him. And then, of course, he did. When the man was close, he took off his sunglasses as Joe got off the tractor. It was Captain Sparrs.

In the open fields it was hard to believe he was the police, a cop. It was all from another world.

"Hello, Joe."

"Captain."

Sparrs looked older than before, his hair whiter, perhaps it was the fresh haircut. The flapping sport shirt made him look thinner. Joe wondered if he had a gun under it. Somehow it was natural not to shake hands.

"How have you been?" Sparrs said.

"All right."

"You look good."

"I've been outdoors a lot."

"Here?"

"Hereabouts. Right here's just for work, a temporary job, that's all. She doesn't know anything about me. I live somewhere else."

It felt strange defending Ellen against the official point of view. He didn't want Sparrs questioning her.

"I'm not interested in that," Sparrs said.

He seemed worried, as if he weren't sure of himself away from the machinery of enforcement, but Joe couldn't tell much from Sparrs' face.

"How did you find me?"

"We service these outlying areas, they don't have their own forces. One of our men got word about a stranger and spotted you. It was simple, an old panel truck."

"I'll bet. He got word, from who?"

"Some gossip. Sounded worked up, didn't leave a name. It was a phone call. Why bother with it? It's done."

"Why didn't your man pick me up?"

"I said I'd make the identification." Sparrs spoke carefully, at least Joe thought he did. "I want the three cons who made it out with you. That was a nice break, a lot of cool heads around."

"For me it was just an accident."

"Sure. Got any idea where they are now?"

"No."

"Or where they were headed?"

"No. They didn't tell me, they took me along at the last minute, they needed a fourth."

A trace of a grin appeared on Sparrs' face.

"How'd they work it, I mean inside?"

"I just know my end of that, Captain, and I'm not even gonna tell you that much."

"Why not?"

"Sooner or later I'm gonna have to live with those guys."

"There are other prisons."

"It's all the same."

"Yeah, it is. All right, an accident."

Sparrs sounded as if he'd settled something in his own mind. They stopped talking, looked away from each other.

"Nice country," Sparrs said.

"Yeah."

"We figured you'd go looking for your three kooks."

"Yeah."

"So we had them pretty heavily covered, even by men who were off duty."

"So?"

"We've worked, Joe, from the day it happened we've worked." He talked slowly, in a low voice, not trying to justify himself. "They cooled it after your trial and started in again on small stuff, two-bit robberies, fights, scaring the citizens, crap like that. We let it ride. After you broke jail they took to having a little more fun, burning barns, torching cattle, with gas, at night, watching the poor things run crazy. We got pictures of the results, and descriptions that can be made to agree. It built up, slowly. We also let the newspapers get a lot of it."

Joe didn't interrupt. Sparrs grabbed a handful of hay and looked at it like a fortune-teller. He spoke to the hay.

"About two weeks ago, at night, one of them got shot by a farmer, a shotgun, not pellets, a slug, sideways through the collarbone, it decapitated him but not cleanly. He was just about to throw a gas bomb at a horse, his second one. So we got some more pictures. It shook the farmer so bad he had to be hospitalized. He thought he was using bird shot. There's always a price."

Joe saw Hank and Tim come out of the house, full of curiosity, and reluctantly go back in. Ellen must have called them. Even from where he was, there was an atmosphere to be sensed.

"Five days later one of them went to a gas station with a hand grenade, called it his credit card. He got the gas. But one of my men spotted him a while later and gave chase. The guy tried to use the grenade, like the movies. Only the fuse was too short. The guy was wounded, not badly. He's out on bail, and there's not much evidence. But we don't give them any peace. They move, we move. And they can't avoid moving wrong. The file's getting thicker."

"That doesn't have to mean anything."

"It means we got a lot of stuff to show they aren't exactly nice people."

"You knew that before."

"Not to put before a judge. It's new evidence in a way, it can reopen your case. Done right, with the newspapers on your side, it could work."

"I'm a fugitive. There's not much law for me."

"Turn yourself in."

"It's too late for that. You're here."

"No. I'm not."

Sparrs put on his sunglasses. "Get yourself organized, Joe. Phone me when you're ready."

He turned and walked away.

Joe watched him as he went down the slope. Diminishing figure, dust, the settling of it, and nothing, as if he had not come. But everything was different.

He leaned on the tractor, suddenly exhausted, and then sat on the ground near the big tire. Grief and danger and flight were over as things past, the grief never to go fully, and the strain, though still present, had lost its roots. The

**278**

cold readiness for killing was being replaced by human realities, and by another kind of struggle to keep them existing. He tried to sort things out as his feelings threatened to engulf him. Somehow he had managed not to choose for death.

"Joe . . ."

The tone was where-are-you, apprehensive. It was Ellen.

He got up to let her see him. He had a story to tell her, the discovery of who he was, and perhaps, if it worked out that way, another arrangement to propose.